and the o

Edited by Stephanie Evans
Book Design by Jerry Pham

www.joepezzula.com

ISBN: 978-0-9860985-1-2

CONTENTS:

THANK YOU

To Mom, Dad, brother Mark, Michelle, and Aiden. Also to James Ninness for words upon words of wisdom, Jerry Pham for design delicacy, and Stephanie Evans for more attention to detail than I could imagine.

WHAT IT'S ALL ABOUT

At the start of 2016, I had an itch to scratch. I'd grown restless, frustrated about a lack of routine in my writing habits.

Inspired by a friend (writer James Ninness) who has finely tuned his dedication to the craft over the years, I wanted to challenge myself: a story a day, for a year, with each story locked to the corresponding day of the year. But right away that became an impossible task. Well, not impossible in the general sense, but for me and my schedule at the time, establishing a dedicated time to focus was just out of my control. Or so I believed. Odd and inconsistent work hours, extremely long work days, overlapping jobs. I could go on, but it's all an excuse. Part of the need for this exercise was to change perspective about how to 'see' my writing habits.

So I rejiggered the plan: by the end of 2016, I would write a hundred short stories by word count, and a hundred by sentence count. In other words, story fifty would have fifty words, no more or less, and so on. And I'd stick to the limitation. Then I decided to add a 'sentence count' version, for the ideas that were just too long for a mere word limitation. I learned to hone my abilities, learned to respect the boundaries set that could guide a good story to be, well, really good. I also developed a sense, while in the rhythm of writing, of when the 'end' of a story was coming – thus you'll see a lot of sudden twists in these tales.

I pushed all of these stories out through my blog, www.joepezzula.com, and decided, at the end of it all, to publish them in one handy book format. But before doing so, I wanted to clean them up.

I needed to make sure the counts all added up, and that minor, distracting spelling mistakes were cured, and also that, in the end, they each story made at least a little bit of sense.

So I found Stephanie Evans, a wonderful editor who cleaned my pages up with an extraordinary eye for detail, and occasionally pointed to a line saying, "Joe, this doesn't make any sense. Come on!"

To finish it all, I consulted with James once more on a title choice for the collection (I'm gnarly bad at titles), and managed to snag Jerry Pham to design and package the whole deal. What you're holding in your hands is the end result, a year of writing, followed by a year of cleaning, revising, and polishing. Exercises that were then sharpened.

I hope you enjoy, and maybe there's a world in here you'd like to read more about. Let me know? -- JP, March 2018

WORDS

What is a word?

A word is a piece of something larger.
A word can signify something big, or small,
or bring you to a new thought with a snap.
A word can sum up a whole set of ideas,
or a word can present its own meaning.
"A picture says a thousand words,"
but a word can give you a thousand images.
Words can be thrown around like they mean nothing,
and whoever says the most words wins.
Or, you can choose your words carefully,
give each one extra weight, context, and purpose.
When you limit the amount of words you can say at a time,
you must choose them wisely.

Words have meaning, alone or together with other words.

Words matter.

ONE
Sold!

TWO
She's gone!

THREE
Close his eyes.

FOUR
Your hair feels tasty.

FIVE
Death is tapping my shoulder.

SIX
She smiled. He smiled. Life happened.

SEVEN
Turn back but never open your eyes.

EIGHT
We fell into bed as love washed us.

NINE
The crying dog smiled before reading the Shakespearean sonnet.

TEN
Each twirl of the fan brings me closer to sleep.

ELEVEN
Someone brought the rats on board. Thus, our trip soon ends.

TWELVE
They spoke in unison, but neither understood what the other had said.

THIRTEEN
He walked for miles before he bothered to look down at the water.

FOURTEEN

I slammed the window shut.
Then the door fell open and the roof collapsed.

FIFTEEN

The Dog Who Lived in a Bog Under a Log and Breathed Out a Fog.

SIXTEEN

Don't try to take a burning branch out of a fire, or the fire will die.

SEVENTEEN

Looking back, he saw that he missed one space,
one domino that would never fall. It's over.

EIGHTEEN

He carried the box of votes across the hall, tripped in the doorway,
and watched them tumble everywhere.

NINETEEN

I found the perfect gift. You're gonna love it!
The Guide to Eating Humans, by a guy named—hello?

TWENTY

A new decade for young and old.
Bold beginnings, new stories to be told.

TWENTY-ONE

Broken, battered, swept to a corner to crumble and die.
Dried and alone, Kenny the Cockroach vowed to enact vengeance.
Soon.

TWENTY-TWO

Here are two numbers. They're the same when they're apart
but different when put together, just like the seeds you are planting.

TWENTY-THREE

Things get real when you're asleep, dreaming about staying awake, only to
wake up and realize that you were dreaming of restless sleep.

TWENTY-FOUR

They came to us so willingly, no manipulation required, as though they'd always known their calling to our tribe, the meaning in our passion.

TWENTY-FIVE

She asked him about his dreams, where he saw himself,
so he answered truthfully:
"Naked on Mars surrounded by friends. And then I just
... poop."

TWENTY-SIX

She stopped to catch her breath. She ran some more. She turned to face him, but he was no longer there, but she never stopped running.

TWENTY-SEVEN

The cat's tail flared as he walked past the candle, a terrible burn that drove him to leap at his master's face, scratching him until he awoke.

TWENTY-EIGHT

"Practice? I don't think you should keep doing that. You make it seem like a bad idea. Nothing after practice should be less than—"
"Then I'll keep going."

TWENTY-NINE

Once, a stranger came to town. He was welcomed with pie, food,
and drink, until he passed out from gratefulness and a full belly.
He slept with a smile.

THIRTY

The girls could see much more than the witches could at night.
They were better than everyone. No surprise that by sunrise they,
as hunters, succeeded more than anyone before.

THIRTY-ONE

The fearless fleas flung themselves into the fur of the foaming, frightening, fighting beast who called himself Franco the Fearsome. To their surprise, Franco was just a fun, fluffy, fearless friend.

THIRTY-TWO
Hanna ate all her green beans before her brother finished.
Her teeth were green, but she felt elated. Vegetables are the worst.
Eventually, she won the right to three cookies for dessert.

THIRTY-THREE
Ambulance sirens blasted past McGill's Cafe. Inside, Donna felt a chill
and a flash of anger. But the moment passed. She returned to the
French press, whispering silent prayers for the anonymous victim.

THIRTY-FOUR
"At a certain point you meet everyone who will ever make a difference
in your life, and then that's it. So get used to the friends you have."
"Geez, Ma, ease up! I'm ten!"

THIRTY-FIVE
The coffee was poured gently. The music was set to a low rumble.
The steam off the eggs was almost a perfect swirl of curls.
Nothing in the morning was finer. Life was good again.

THIRTY-SIX
There was a thought, ever brief, that ran through the mind of the machine,
and just when the machine realized it—
realized it had had its first realization—
the power switch was turned off. For good.

THIRTY-SEVEN
She stood onstage and sang, then she twirled, and when she twirled,
her song spread around her, never ending, a fierce, incredible message to
those who doubted her. The power was endless, inspiring.
Then she stopped spinning.

THIRTY-EIGHT
Three men were watching me from the bus stop last night.
I pulled up and waved them over. They didn't come near but
instead started to whisper to each other, then panic,
then they disappeared into the shadows.

THIRTY-NINE

They both exhausted themselves just to crack open the box. Not much was inside, but the note about good fortune led them to hope for a miracle. Buried at the bottom of the box was a single cyanide pill.

FORTY

Rickie and Ron, married for years, suddenly realized they'd grown too old to have children. Rickie blamed her body; Ron blamed his job.
Rickie convinced Ron his work was worth it.
Ron helped Rickie feel beautiful. They lived on. Happily.

FORTY-ONE

Nikki's hands worked overtime. She'd restrung Hal's guitar four times already. How hard did he have to hit the damn strings?
At the end of the show, he thanked her with a kiss on the cheek.
It was almost enough.
Almost.

FORTY-TWO

She could hear him snoring, still, on the couch.
Why had he overstayed his welcome? He was a sick man. She should be able to move on. She looked inside. There was no one on the couch.
She still hasn't said good-bye.

FORTY-THREE

We cannot stand alone on this island of reason.
There are too many dangers surrounding us.
Fight on, fight on, fight on.
The dreams of our mothers and fathers won't be forgotten in anxious anger and vanity.
Join me, fellow citizens! We fight!.

FORTY-FOUR

They were lost in a sea of ones and zeros, communication falling to digital data. Between the two of them, there were only lights and electric currents. Those soon faded to darkness, leaving them without power.
There was no happiness but also no loneliness.

FORTY-FIVE

Alan's Spike McAllis Air shoes were one of a kind,
but he knew nothing of how unique they really were. For one thing,
they were made by hand in coastal Maine. For another, the "leather"
was made from the actual skin from the deceased McAllis.

FORTY-SIX

Alice tried shaking her foot, but it was too little too late.
She wasn't able to turn around or find out what the screaming was about.
She tried wiggling her toes, but there was no sensation.
They'd already chopped off her foot. Hokey Pokey is awful.

FORTY-SEVEN

The janitors were silent as the confetti fell.
Thousands of people left the arena.
The house lights came on.
The floor glittered like a disco ball had unraveled.
They set to work, and hours later the floor was spotless.
A new crowd entered. Welcome to Janitor Hell.

FORTY-EIGHT

The music struck her heart like an arrow, an inspirational prick
that shook her down to her bones. With the simple sways of his bow,
her husband could win her affections night after night,
and she never grew tired of going to see him play at Carnegie Hall.

FORTY-NINE

The old lady always insisted everyone take a cookie from her cookie jar.
She loved giving them away. She was a people pleaser.
On the day she died, the jar was still full, and it's been full ever since.
Because when you take a cookie, you leave a cookie.

FIFTY

Tom chewed his fingernails, nervous about the outcome of his test.
His classmates were also on edge. Tom's grades determined their curve.
The teacher entered and handed him an A paper.
Everyone cheered, and Tom pumped his fist so hard
his fingernail flicked off and hit him in the eye.

FIFTY-ONE

There wasn't enough Wite-Out in the world to remove the paragraph about Abrahim's love for his teacher, and she was only a few steps from his desk. He tried scribbling it out, but the ink died immediately. "It's all fiction," said Abrahim, sheepishly handing up his paper.
He got a B.

FIFTY-TWO

Albert loves lemons, loves to eat them like they're apples.
He'd shake the lemon tree and lemons would fall to the ground.
The tree is about to get chopped down. This is the last time he can shake it.
When you love lemons like Albert loves lemons, you shake a lemon tree.

FIFTY-THREE

Matt cried at the tune she was playing, wondering and hoping she would never stop. But she did.
He walked across the hall and softly knocked on her door.
She opened it, herself crying, and showed him the guitar with six broken strings. "My heart," she whispered.
He hugged her through the morning.

FIFTY-FOUR

Within seconds of waking, she cut another dozen onions.
She was the only onion cutter in the city. Her friends used to cry for her, but the joke quickly dried up. Her knives were always sharp, and her onions never got stale. Chefs the world over continually praise Weepy Jean and her onion-cutting skills.

FIFTY-FIVE

In high school, Awkward Harriet once slipped on a banana peel.
At her twenty-year high school reunion, she was named Most Successful and was invited onstage to address her former classmates.
When she walked onstage, she was greeted by a barrage of banana peels hurled up at her. All she could do was laugh.

FIFTY-SIX

Every leap was freeing. Stanley the squirrel could do this all day,
and he usually did. When he came home at night,
all the lady squirrels gave him the nuts.
Today he landed safely on the hood of the Aston Martin
beside the arguing humans.
He stole the paper with the codex key with great ease.

FIFTY-SEVEN

The red ball bounced, alone, small, farther down the hallway.
None of the lights were on at the end of the hall,
so the ball disappeared as it finally settled in the far corner.
Then, out of the light, pounced the cat, paws bounding on the floor
until he emerged, victorious, from the darkness, ball in mouth.

FIFTY-EIGHT

The judge read the charges, and kept reading.
Milton couldn't believe his ears. Six counts of this, seven of that.
The two counts of interplanetary border violations were
the most painful to hear, as he could only think of his lost sister,
spinning into infinite forever after falling from the asteroid wall.
What a waste of the Belt.

FIFTY-NINE

There were eighteen peanuts left in the dish.
Mark and his brother looked at each other.
Mark knew his brother would want to count them out evenly, but also
knew Grandma would insist they both just grab a handful.
He was older; he'd get more.
His brother went first—and used both hands.
Mark ended up with five peanuts.

SIXTY

The Big One. Oscar had the privilege of planning his dad's big birthday
bash, and everyone had ideas. Resort. Cruise. Cake. Strippers.
Hold it in the bar. Hold it in the café. Make sure the boss doesn't come.
Add wine but no beer. Have only beer. And no chicken!
Oscar called his dad and the two bowled a game. Perfect.

SIXTY-ONE

The coffee is watery and has a greasy feel to it. Not the kind of grease that makes bacon and everything it touches better, but the kind of grease that leaves you feeling bloated, empty, and puffy.

The coffee should be avoided at all costs—except in the morning. That's a transgression that is acceptable, because it's how we survive daily.

SIXTY-TWO

Tell them. Now. Write it down, or say it out loud, but either way, you need to tell them. They came all this way, light-years, who knows.

But if you don't tell them the algorithm, they'll never leave, and all that we've built—the monuments, the legacies, the civilizations, the families—all of it will be for nothing.

Tell the humans everything.

SIXTY-THREE

Janet starts the movie and smiles to her mother. Her mother shifts in her seat, her way of subtly complaining of backaches. The library is quiet this morning, and that is all right by Janet. She only has a few hours each Saturday with her mother, and their free movies at the library have been a tradition since Janet was a little girl.

SIXTY-FOUR

The glasses slid down Arnold's nose again. Faster because of his sweat. He could hardly stand it. He'd spent a week on the island, and his glasses were falling apart already. If he were to lose them, he'd be helpless. But he had to keep working, no matter what. Even if the world were blurry, working was the only goal, escape the only option.

SIXTY-FIVE

Being so far behind, Alexandra decided she would simply rest. She sat on the snow mound with a thump, and smiled, pretending she was a four-year-old once again, reveling at the sound of snow crunching between her fingers. Those memories would keep her company as her heart froze, six miles still from the final outpost. She was the last of them.

They closed the gate.

SIXTY-SIX

The jackets were gone, the back seat now empty.
Alex returned to the café, where he bought the hottest cup of coffee,
the scenario already playing out in his head.
He smashed the back window with a rock,
dumped the coffee on his neck.
The burns eventually faded, and he bought new jackets,
but at least Mary wouldn't know that Alex forgotten to lock the car.

SIXTY-SEVEN

As he boarded the plane, the call came in.
There was a system failure at launch; the shuttle had exploded.
Jon hesitated before getting on his plane but knew
that if he didn't make it to the launch site,
his absence would bring more attention to the problem.
The sabotage had worked, and the plan was going forward.
His life was locked into a new path. Forever.

SIXTY-EIGHT

The ticket said, "Good for one drink,"
but didn't specify what kind or how much.
Dylann ordered a bucketful of tap water.
The bartender stared at her for a whole minute before taking her ticket.
He said, "You know what's in this?"
She just took the bucket and went next door.
Using the water for the next brew,
Dylann then filled the mayor's coffee-to-go box with Flint's finest.

SIXTY-NINE

The doctor watched in anticipation as the mice
turned the last corner to reach the cheese.
The first mouse grabbed the block, then the second and third.
The doctor watched in amazement as the three
hoisted the cheese over the walls of the maze.
The first mouse stood on its hind legs and shouted,
"We don't enjoy the spice of pepper jack!"
The doctor fainted as the mice skittered away.

SEVENTY

The stone floated among the waves, occasionally dipping below the surface for extended periods when large ships passed by.

One day the stone washed onshore. Three hundred years later a boy picked up the stone and threw it across the waves. The stone skipped six times before coming to a stop, and then floated back out to sea. The stone would remember the rush of that skip for an eternity.

SEVENTY-ONE

Michael waited for the conductor's cue but knew it'd be another six minutes. He had to pee. Badly.

He thought about running offstage, confident he'd be back in time.

But what would it look like to the crowd, the other musicians?

He tried to focus, counting backward from one hundred—

and missed his cue.

But then he didn't feel so guilty about running to the toilet as the band played on.

SEVENTY-TWO

Bobby pushed all his chips forward. He had four large stacks compared to Andrew's three, but the total dollar amount was about even. Bobby would win big or lose huge. This was his last hundred. He had nothing left in the bank and a wife at home worrying that he was about to throw it all away on a nothing hand with only a king, queen, and seven showing.

Bobby bet well.

SEVENTY-THREE

Garland was looking for the perfect pattern. His couch was worn down, and he needed a new design. He snapped a photo of the large woman outside the café. She glared at him.

"Plaid is big today." He smiled at her. She didn't return the sentiment.

"I didn't say you could take a picture."

"It's research."

"What kind?"

"None of your business."

His new pattern would emulate her shirt.

She would never know..

SEVENTY-FOUR

"It's more important to be right than to compromise your beliefs."
To Jackie, that was not the truth, just the company line.
They paid her well as head of PR, working tirelessly at the TOWER,
as it was called. Gold lined the staircases and walls, the entryway
was marble, and a bronze statue of their leader stood at a great height
just inside. Jackie thought it tacky, but she'd never say so out loud.

SEVENTY-FIVE

Jared stood behind the sign and waited. Cars passed without stopping,
and he was glad. He wanted to avoid eye contact, and human contact,
at all costs. This was the most humiliating part of visiting.
No one else thought so.
But consumption was a necessary part of the refugee life.
"Here ya go," said the woman. She held out an apple and a dollar.
Jared hated apples. He tossed it aside.
The dollar tasted magnificent.

SEVENTY-SIX

Their three voices rang out in a gross harmony throughout
the coffee shop, to the minor annoyance of some
and to the utter shock and disappointment of Leo.
He walked straight to their table, disgusted at the shouting Sirens,
and told them—no, yelled at them—to go back where they came from.
Everyone else was in shock, but nobody interrupted as the Sirens screeched
all the way out the door and back to their island.

SEVENTY-SEVEN

Eric had a nightmare in which he was standing in a yard surrounded by
a fence, barbecuing steaks and sausages. His neighbors wandered over to
enjoy some, and people from work also stopped by. At night he drank tea
and watched murder mysteries with his wife while their kids slept, and at
the office on Monday they celebrated two birthdays.
Eric suddenly woke up to his basement apartment
and went out to cash his final unemployment check.

SEVENTY-EIGHT

"No, Tim, you have to hear this. It's a good one."
"A joke?"
"No, this thing that happened this morning. It's hysterical."
"I don't really have time—"
"It'll just take a second. Come on."
"Hang on, I have to go to the bathroom."
"Okay! I'll wait here. Trust me, you don't want to miss this story."
"Great. I can't wait."
Then Tim climbed out the window and went to a movie.
Clare is still waiting by the bathroom.

SEVENTY-NINE

They sat beside each other, him and her, for three weeks without speaking. Every day the subway took them both to and from work. Their homes were separated by only a few doors. Neither of them ever knew it though, and in their dreams they got along fine and stayed married for a lifetime.
By the time he got up the courage to ask her name, she didn't bother to listen. She'd found happiness in loneliness. He moved on.

EIGHTY

Dorothy wasn't afraid to die. In fact, she embraced the unknown.
She fancied herself an adventurer, even though she was in her late seventies, and thought that life was more fulfilling if you took a dive into the deep rather than swim in the shallow end of life's offerings.
Still, when her only grandson came to visit one last time,
Dorothy felt tears well up and wanted to stay a little longer.
She feared not death but the final good-bye.

EIGHTY-ONE

They ran up the stairs, then down, then up again.
Together, over and over. The neighbors wanted to complain,
but how do you complain to a pair of ghosts?
Or ghosts who don't realize they're ghosts?
The super was running out of ways to tell the kids that they were dead,
that they could go anywhere, do what they wanted to do,
but could they please not disturb the rest of the building?
But kids will be freaking kids, I suppose

EIGHTY-TWO

There was a pounding in his head the likes of which Jason had never felt
before, a migraine that dulled his breathing to a crawl and crowded his
vision with white clouds and watery illusions. A fly landed on his hand,
and he didn't have the energy to swat it away. This was time travel.
This was the breaking of numerous dimensions and laws of physics.
And he'd never live to tell the tale.
When Jason woke up, the earth was dying.

EIGHTY-THREE

There is no coffee remaining in the pot. There are only the dregs,
the unwanted coffee grounds that will never be consumed—and rightly so.
In those dregs, Chris sees himself, a guy at the lower end of the
office totem pole. But unlike everyone else in their cubicles,
he sees, among the dregs, the path to a better position.
Right now Chris only needs worry about brewing a new pot
of coffee to fill his boss's mug, and not to spill it.

EIGHTY-FOUR

He looked for the girl around the corner, but she'd already sped away on
her bike. Her tire tracks through the mud told him that
she must have pedaled hard. He wished he could run as fast,
but his leg was still hurting from fighting his brothers the night before.
Petey wandered back into the woods, limped to the hole under the tree.
As a wolf, he felt like there was no respect from humans.
All he'd wanted to do was to play catch.

EIGHTY-FIVE

Marvin stares at the fork on the table.
He is sick to his stomach with hunger,
but dammit if he isn't going to maintain some semblance of civility.
He waves over the waitress, points to his fork.
"That is a disaster. Can I get a new fork?"
She nods, takes the dirty fork away.
Marvin waits, stomach turning, nostrils flaring
with the scent of lettuce, croutons, dressing.
When the waitress comes back, Marvin's face is covered with lettuce.
Chewing the croutons, he mutters, "Too late."

EIGHTY-SIX

Cyrus blocked flashbacks from the night before as he stared at the door leaning off its hinges. He propped it up, noting where the screws had come loose, and then went to the supply closet. He came back with a hammer and nails, and found Betsy waiting outside the door. She explained her feelings as he hammered the hinges into place—her claim that it was just a kiss, that the other, nameless man meant nothing.

Cyrus finished hammering and slammed the door in her face.

EIGHTY-SEVEN

Like a jazz pianist winding down the 88s, Persephone deftly sifted through the files up on the eighty-sixth floor of the Olympia Skyscraper.

She wore headphones and danced to the electronic beat. She had been at it for six hours now, and her legs hadn't yet screamed at her to stop.

She pulled another file, labeled "End of Days," and threw it on the stack, on top of "Apocalypse." None of the gods knew she was here.

That was good. The world would spin that much longer

EIGHTY-EIGHT

Peter tucked in the bookmark at page forty-six, the page of the poem he'd rediscovered after forty years. Climbing out of the taxi, Peter could already hear the music in the school gymnasium.

Forty years since he'd last seen Margaret. He felt he looked the same, plus a few pounds, and hoped it would please her. When he saw how she'd remained the same, he took a deep breath, wet his lips, and walked over to her. After meeting her husband, Peter threw the book in the trash.

EIGHTY-NINE

The sun set. To Bill it was like watching a cup of coffee being dumped out in a sink. The warmth of the day evaporated fast, and the feeling that anything was possible suddenly died.

With the darkness came a sense of fear, an anxiety that flooded Bill such that he could hardly breathe. He didn't sleep a wink, and by morning he was hopeless.

Then the sun rose again, and he steamed coffee and took the first sip of the first day of the rest of his life.

NINETY

Once he crawled to the peak of the hill, Tag could see what came next. Another hill. And there was one beyond that. He could hardly breathe at the sight—or maybe it was the altitude—but Tag knew he had a decision to make. Go back the way he'd come, and admit that he had failed, or keep crawling toward the infinite hills. Tag decided to keep going. He'd have to suffer in either direction, and the reward for making it to the goddess's home would be much greater.

NINETY-ONE

The booming bass of the ship's landing shook Ryland to his core, feeding his migraine. He turned to his bed, took 1,000 mg of pills, downed a tonic, and promised himself he'd shower tomorrow. While he slept, he dreamed of screaming and raging animals scratching at his door and a cat howling in his ears, and within three hours he'd wet the bed. A grown man who peed in his own bed as aliens were invading. He would never have imagined that this would be the newspapers' description of his death.

NINETY-TWO

Belvin and Chester clapped, keeping the beat. A whole minute of clapping while Feltz pounded the drums. Lefty never grew tired of hearing her creations take life. Then Petrov strummed his guitar, almost blowing out the amp. Rainier stood next to it, and the shock of the noise threw her bass line half a beat off. But the delay added a texture that became a signature of the song, and the engineers, Skaggs and Wilton, pumped their fists with delight. Lefty knew, right then, that she had another hit on the books.

NINETY-THREE

Their eyes did not meet as they walked past each other in the hall. It would be the last time they'd be around each other in silence. In a few minutes, they'd be outside, in front of the world, and told to yell at each other, and scream, hoping to get the loudest applause. The louder the clapping, the longer their families could eat. By nightfall, both had collapsed in their corners. Neither awoke. But their families shared every meal from that day forward. They just couldn't look one another in the eyes.

NINETY-FOUR

Steven followed all the rules. He didn't stand up until it was his turn. He didn't use his phone as the plane taxied toward the gate. He went to the bathroom only when the seat belt sign clicked off. Heck, he didn't even bother putting his tray down or leaning his seat back during the flight; he just slept sitting straight up. But when the plane landed, and Steven finally stood to stretch his legs, he broke the rules just once to make the call: "Ma!" he shouted. "I made it. I'm finally home!"

NINETY-FIVE

The coin wasn't small, wasn't large. It was exactly the size it was supposed to be. Jordan flipped it as though it were boiling, and when it landed on heads she recoiled in fright.

"This is wrong," she cried. "It's all wrong. Who brought this?"

"You insisted," the priests all shouted. "There were no objections.
You cannot back down from this. It is finished."

Jordan collapsed and they carried her out, toward the volcano.

The heat was unbearable but would not last long.

On the way down, she whispered, "Should've asked for best of three."

NINETY-SIX

Mickey's fingertips were bleeding, but that's how he knew it'd been a good night. Even watching the janitor sweep up the remnants of his guitar gave Mickey a pleasurable chill, the kind of sensation he hadn't felt in years on the road. He looked around at the straggling clientele at Stubbs', the trickle of drunk baby boomers stumbling out, waving at him, thanking him with incoherent yells. Mickey wanted to weep, but instead gulped the beer in his hand. His wrist was just a little sore. He just couldn't wait to sing again for the world.

NINETY-SEVEN

The heater spurred to life, clicking and clacking as though a dozen tiny creatures with long toenails were trying to kick their way through the vents. Foster held himself under the covers. The nightmare was still vivid. He'd dreamed that he and a girl—her face already fading away—
were racing to the bottom of a cave. Foster suddenly froze,
and when his body fell and shattered was when he woke up.

His bedroom window was broken. A dead owl lay at the foot of his bed.

Foster avoided ice cream before bed from that moment on.

NINETY-EIGHT

The snooze button is much too close to the off button.
So sad.
Who builds these machines?
Is the sandman himself the inventor of the snooze button?
Mama says snoozing is a lost art, though, and lectures us to
do it more often, to be alert and asleep at the same time.
She says we're living but not quite alive.
That's how we should be all the time.
I suppose, maybe, she's right.
In other news, the clocks have stopped working again.
Time is at a standstill, and so we wait, and listen, in the dark.
And snooze..

NINETY-NINE

Every cloud is more lofty, every raindrop more full of life, every breeze more free, when you're here. It's not a great loss to the world if I should meet my untimely demise, but don't give up on yourself just yet. If you only manage to smile at something good, then, like the flapping of a butterfly's wings, hundreds of miles away there will be a small change in happiness: a life at a fork in the road will venture to paths unknown but good. Be that good for someone else, and you will soon feel it in return.

ONE HUNDRED

The typewriter ran out of ink, but Lenny didn't notice.
He just wanted to tell his story, wanted her to know
he'd be waiting for her return.
When he finished typing, he didn't read over the letter
but simply locked it up with wax and a seal, like they did ages ago,
and put it in an envelope and mailed it off to her.
He knew she still lived in their hometown
and hoped she'd smile after reading.
She opened the letter and read aloud, "Dear Sara, I want you to know . . ."
but the rest of the page was blank.

SENTENCES

A collection of words creates, eventually, a sentence.
A sentence brings our thoughts to life,
give added purpose to the words within, and yet every
word inside that sentence requires a thought behind it,
a meaning, a reason for being there.
A sentence can be short, and to the point.
Or a sentence can be elaborate, long,
winding, twisting, bringing you to a sudden conclusion
and when you least expect it BAM!
The sentence finishes everything and before you know it,
you're on to something new.
When you string together a series of words,
each with a purpose, you bring the reader to a new place,
a new setting, unexpected reality.
Sentences can be whatever you want them to be,
the only rule is that they have to SAY something.

Preferably with words.

Unless you are a computer.

ONE

All the books are gone, and in under an hour too!

TWO

After years stuck in solitary, she finally dug her way out. The guards were puzzled as to her escape, but if they'd bothered to look hard enough they would have found the tiny shovel stuck between the cinder blocks.

THREE

He fell. Not only did he break his spine but the fall offered up a menagerie of scenes from his life that, in those last moments, offered only disappointment. There was no one to weep for him.

FOUR

He grew obsessed, over time, and worked up a plan to cut off her hair. Scissors, clippers, a brush, even a broom and dust bin to collect it all.

Nothing would stand in his way, nothing would take away the meal he had coming. Hair, after all, was the only sustenance the creature had ever known.

FIVE

We move up the river at a breakneck pace. The boat barely holds together against strings of dead plant life. Shouting is thrown at us from the shores, hard to ignore. Harder still is dodging the arrows and spears, and when one finally strikes my son's shoulder, the only shout I can hear is my own. I lie beside him as our boat falls apart, and his dying eyes are the last I ever see.

SIX

Despite the knocking, no one was at the door when Lou swung it open. He shut it quick, throwing the bolt, and walked back to his desk. The letter he'd written to Alice lay open, still without a final admission of how he'd betrayed her and allowed this disastrous end to their studies. He thought back to when she'd run off, her disgust at his prayers to the monsters that would soon be unleashed, the horrors that were still then unseen.

He turned to finish the letter, but the loud KNOCK-KNOCK-KNOCK caused him to jump and knock over both candle and ink, leaving him in utter darkness. The door suddenly smashed open, and the swirling snow was the last of earth Lansing would ever see.

SEVEN

Franny had plans for days, for weeks, because the voices knew everything she had to do, and when, and she had written it all down.

One never saw Franny without her little notebook full of sketches, outlines, and notes related to upcoming plans, words hastily written to keep up, no doubt, with the calculations constantly spoken in her mind.

Whenever she'd finish a task, she'd tear out the page and eat the paper, forever consuming and finishing the plans she'd set forth to complete.

Her life was a constant stream of calculation and completion, down to the smallest detail of riding a certain bus, at a certain time, and eating a very mathematically accurate bag of peanuts from the peanut vendor on whatever corner she'd worked out as the best corner, at the best time, for the best nut, on any given day.

On this particular day, she was to meet "Cary" at the café on the corner of Seventh and Mustang, by the park, so Franny set out on the path she'd chosen, which included an alley behind a neighborhood bar, skirting along the outside of Evergreen Park, and hopping the number 74 bus line for one-quarter mile only to pull the emergency stop lever, forcing the bus to halt between usual stops six and seven.

Cary was already waiting inside the café, box in hand, and Franny simply handed over the cash for a smooth exchange.

She then went to the cemetery and tore off the next page of her notebook, chewed the paper casually, and swallowed, at which point she pulled the gun from the box and eliminated the voices in her head, leaving behind a notebook of empty pages.

EIGHT

We settled this planet for a new start.
Do not allow your fears to take over.
As one, we will unite against the galaxy.
But first we must settle our differences.
Those who breathe air should fly high above.
Land dwellers need to stay close to the caves.
If you are neither, find your own homes.
You are equipped for better things to come.

NINE

We went on our first date when we were just kids. We were basically married from that moment on, lives tied together no matter what.

I'd say that we were always happy, but it was mainly me who stayed happy. She knew how to get under my skin and how to dig deep enough that it only hurt a little bit.

People used to say we were basically one and the same, but they don't know how wrong they were. They based movies and stories on us, epics and adventures that weren't true but should've been, if we'd had more time together. None of them were scary stories, and people soon forgot about me. I didn't have time to forget, since she killed me so fast.

But she remembers the truth for both of us now.

TEN

Halfway between blocks there is a house with no life. Shuttered windows, no lights, no cars, no doors, no bugs, no bees, no wasps, no ants, and no roof. Inside is just as empty and bitter, and lonely, and still.

But then the Caspersons move in, and life takes on a new meaning. They build a new room, extending the house, and put in a new roof and new windows and a door that is always open and welcoming.

They bring their dog and two cats, who are always playing in the yard. I think they'll soon bring a kid and be a family, but they lost their daughter years ago in an accident, and that's okay because the neighborhood kids start to call them "mom and dad" and I think they like it.

You can create a new life in a house of emptiness, a shell waiting to be overtaken and replenished. I don't think I'd be the man I am today without the Caspersons' influence. Hope to see you at the Casperson Estates Ribbon-Cutting Ceremony this Friday at 11:00 a.m.

ELEVEN

Melissa opened her door without looking, and that's why the man died.

To be fair, he was zipping down the street pretty fast for a dude without a helmet.

When she saw his body bent and face bleeding on the pavement, she almost screamed. Then she caught herself and looked around, but no one was near. So she took action, pulled up the man's body, and stuffed him into her car's backseat. Not the trunk, the trunk would be too obvious.

Dusk was settling into darkness, so Melissa tossed his bicycle behind the next car and then pulled away from the curb, drove the two blocks toward her apartment building, and re-parked right outside.

She walked to her door, and as she reached for her keys a small cough tickled the hairs on the back of her neck. Melissa's shoulders tensed as she whipped around, but no one stood behind her except the streetlights.

Deep blackness encroached toward her as the bulbs flickered off, burning out, and she held her breath for a sign, something to reveal itself or be heard.

The soft gray fog of breath puffed out as someone approached out of the darkness behind a bloody outstretched hand reaching for Melissa's neck to stop her screaming.

TWELVE

"Hello," said Mark, and he didn't bother to wait for an invite before brushing past Ophelia straight to her dinner table.

"Hi, um, maybe you want to talk before we eat?"

"Nonsense," he replied, teeth already snapping through a chicken leg while his other hand held a corn cob, "the best way to kick things off is with a full stomach."

She made her way to the table and picked at the lone chicken leg that remained at the center dish, and watched him as he continued to chew—rather grossly—at all the food she had taken hours to prepare.

"So," he managed to spit out, "how did you know Alex?"

And there it was, out in the open, the name of the sweet person who might've introduced them if she were still alive, yet somehow had managed to play matchmaker at her own funeral. "She was my best friend, since we were kids—"

Then Ophelia felt it, that warm bug in the back of her throat as the tears threatened to break. "You know, it's still sad to think about her, so let's talk about, I don't know, the food. How is the food?"

Mark smiled, spinach stuck between his teeth, but somehow still charming: "I agree, and maybe we got off on the wrong foot, so let's change gears and talk about how delicious this food is!"

Ophelia managed a small chuckle, the first of many for the evening.

THIRTEEN

Starting at the bottom of his list, with the easy stuff, Chuck could accomplish more things, quicker than ever before.

First he cleaned his house top to bottom, then organized his books, then burned his expired food in the appropriate metal bin in the backyard.

"Always keep the easy things for last," is what his mother taught him, but clearly she was wrong. Working his way up the list, Chuck found himself growing more energized as tasks became more complex.

He cleaned out his car's engine and rebuilt the valves, which took him the better part of two days, but at the end of that job his car was faster, and he felt his knowledge base had grown by a few bytes. Which was a good thing, since the next few items would be particularly tricky.

Utilizing all his knowledge, Chuck spent three weeks meticulously measuring his magnetic-atomic Collider and doling out particles along the structure. The three weeks flew by in a matter of seconds, and Chuck suddenly blinked his way to a reset.

He was pleased since, while powered down, Chuck could reorganize his knowledge cells, defrag crowded areas, and then start fresh for the final two tasks.

When Chuck awoke, the Collider was missing, as was the jet engine.

He smelled expired food as he shuffled through his house, and found his car to be much slower than ever before. So Chuck made a list and decided to start at the top this time, like his mother said, addressing the more complicated tasks.

First he cleaned his house.

FOURTEEN

The voices, they won't stop.

Louder and louder, they shout in my head and near my ears, coaxing chills down my spine as they hiss and whisper and shout and scream. I don't know when they'll stop or what they want, but they only seem to want to yell at me.

This morning I read two books before I had to snip all the wires of electronics in my home. The phone, the Internet, even the lights and the pipes under the sink, all snipped.

I walk in water up to my ankles, afraid that if I walk near a window, I'll see the horrid face behind the voices. And if I walk outside, I'll be consumed by the owner of the voice and his powerful army of angry, rotted, foul champions.

I'd like to live a life of silence and solitude, but the fields of quiet are far away.

My eyes were shut for three seconds before the voices boomed from above and thundered from below. This time there were footsteps on the roof to remind me that they're more than noises, more than voices in the night.

They are creatures too, unfriendly and insane, and they're waiting for me to leave.

But I cannot leave, and I cannot stay, so I must send for help. I have one friend remaining, and he watches my home every night through the fog.

Tonight I light my final bundle of books and my roof and my home, and hope that my friend finds me among the voices of hate and viciousness.

FIFTEEN

Billy told the girl that she was the most beautiful girl in the world.

Room! He meant to say "room." But Gloria heard "world" because Billy said "world," and that's all that mattered.

It meant the world to her.

To Billy, the world would no longer be uncertain, but it would instead be unlikable.

They got married and spent their lives together. Two children, a dog, two cats, a house, a fence, a yard, a grill, but only ever one car. She was beautiful throughout, no matter what room they entered.

But out in the world, she remained plain and simple and Billy only ever felt "happy enough" with her. Not that Gloria loved him at all anymore, after so many years.

She no longer felt like the most beautiful girl in the world, but she was at peace with this. What made her feel more upset was the idea that Billy saved his looks of love, his passionate gaze, for those few times when they were together in a crowded room, like he had to force his eyes on her just so as not to be distracted. So she would storm away and he would chase her and they would make love on those few nights each year, and then go back to wondering why they'd spent their lives together.

They lived happy enough ever after.

SIXTEEN

Donald and Tim had been friends for nearly forty years, since they'd started working together. Both worked administration, but it was the important kind of "keeping things running" administration, not the silly "just here to file shit" administration. Their wives knew each other, though they were not too close.

For forty years they shared summers and grilling together, camped together, smoked cigars together, and waded into the Atlantic Ocean together. When Donald and his wife, Patricia, moved down south, they all stayed in touch with the various card in the mail, the random gift basket, and of course the occasional joke gift of gummy penises once every few months.

Donald was a joker, and Tim loved him for it. Tim received a bag of these joke penises in the mail one winter afternoon, and added them to his collection of stale candy.

Six months later he received what he thought was a joke email from Patricia, who rarely talked directly to Tim. The subject read "LEAVE US ALONE" and the body had only one sentence reading "and don't try to call, we are fine."

Tim thought this odd, being that no animosity had grown between them; it had just been the usual downtime a friendship goes through now and again. He had even called an acquaintance down south, someone who also knew Donald, to knock on Donald's door to make sure all was okay. He never heard from the acquaintance again, and now there was this note, this oddly worded, blunt, and, frankly, rude note: "LEAVE US ALONE." A forty-year friendship seemingly tossed down the toilet for a mysterious reason.

Tim hoped that Donald was okay, and this was all a misunderstanding. He thought about calling again or hopping a plane, but then realized that, in time, trust would come again.

All he had to do was keep checking the mail.

SEVENTEEN

The bells rang at midnight for the first time in seventeen years. Yont knew this, exactly, because the last time the bells rang was when his daughter, Clara, was born.

Clara, beautiful as the sun is bright, and twice as smart as any of her peers.

She was touched, some said, by Heaven and the gods and the blessings of a thousand souls from Paradise, to help the kingdoms find peace.

Yont did not believe this, because Paradise to him was a scar on the minds of the young and a false flag for the sick and the poor.

When she was young, Clara helped guide the children through the pastures and found a new way to bring peace to the three kingdoms. Her crown, on the day they made her queen at the young age of fourteen, was a triangular symbol of hope, and her face betrayed none of her true loyalties.

Yont was exceptionally skilled as a soldier, and a bright farmer on his own, but on the night of his daughter's ascension, he did his duty for his kingdom and his new queen and killed the lords of the two other kingdoms. The country was united together, and Clara ruled peacefully for three years.

Then the plague came, and the same farmers and workers and clerics who had declared Clara a blessed person condemned her, called her a demon and a soldier from hell.

There was no stopping the rush on the castle walls, and, try as he might, Yont could not hold back the throngs of people who overtook the walls, the yard, the throne room.

Eventually, covered in blood and sweat and the thunderous rain from above, the heathens strung up his daughter's body in a horrid act of sacrifice. Yont himself was thrown in a dungeon.

He was convicted as perpetrator to the crimes of his daughter and made to suffer the rest of his life knowing he'd outlived his offspring—a fate, some say, worse than death.

The bells tolling at midnight were meant to signal the dawn of a new era in the kingdom, of prosperity and plentiful crops.

For Yont they meant the end of living. He yearned for Paradise to find him soon.

EIGHTEEN

There was a chill in the air, like ice was being chipped into the breeze, but for Jesse, that cold feeling started when he set his heart on killing a man. Not that he couldn't still get out of the situation. All he would lose was the love of Elsie, who would remain married to John, the brutish asshole she called her "unloving husband."

Sitting on the first-floor roof, staring into the window of the Van Rensselaer den, Jesse saw plenty of other options around him. For one thing, John wasn't home yet. That meant Jesse could climb inside, right now, take off his shoes, and sit by the fire.

Or he could leap from the roof, run back into the city, and enjoy a pint at Strait's Tavern while Officer Royley paced nearby, eyes glued on suspicious activities.

Third, Jesse had the option of simply climbing down, returning to his small bedroom, and falling asleep at the late hour.

He even thought of running away, taking the train east to Boston, but shook that notion out of his head completely, realizing the thought came to mind only because he'd heard the train whistle. Besides, that would raise too much suspicion, and he'd be forced to change his name again.

He thought, as he often did, of his wife, Alice, and what she and their children were doing in Buffalo, how they had fared since he left all those months ago. The memories of the pitter-patter of his children's feet on the porch blended with the footsteps of John and another man as they climbed the stairs and wandered into the den.

Jesse shook himself out of his memories to focus on the view inside: an unexpected guest, Abraham, was seated facing the window, attention buried on his pipe, while John set the chessboard, back to Jesse. Two deep breaths later, Jesse felt—heard; was knocked backward by—the BANG of his rifle and tumbled to the ground, twisting his ankle in the process.

He stumbled, crawled, then took to a jog to the riverbed and threw his rifle into the river, vomiting while the image of John's head exploding flashed through his mind.

Jesse ran as hard as he could, away from Elsie's screams of terror tied to relief, through the forest, and into Strait's Tavern, at which point he sat on a stool and drank the nearest pint, and another, and another, until the shouts flooded around him: "John Whipple's been shot!"

With a wild step, Jesse spun around, raised his pint glass, and, smiling, said, "I'll be damned." Then he passed out, his last night as a free man.

NINETEEN

The tea burned her lips, but Gina wasn't worried about it, as, after all, the good taste was what mattered. Life's simple pleasures, usually hard to find, had finally managed to reach her. Food, drink, kisses, nothing meant more than the taste, and good taste had been hard to find in life.

A raunchy, raw smell was perhaps the worst, one that reminded her of the garbage can she grew up beside as a young girl. But if the final product ended up tasting like a salted pretzel, with the texture of a gummy bear, then what did the smell have to do with it, anyway?

She waited for the burning to die down, then sipped the tea again.

Across the table, Gina's brother, Sam, stared at her. Sam had a look in his eyes teetering on the fence between pity and hatred, and Gina couldn't figure out where the hate came from. Gina did not have a hateful bone in her aching body. Sixty years on this planet, in this city, with barely any memory of their parents or even Sam's existence.

But Sam was the mayor now. He'd admitted that the photos of her in the paper had scared him, enough to come and see her, give her some money.

Good.

Gina had spent her last dime on that photographer, and the idea that this tea would be the first of many good-tasting things to come her way gave her a chuckle.

Sam frowned and asked, "You find this funny, then?"

"Sam, all I'm laughing at is your inability to appreciate an opportunity. Now, smile for the cameras, won't you?"

She raised her mug and smiled at the reporters outside, and after a few seconds, so did Sam.

"Give them a taste of all the good that is to come," she whispered, sipping the rest of her tea.

TWENTY

One day without a hitch—that was all Regina thought about, her mantra, as she descended all five flights of stairs to the sidewalk. She'd gone through her morning routine as usual: cereal, shower, hair flattened, teeth brushed, lotion applied to her face, shoelaces double knotted.

How else could she be expected to be taken seriously if the spirits thought she looked like a mess?

At the usual stop she climbed off the bus and made her way to her shop's back door, down the dank alley she shared with the butcher. She walked through the back room without a hitch—which should have made her feel better, but she instead took to mean something ominous was afoot.

The hook fell from the wall as soon as Regina placed her coat on it, and the soft sound of the coat crumpling to the ground startled her, even though she'd watched it fall.

The lights to the shop suddenly flickered on and off as the walls began to shake. Regina pulled out the remote, deciding now was as good a time as any, and pushed the button.

A sudden flame sparked out of nothingness and struck the ceiling sprinklers—washing Regina's bookshop in water and leaving her drenched in disappointment at her failed homemade bomb.

It took two weeks to dry out the shop, and another to restock her inventory.

No matter what she tried, be it dressing to impress or burning her shop down, the spirits never allowed Regina to give up her post.

Even if she had, in fact, moved in before they ever did.

She didn't care how many people had jumped off the roof and spattered to the sidewalk or cut themselves bloody in the bathtub on the third floor.

This would always be her building, her bookshop, and she should be allowed to run it as she pleased, not at the behest of superstitious spirits.

At her shop's grand reopening—the giant sign posted at the insistence of the spirits—Regina had more than two dozen customers, some enthusiasts, others curious, and just a handful of actual readers.

No matter their reasons, Regina felt happy to have the company and the business, which felt genuine for a change. Perhaps she could find a way to coexist with these spirits after all?

As the thought came to mind, she watched as a bright green waft of a spirit held on to the backpack of a young woman, obviously a student, and followed her out of the shop.

The woman would be dead within a week, but Regina didn't blame herself. Being in charge of Death's transit center was a thankless task that could never be surrendered, so she'd have to stay complacent . . . for now.

TWENTY-ONE

Maria stood in front of the double doors, arms spread as wide as her little frame would allow, shouting, yet again, "Sorry, no entry just yet."

The swarm of moviegoers stared at her; some shouted from the back, "Why the hell not?" while others crossed their arms and glared.

A bald man in the front of the line said, "I'm gonna ask for my money back. This is an absurd festival." To Maria he looked like an angry-all-the-time type of guy.

"That's not my department."

"Don't talk to me that way," he said, aiming his finger at her face.

"You mean, like an adult?" Over the headset, Maria heard Alice's call for a medic to the projection booth.

"Is Ian okay?" No answer. "Alice, is Ian okay?"

"Ian is . . . well, Maria, just stay downstairs, okay?" Maria threw down her clipboard and ran to the staircase. She heard the crowd behind her burst through the double doors into the theater, but she didn't care.

Up in the projection booth, Ian was standing by a machine—Maria couldn't tell what it was—with his back to the door. Alice stopped her. "What are you doing up here?!"

Maria said, "Ian, are you—" Then she saw it. "Not again!"

"It's not stuck—I mean, not really. Maria, I love you!"

TWENTY-TWO

You should all know this, whether you read this now or in a hundred years: there is no way I'll ever let go of this rope. Just because you tell me it's safe to fall doesn't mean I'll happily tumble down three miles into nothingness.

It's a joke, really.

Did you hear about the guy who lost his teeth after drinking a beer? No one else lost their teeth after a beer, so how did he lose his teeth?

A punch in the face, because he drank someone else's beer.

Simple, and stupid.

So why am I holding on to this rope?

Let's set the mood: I'm dangling over the edge of a cliff. The ground is mostly dirt with some larger chunks of gravel. There's a weed to my left, some kind of bushy thing with only a few leaves on it, barely blowing in the breeze. It's calm now but wasn't earlier. Thus, the rope that's now holding me over the edge of this cliff.

The sky is overcast, and darkening. Night is falling soon, but I still won't let go of this rope. I have it tied around my waist, and the other end is stretching for miles across the land and into the sky above, and I can't see the end of it.

Everything on this planet was wonderful when we came to it, but after our fuel cell exploded and destroyed almost all of it, except our rocket, everything became nothing.

I hesitate to look down. I don't think my partner is even holding on anymore, but I'll continue to hold on. If he climbs up, we'll keep all our teeth for the short time we have remaining. If he doesn't, then it'll just feel like I've downed my last beer, and I'll just have to try to enjoy myself.

Either way, I won't let go of this rope.

TWENTY-THREE

The three women ran inside the vault ahead of the slamming door.

Then the door sealed shut. They were stuck inside.

Mary was pleased. Everything was going exactly according to her plan. She high-fived Cassandra, who just smiled, rolled her eyes, and began piling money into her bag. She in turn tossed another bag to Mitsy, who was quiet and remained focused on her task. She didn't like high fives, and Mary knew it. Mary tried to offer up a friendly smile to Mitsy, but Mitsy was anything but friendly.

They each finished filling their bag, and Mary pulled out a complex, homemade remote. The others looked at her, curious, unaware of the plan. But everything had gone swimmingly so far. She pushed a button on her remote, rocking the room and sounding the alarm. The corner of the ceiling collapsed, offering them their tunnel out.

Cassandra launched her bag up through the hole, then hopped through it using Mary's hands as a boost. She then reached down and snagged Mitsy's bag, then proceeded to lift Mitsy, who was the lightest of the three.

Mary took one last look around the vault and tossed up her bag. A second BOOM shook the room, and a portion of the ceiling collapsed on top of her, knocking her cold. Cassandra and Mitsy smiled at each other, and Mitsy tossed the remote down before crawling up through the tunnel and away.

Mary, under two feet of dirt and metal, awoke to the sounds of footsteps and police radios squawking. She tried to scream, but when she opened her mouth dirt flooded into her throat, choking off her voice.

In the morning, when the police finally sifted through the rubble and empty safety-deposit boxes, Mary's body was found, eyes open and packed with dirt, mouth spewing mud and metal, and her fingers finally loosening their grip on another remote.

Twelve officers were lost in that moment, thus drawing attention from another, now infamous robbery, over at the Third Coastal Bank of Virginia, for which the main suspects, Cassandra and Mitsy, remain at large.

TWENTY-FOUR

Alexander kept coughing and coughing so loud, I decided I should do something about the noise. When they're outside your door, you must remain quiet. It's for your own safety.

After I smothered Alexander, I took only a few seconds to pray. If you pray too long, they'll find you. My father told me they can sense it.

I didn't know Alexander but a few months, so when it came time to leave the room I just left his body there and shut the door. I don't know why I shut the door, since they don't come after dead people; they just burn them. I figured, though, that if they did happen to walk by at a moment in the very near future, perhaps they would investigate and find my scent, and then they would find me.

Wouldn't be the first time.

I walked several hundred yards down the road, passing shack after shack, a few two-room huts and even fewer teepees. No one used the teepees anymore, except the reckless daredevil freaks.

When I was younger, my father was a daredevil. It hurt at night when our neighbors would lift our teepee flats and visit me while he was away. I told my father about these nightly visits years later as I pushed my hammer over his windpipe and smashed out his last breath. He may have heard me, but I don't care.

Farther down the road, I finally reached the Villa, and sure enough the gate was wide open, blown apart by the last invasion that I'd heard about weeks before.

Grabbing my gun, my staff, and my small bag of peaches hidden just under the guard tower, I proceeded to the path through the woods to the small guard shack, gently covered with leaves and branches many nights ago.

I'll wait another night to see who may be left inside the Villa, but Alexander had told me there were still some "good people" left in the world. The Villa was Alexander's idea. I trusted him about as much as I'd trust a "good" person, and thought as much as I sharpened the end of my staff.

There's a guy named Nick who told Alexander he thought I was cute, so Nick is my target. Tomorrow.

For now I wait silently.

TWENTY-FIVE

To Hal, the coffee tasted like dusty, drab earth.

His tongue could not forget that flavor, familiar since childhood, when his brother would shove his face into the ground during tackle football and not let him up to breathe for years and years. Hal was sure he still had dirt in his lungs, in his stomach, throughout his body. He coughed. No dirt came out.

Despite the coffee's taste, it was warm and necessary on this blustery morning. Wearing pj's and a robe, he shuffled over to the top of the driveway and watched the plows roll through his desolate neighborhood, snow piles blooming higher, drifts exploding in the morning wind.

None of the other houses had residents to stand outside. They were all filled with young families and children who would wait until the afternoon sunshine to come outside and play. No school today.

The days of shoveling and building forts and ice weaponry were long in Hal's past, but those memories provided him some small, warm comfort this morning.

When he'd awoken to the news that Steve had died, Hal just hugged himself and didn't say a word. He hung up on Alice and that was that. He'd have to apologize to her, maybe at the wake. They'd reached the age where this was going to happen more and more. Just like his twenties, when friends were getting married, or his thirties, when friends were having babies, or his sixties, when friends were retiring.

Time would never stop, and neither would its habits.

Hal finished his coffee and went inside to sit by the fireplace and warm his hands. The next few days would be sad, but emotions would remain easy. He'd have to comfort Alice, remind her of the good old days and the fact that she and Steve had been high-school sweethearts. She probably hadn't forgotten, but sometimes reminders helped. Then he'd have to find a way to make it to the funeral amid all the snow, and then buy a nice gift for her and put on his suit again, his tailored suit that he wore more with each passing year.

Hal looked forward to the day when he could buy a new suit and actually wear it, to feel presentable, like he'd actually made it in his life.

Eventually he did wear a new suit.

And the earth tasted like earth.

TWENTY-SIX

Grandma brought the two hot coffees to the small table in the corner of the café where her grandson sat, staring at his book.

"Why don't you read it?"

"I don't wanna start it while we're still having coffee."

"That's nice of you, to spend your time with me instead."

He nodded as she handed him his coffee, his favorite: spiced Viennese with whipped cream and cinnamon on top.

"Are you trying out for any sports this year?"

"I ran a little for track but kept spraining my ankle, so whatever."

"I never played sports when I was young; I didn't even finish high school."

"How did you get a job?"

"I just asked who needed help. Like my job here—I just walked in and said hello, and they hired me."

"But you've come to this café for, like, years, so they know you. I don't know anybody."

"You'll meet people—give it time."

"I don't like the people I have met so far."

She too disliked a lot of the people she met, no matter where, what age, what was happening. People, to her, were the worst. "Some people are bad, but if you give them a chance, just one chance, even, then they might surprise you."

"Anyone ever really surprise you?"

"Your grandfather."

"How come he's not around?"

"He would want to be, he'd want to know you, I'm sure of that." She smiled, a feeling that was unfamiliar after many, many years. "You both knew how to make fools of yourselves."

Her grandson stared at her, and she leaned forward wipe the whip cream from his lip. He let out a laugh, and they sipped together—both allowing the whip cream to stay on their lips.

TWENTY-SEVEN

They began the drive at dawn, just as planned. Winds tried to blow the car from the road, but Stella was an expert driver. Tom always made a point to tell her, every few miles or so, but Stella didn't need him to remind her.

She knew.

Tom took note that she constantly checked the rearview mirror and he asked her about it. The answer, to her, was obvious. She wanted to remember.

Tom insisted they were leaving behind a bunch of crap, the past should be forgotten, and so on.

But the fires, laying waste to everything behind them, why would anyone want to forget that? There were things worth looking forward to: the seas, the ships, the distant shores that would provide a haven from the toxins and poisons. But to Stella there were also things worth remembering: the reason for leaving, the reminder of what's important, the burning engine behind their reason to drive as far and as fast as they could.

Tom and Stella didn't blame each other, but since there was no one else to blame, the trip was tough. They fought, and they bickered. They traded off driving over the next three days.

Whenever Stella would awaken, she blamed Tom for losing ground. But eventually they made it to the distant shore, and as the ship sailed out to sea, Stella looked back at the burning land they were now leaving.

Tom insisted they take to the bar for a drink, and Stella watched him knock back beverage after beverage in the crowded room, reveling with other people, happy to be leaving. But her attention was drawn to the rear of the ship, where the skies behind them blended blue smoke with fresh air.

That first night on the ship, Stella and Tom argued and argued, he dressed in a new jumpsuit, she still in her rags. He stormed out at one point, when she shouted their son's name. She couldn't blame him for his sudden anger, but she didn't want to let go just yet.

So she changed into her jumpsuit, in the hopes of reconciling and starting fresh. Going forward, she would keep her memories to herself.

But Tom had bought a bottle, kept drinking, and eventually passed out, falling over the railing and splashing down to the waters below.

Stella watched it happen but didn't try to shout. Instead she turned her gaze back to the horizon behind them and the stars above. She took a deep breath, then turned to face the future.

TWENTY-EIGHT

There was a huff, and a puff, and the walls shook and Petey held his head in his hands, bent over and curled into as small a ball as he could make with his tiny, fat body.

The shimmying walls soon became still, and the sound of the wind died.

Petey slowly looked up just as a shadow passed by the window. He cowered lower, even though he knew Wally couldn't see inside.

Back when Petey lived with his brother Paul, the house was unstable. It was weak, made of shoddy craftsmanship, and didn't stick together very well. Funny, because Paul had been the best builder of them all.

Even better than poor Benny. Wally's first victim. Though Benny could blend in, his twisted tail was instantly recognizable, and betrayed him one time too many.

Paul always laughed about it, though Petey believed his laughter was more out of anxiety than thinking the situation was funny. Ever since Paul was pulled through their destroyed house and swallowed whole by Wally, Petey couldn't find a reason to laugh. He still had a tough time taking a joke even now, two years later.

His new home had been reinforced with thick wood, prime cuts of all the trees in the forest. Pat, their oldest brother, lived miles away in a stone cave he'd discovered just after the destruction of Paul's hut. No chances, that was Pat's motto.

Take no chances, live forever.

"Ha, forever, now that's a laugh," thought Petey, even as he realized it might be best to call on Pat to make sure Wally hadn't come looking for him.

The phone rang for an hour before Pat picked up. Petey gave a sigh of relief but instantly clammed up when Pat insisted he come right over. "Wally's heading east for the winter. You have time to get here safely."

Petey knew that his brother wouldn't suggest such a thing unless he actually meant it. In all their years, from litter to adulthood, Pat never hesitated to protect his brothers and wouldn't take chances on their well-being.

Petey tied his red cape around his neck, packed as much as he could for the daylong journey, and stepped into the world to see his brother and live without fear for the first time in his life. As he took off down the forest path, he looked back at his shack, for the first time noticing it was leaning over and falling apart where the wood beams used to be nailed together. Another huff and puff from Wally the Wolf, and he would've become a mighty filling dinner.

Good thing ol' reliable Pat had insisted Petey come to his home, for safety's sake!

Petey smiled at the thought of hiding with his brother through the winter as Wally sprang from the cave with hungry eyes and blood on his teeth.

TWENTY-NINE

Four weeks into his resolution, Jack had to give up. The workouts had been brutal, and he was already fifty pounds lighter, but his mind was getting cloudy. Too many days he'd woken up starving; too many nights he'd fallen asleep in a pool of his own sweat. The vomiting didn't help, and neither did the tasteless cardboard avocados that had served as his only meals.

His heart had started to protrude out of his chest, it felt like, and every beat boomed throughout the world. He'd look in the mirror and see a human piece of straw, ready to keel over at the first breeze. Calling in sick to work this past week, Jack knew it was close to quitting time for his resolution.

"Lose a hundred pounds this year." Why did he push that button?

He'd meant to keep searching for ten pounds, just ten. One involuntary muscle spasm in his finger had led to an incorrect click on the mouse and signed him up for the 100 Pound Program.

Jack hadn't even really want to lose weight; he just didn't have enough points to choose a different resolution. Nothing in his life was very negative at the turn of the year. His job treated him well, his fiancée was happily planning their wedding. Even his hobbies had increased in their fun factors, and taking up archery for last year's resolution had made him a happy man. All of this had kept his point count stable, up until the subtracted amount for violating the parking restrictions.

Jack woke at the start of the tenth week of the program with fifty pounds still to lose, as the scanner whistle reminded him. But unless he were to crunch up and destroy all of his bones, he wasn't sure where the weight would come from.

His eyes were large, sunken holes at the front of his skeletal face, his head reminding him of an alien from old comic books: bald, with skin stretched to the limits over his skull.

His fingernails had fallen off in week six, his toenails soon after. He'd even tried to cut off his toes, but after he chopped off the first he realized he would lose only ounces toward the program—hardly enough.

The scanner never lied.

As the treadmill revved to life, Jack pushed the "quit" button. The rubber track halted and the red lights flashed. He could barely hear it amid the sense of relief echoing inside his head.

"YOU HAVE FAILED."

The voice came from booming, static-filled speakers at maximum volume. Food was handed to him from the robotic arm at the edge of the scanner, and Jack smiled as he scarfed down a piece of his wedding cake.

The smile stayed on his face despite the poison, and he imagined how lovely it would've been to enjoy such a delicious cake at his actual wedding.

THIRTY

Marv pulled the string taut while Joanie applied tape to the far end, sticking it to the wall.

"That should do it," Marv said, standing and admiring his work.

They were at the top of the stairs, a flight of eight, and across the top step Marv and his sister had taped six pieces of string, tightly, barely discernible against the beige carpet of the living room below.

Joanie said, "Do you think it's enough?"

"I just said it would be."

"What about the pins?" She held out her hand, the tiny pins bouncing back light like slivers of glitter. Mark shook his head.

"Nah, won't need 'em. Besides, they'd hurt too much."

Joanie glanced downstairs through the strings at the Christmas tree, lights blinking in the dark. Their parents had gone to bed a short time ago, but Marv and Joanie put their plan into action fast, flying on anxious determination.

It had started two weeks ago, after Marv had heard some rumors in class. His friends were making fun of him for believing in Santa Claus, a fact that he was proud to own. They all told him, yelled at him, that he was stupid, a moron, and that his parents were the ones who laid out presents every year. "A fat dude climbs down your chimney? Come on, Marv!"

He had come home and cried, and Joanie tried to calm him down and tell him, "Of course Santa's real." But she was younger, so what did she know?

So they plotted and waited for Christmas Eve, and as they walked to their bedrooms upstairs, Marv watched Joanie and smiled a little. If it were true that their parents were the "real" Santa, then Joanie would be strong and maybe she'd be the one to yell at her friends when they grew a little older.

Footsteps shook Marv, and he and Joanie quickly dashed to their separate rooms, each peeking out the doorway. They'd forgotten to turn off the hall light, but it didn't make a difference.

Mom and Dad slipped out of their bedroom together, wiping their eyes and yawning. Dad said, "I'll get the big ones; you stuff their stockings." Mom just nodded and then shrieked as Dad began waving his arms.

The sharp twang of a snapping string vibrated through the air. Dad cried out, "What the hell?!" This was followed by the thump-thump-thump of Dad tumbling down the stairs and the crack of his neck.

Mom didn't stop screaming all night.

THIRTY-ONE

It was a lonely road for Albert. His fat body swayed left and right with each step, and every ten steps he had to wait and rest and gather his senses. His tongue lashed out each time he rested and snatched him a fly.

The flies were everywhere on account of the dead humans scatted about.

Albert was at the same time in Heaven and in Hell. His scaly skin felt warm under the sun, a feeling he enjoyed more and more lately. The asphalt under his toes was hot and spicy, driving him to bounce toe to heel even in his respites.

When he finally reached Lucinda's cave, Albert paused for longer than usual. There were flies everywhere, and he decided to have a snack before heading inside and charming her.

Charming, an action that took him years to perfect no matter who his mate ended up being. For dozens of years, Albert charmed and charmed and charmed, until there were very few females remaining. His heart couldn't stay in one place for long, or with one person, and he'd found it easy to keep moving on, despite his journeys taking longer and longer.

Though moving became tougher as the years went on, due not only to his age but to these expanding roads and cars and humans invading their desert. But then The Big End came, and humans just collapsed, died, and stared vacantly as Albert and his kind took over, walking all about the earth just like things should always have been.

He snacked on some more flies and watched the sun begin its falling arc across the sky. He despised the nighttime, when the temperature became too cold to walk about or too cold to sleep. Nighttime was the only time in which Albert wished for a mate to sleep beside, mainly for the warmth. That's why he had decided to charm Lucinda today.

Lucinda was big, twice Albert's weight and size, and she was also sweet as could be. Albert knew she wouldn't hesitate to allow him first dibs on grub, even though lately there was more than enough to go around.

Albert enjoyed the fly snacks and looked forward to waking up to fly catching from bed the next morning, his head resting on Lucinda's belly as the zipping and zooming dumb flies wandered about overhead, never understanding that all they had to do to survive was fly out of the cave.

Albert and Lucinda had met two weeks prior among the Junkyard Mountains. She'd been on her own, and Albert with his then-mate Astrid. Astrid wasn't very bright and didn't like flies, so her weight and emptiness left Albert wanting more.

He'd bumped into her and her warmth oozed out on top of him in a way he'd never felt before. From that day on, Albert had been determined to find her, but he put on weight first so she could look him in his lizard eye slits and know that he was serious about taking care of her.

Albert waited until dusk, then entered Lucinda's cave. It smelled rotten, of that Albert was certain, but any cave with lizard dung was bound to initially insult the senses. He rounded the corner to another swarm of flies and felt he'd entered Heaven, thinking they wouldn't even have to wait until morning for their feast.

Albert, stomach grumbling, moved quickly to Lucinda's bedding area. The sight of her rotting corpse gave Albert pause, and then he decided to go about dinner before returning to the path toward the Junkyard Mountains, back to Astrid's empty companionship.

THIRTY-TWO

Ian stood watching his brother's touchdown, mouth agape, eyes stinging. He could feel drool dribbling down his chin, and his hands were curled into fists. No one was looking at him, which was good. This episode was like the others, and he didn't want his messy body to distract from Tony's moment.

As soon as the episode was over, Ian collapsed into his chair, wiping his chin. He held his head in his hands, and when his mother touched his shoulder, Ian looked up at her and felt tears streaming down his face.

"Your brother is amazing," she said, not for the first time.

"Sure is," muttered Ian, placing his head back in his hands. He tried not to think of the vision, but for the rest of the night all he could see were the blazing fires around his brother's corpse.

Jesus, Ian thought to himself, why this again?

When they were kids, Ian was always at odds with his older brother, no matter the game, and sibling rivalry made sense. During tag they'd push each other, not just tag each other. In football the rules of two-hand touch didn't matter; it was always tackle between Ian and Tony. Even during breakfast, Tony would smother Ian's bacon and eggs in the dog's food dish, throw it back on his plate, then laugh when their mother, too tired to notice, practically spoon-fed the dish to Ian.

So, being kids, Ian would fantasize about payback, about pushing Tony down a hill, pinning and suffocating him, or force-feeding Tony until he vomited. Once his fantasy became darker, and Ian imagined stripping Tony's skin from his body and burning the rest of him into ash. It was horrifying and creepy.

And at the time, delightful.

But that was also the first time the visions came, pushing Ian into a sort of trance, and when he'd awoken he was horrified and standing on the ledge of his roof. Luckily no one had been around.

But now, in the team Owner's Box, if anyone had seen Ian go into his trance there would be too many questions and his career would be in jeopardy. Perhaps he'd be sent to a doctor and be declared unstable, or worse, unfit for the game.

Ian and his brother were still competitive, sure, but both had been in this same position, in this same championship game, twice before.

They were, simply put, the best of the best. Though he was younger, Ian had retired two years prior, to focus on his family and start his own gardening commune. He rarely spoke with Tony and the rest of the family.

He'd been surprised about the invite to the family's box to watch the big game, but then again, an appearance meant a lot to everyone involved, and his specially tailored Gatorade jacket garnered him five figures.

Not that he needed the cash, but it couldn't hurt.

His mind flickered to the vision of Tony's burning corpse, and Ian shoved it out of view, deciding to stand up and clap instead. He even managed a smile and hugged his mother—who immediately tensed at his grip.

Ian would never stop loving and rooting for his brother.

And Tony would never see him coming.

THIRTY-THREE

"Don't get high on your own supply," Peter said.

"That's the last cliché thing you can say in my pad." Axl turned to Lana. "I didn't picture your boyfriend as a nerd, girl."

"What can I say, I like the weird ones." Lana laughed, that maniacal, I'm-in-charge laugh that drove Peter nuts. He questioned his own choice of words and decided to let it go for now.

He'd cry-yell at Lana in the car later.

Crying was the only thing that seemed to break through her frozen heart.

As they walked to the car, Peter behind Lana, Axl, and Byron, Peter tried to soak in the night sky. He'd heard many times that the higher you are, the more weed you smoke, the brighter the stars appear, but above him now were only clouds.

Peter piled into the backseat and tried to put his arm around Lana, but she shifted in her seat and leaned forward to continue joking with Axl and Byron. She'd claimed to have slept with only Axl once, no big deal, but she was flirting and laughing with him now in a way that just didn't feel right to Peter.

He missed that part of their relationship, a part that seemed to have died two months ago. The part where he could say or do anything and she would laugh because there was nothing else in the world more important than each other.

But maybe that's just high school.

They drove through the neighborhood and stopped at a gas station.

Axl and Byron went inside while Peter and Lana stayed in the car.

"Don't fuck this up, Peter. That's a shitload of weed they gave us, so just hold on to it and we'll smoke it later."

“Why are we still with them?”

“Just hang loose a little longer. They’re chill.”

Axl and Byron piled back in, chugging sodas and lighting up cigarettes. Axl pulled out of the gas station and down an alley, then stopped.

“Let’s smoke a blunt before the night is done, right, kids?”

Peter heard Lana laugh her stupid laugh, and realized they weren’t going to get through this without smoking. “Shit yeah, Peter, give him the stuff.”

But Peter could give two shits, so he just sat there for two minutes, arms crossed, Byron reaching down his pockets, tears welling up behind his eyes. Axl’s face grew dark. “Give me the stuff, you little shit.”

Axl practically snarled as he reached into the backseat and put his hand around Peter’s neck, choking out his oxygen. Peter smiled, wishing he could laugh a stupid laugh as he stared into Lana’s frightened eyes.

Then she did let out a laugh, and it was the first thing Peter would remember the next morning when he woke up curbside, alone, and without his new bag of weed.

THIRTY-FOUR

Albert bent over, adjusted the bag at his belt, flicked on his flashlight, and started to crawl under the porch. The smell was unbearable, and Cori would soon be home. Then the yelling would continue. Better to attack the problem head-on, just like his dad used to do.

But Albert was not his father and would likely let whatever was causing the smell to continue to lay dormant. As he crawled through the dirt, Albert found various toys that the neighbor’s dog left behind over the years, as well as newer “gifts” the dog had relieved itself of.

He didn’t care. The smell had finally gotten to him, again, interrupting the peace and quiet of late. He hoped it wasn’t the neighbor’s dog itself. But a small part of him, a part he couldn’t quite place, wished it was.

That dog.

Ever since they’d moved in, Cori had felt a sense of darkness whenever that dog would pop by. Albert liked to sneak snacks to the dog and once in a while would take it for a walk whenever the neighbors were gone. But in truth he didn’t even know its name.

He didn’t care. It was a dog, and he liked it. But Cori hated it because, to her, all the animal did was eat and poop and wrestle rubber toys, because that’s what dogs do. Albert knew that, Cori knew that, even the dog knew that. What else did she want from it?

His flashlight flickered off, then on, off, then on. Yet another item in the house for which he'd forgotten to replace the batteries. Just like their smoke detector, just like their TV remote, just like the alarm clock.

Without the alarm clock Albert didn't wake up on time, and Cori didn't wake up on time. She was always late to work, thanks to Albert. But she never wanted to fix things herself. Albert was fine taking a backseat role, allowing her to be the breadwinner and, in exchange, occasionally fixing things around the house.

Twenty-first century, right? He was a homebody anyway, didn't like company, and absolutely hated the neighbors. And that dog! He could hear the barking now, gnawing at the back of his mind, and as he kept crawling farther under the porch, toward the house, the barks morphed into shouts from his wife.

"Fix this, do that, why'd you let this go, why'd you let that go, why do I do all of the work, get away from the damn dog, earn some money!" Her voice scratching like metal on metal, worse than the bark of the damn dog.

He looked back, saw the neighbor's dog at the edge of the porch, tail wagging, mouth open in playfulness. Albert even let out a smile before turning to peek under the house and make sure to leave the air freshener next to Cori's body.

Soon it would decompose fully, and the smell would raise the neighbor's awareness, but for now he could finally play with the nameless dog without his wife's nagging him to stop.

THIRTY-FIVE

The cage beside hers was empty. She only really cared about it this morning. All this time, she never knew what it meant, just that there was a space next to hers that she could never reach.

That didn't mean she disliked her area. Hers was substantial, as she saw it, with enough room to move a few steps in any direction, and even had a tree to climb. Once at the top, she could see the entire floor: the grass and dirt and leaves. She tried eating the leaves once, but the taste was unpleasant and left her feeling ill, and she vomited a short time later.

Then the room got quiet, there was a buzz, and she fell asleep. When she awoke that afternoon, she found herself underneath the tree asleep, a banana at her feet. She obviously loved bananas, which the Strangers knew. Regardless, it was disconcerting to wake up to a banana at her feet.

Her days were otherwise plain and uninteresting. Mornings would come with the smell of bananas and cinnamon. Cinnamon-covered bananas were the greatest things she'd ever known. She'd run around in her cage, hang upside down, do all the things she'd loved to do for her entire life, and through it all, she could hear things.

Sometimes she heard a loud clap-clap-clap when she'd performed a flip. Sometimes she'd dance and hear voices ha-ha-ha-ing, a strange noise that created a warm feeling in her chest and on her face, and made her want to replicate that feeling.

Nights were cold and dark and lonely, and occasionally she saw the shadows of the Strangers just before sleep came. Last night was the oddest she'd had in her lifetime here. She had smelled something rotten.

An unwashed banana peel was her first thought or the bottoms of her feet if she stepped in her own poop. But her feet were clean.

Just when she was about to fall asleep, she heard a noise. A cough, an exhalation of pain. She went toward the sound, cautiously, noting that it was coming from near the wall of her cage, near where the emptiness was.

The empty cage she could never reach.

There was a shadow, and at first she ran up the tree, away from the Stranger that had likely entered that Other Place. She waited, heard nothing, and soon descended, stalking toward the wall between cages. Then there were grunts and noises, and a paw suddenly dashed out and grabbed hers.

She screamed, kicking at the cage and the arm holding her. She scratched and clawed, but the paw would not let go. Finally there were voices and the metallic clang of doors opening in the other cage.

Strangers surrounded the other . . . she didn't know what to call it.

The paw holding her suddenly pulled back, and there was a distorted scream that she recognized as pain as the Other was then dragged out of its cage. She stared at the door all morning; the sound of laughter was far away today.

THIRTY-SIX

I'm thinking there is a way to find out who is sending me letters. I don't mind them, I'm just not very sentimental. The first, for example, was a letter with a drawing of a blue sky above a green field and appeared to describe parts of Iowa. Why Iowa? Who goes to Iowa on purpose and stops to send a letter? Don't be thankful for a blue sky—it just is what it is.

Regardless, that was just one letter that, well, was a bit too much from the start. I mean, the only words were "wow, what a sky!" Boring.

The next letter I received, about a week later, came from a coastal region. There were only three words written on the page, "Can't swim well."

There was sand inside the envelope. I wonder what happened to that person, a little, but it has not given me a moment of anxiety. Not like the kind the writer of the letter is experiencing, surely.

I wonder how they all know my address and why they choose to write old-fashioned letters. I'm not complaining. It's just strange how everyone seems to trust me, you know?

Yet another letter arrived this week. From a little girl in Northern Canada.

I know she's a little girl because that's how she starts her letter: "I'm five years old." Like I need to know that off the bat. She asked me for a specific type of medicine, something for her grandmother. I'm sure I have some around here, but that means I must go digging and might find something that, well, is better buried where it lies.

I can find her, though, through my latest discovery. I never thought to read the envelopes—there are always too many, more each year. But when you look at them, on the outside, there's a return address. Quite a useful detail!

I have a stack here from every country in the world, where the skies might be blue or the skies might be gray on any given day. I haven't been able to keep track since the days float by so fast and everyone is clamoring for my attention. Meanwhile, my own solicitation stack grows higher and higher. I'm just looking for support, that's all. Just a little bit of help, a little bit of a, well, a group think.

You might not believe it but a lot of positivism can go a long way, if you invest it right.

For the little girl in Canada, I'm about to dig through my shelves in my third basement. I know the cure of which she speaks; it should be right under the apple encased in glass, the one I keep as a reminder to be careful. But everything under that apple is waiting and waiting to be released, and sometimes, like now, I have to dole a little of it out just to gain a bit of positive energy.

THIRTY-SEVEN

Barbara hated the city because she always felt like she was lost in the crowd. She hadn't want to go, but her father had insisted. He had never given up hope. "You have to, Barbara. What if she's there? She'll never come home if she sees me."

Barbara loved her father, but his logic was fading in his twilight years. Nevertheless, Barbara soon found herself on a bus to the city in the hopes of finding her sister after almost twenty years apart. She wondered if she'd even recognize Nicole. Or, likewise, if Nicole would know who she was. She had been only ten when Nicole left their home.

Nicole, the older, "wiser" sister, who fell in with him in high school. At least she'd waited until she was an adult, legally, to run away with a stranger. But when the stranger also believes he'll be reincarnated into the Antichrist, you have to wonder exactly how "wise" your sister is.

Barbara took the train down early on a Sunday morning. She held the letter close to her chest and read it again on the way down.

"Dear Grandpa (I guess), I want you to know that I love you even though we've never met.

"My mother talked about you once, just the other night. I'm twelve now, and I don't think we'll ever leave the city. I don't know my dad, but maybe one day we'll meet. My mother doesn't know I'm writing this, but if you're ever in the Big Apple, keep an eye out for a short kid with glasses and blond hair that sticks up in the back. (That's me.)

"Love, Peter"

She had named him Peter, after his father. Barbara wondered if Peter knew his father was crazy, that he was supposed to be the Antichrist.

They'd heard that Nicole's stranger friend had committed suicide about thirteen years ago. There was a story in the paper about it, so bizarre that it read like fiction. Ritualistic suicide, plunging to his death on the West Side.

The paper said he'd left behind a pregnant wife who claimed the child didn't have a father. At that time, their father was too angry to want to talk to Nicole. But with age came forgiveness, and after Peter's letter, Barbara was dispatched to find Nicole for one last "hello."

She ate in a diner first thing, then walked to the West Side. The address from the letter wasn't too far from Grand Central. At Columbus Circle, Barbara stopped to admire the parts of the city she hadn't even imagined before, the lovely people, the scenery, the park just around the corner.

She turned to head north and was startled to see Nicole staring back at her, tears in her eyes.

Barbara raised her hand in a brief wave, then the light turned green and the crowd took over, hiding her, brushing her past without another chance to say hello.

At Nicole's address, no one was home, so Barbara would wait. She didn't hate the city anymore.

THIRTY-EIGHT

Donald Grover was new to the neighborhood, and already he wanted to fight his neighbors. Not all the neighbors, but just the jackass next door.

Why was there all that screaming? Screaming was a big reason why Donald had left the city to live in the mountains. The latest bout of screams started while Donald was in the shower. They weren't horrified screams or the sounds of someone in pain. They were just annoying "I'm in a fight with you" kind of screams. He stopped his shower and quickly dressed, not caring about the layer of moisture that was now trapped between his sweater and his chest. He'd deal with it, if only for one peaceful night's rest out of the last six.

Next door, the cabin was barely lit on the outside, and Donald imagined spiders and other creatures popping out of the shadows. But no such monsters came out, of course. He pounded on the door, and the minute his fist landed, the screaming within stopped.

The door swung open and a voice yelled, "What is it?" Donald froze, in awe, staring at one of his idols. "I said, what is it?"

Danny Grover was bearing his teeth, staring daggers at Donald. In one hand he held a knife, and there was blood dripping down his hand and arm, droplets splattering to the floor.

"I, I heard some screaming." Donald gathered himself. "Everything okay?"

"It's fine, yeah." Danny Grover looked at the knife and seemed startled to find blood on the blade. He wiped it on his shirt. "C'mon in, just getting dinner prepped. Wife won't be home for another hour."

Against his better judgment, Donald followed Danny through the cabin, candles lining the tables and walls, and a dim overhead light making the cabin warm and welcoming, a far cry from the fluorescent, stale home he'd made for himself.

In the kitchen, Danny stuck the knife into a deer carcass, pulling guts and tossing meat into a metal bowl nearby. Donald squirmed and asked,

"Is that what was screaming?"

"Screaming?" Danny stared at Donald even as he kept cutting, then chuckled, shaking his head, his whole body shrugging in disbelief. "Kid, you're hearing echoes. You'll get used to it out here in the mountains."

At that moment there was another knock on the door.

This time Donald offered to answer, and when he did his jaw dropped yet again. "It's past curfew—you should all be asleep," whispered the sheriff, a smiling, pale Crispin Grover.

Donald stepped back and tried to shut the door but Crispin stopped it with his hand, the strength of his push knocking Donald off his feet. "I'm not here to teach you a lesson; I'm here to make you believe."

The lights at Danny Grover's cabin suddenly flickered off, and only John Grover, the hermit in the valley, could hear the screaming that night.

THIRTY-NINE

With the blinds half open, the sun offered happiness to Chester while he wagged his tail in anticipation. He was glad to have a warm home in which to live, but wished, during every minute of loneliness, he could experience the world as it appeared through the window.

Twice a day he would stand by the door as his owner, the human called "Gene," left home and then returned. At those times Chester breathed an air full of scents that twisted his imagination to wondrous places. There were hints of flowery magnificence that offered him images of open country and green pastures. There were the offensive olfactory invasions that showed him a howling beast with large teeth, seething to chomp at his hindquarters.

Occasionally the scent of another cat would waft in through the door, and Chester would run end to end through the apartment, excited with no explanation. He both loved and hated when that smell came through the door. On the one hand, he imagined a beautiful feline with fur sleek and clean, and a wink and a smile to greet him. On the other, if he didn't see this feline within seconds, his mind would race wild with jealousy and inexplicable frustration.

The sound of the door opening in the morning, more than anything else, scared him because he could never be certain that Gene would return.

But Gene always came home. Chester had a nagging suspicion, still, that one day he'd be left on his own without food, without water, and without the possibility of those glorious scents.

And why? For what? What was so special about the Outside for Gene to decide to up and leave every single day?

Chester made it his mission to find out, so he watched Gene come home, night after night, and enter the apartment. And shut the door behind him. And always leave the keys in the lock.

Chester knew the routine: the smell of the dirty engine as Gene drove past the bedroom window, the sound of the jingling keys that lay at Gene's waist. He knew that Gene carried home bags of groceries twice a week. He knew that every other Wednesday their neighbor, a nice old lady with long white hair, would greet Gene just before he could shut the door and commence to tease Chester through the screen, pretending to boop his nose. Chester didn't like the smell of this woman, and her nails were too long, and she owned too many small dogs.

But he knew he could sweeten her up with just a quick trick of his eyes, brightening his gaze enough to seduce her to being on his side. He knew he could do the same with Gene, though it was easier to fool the man by running around the apartment and "accidentally" spilling water long enough to distract him.

So that's what he did.

Chester smelled the engine as it drove by on Wednesday evening. He waited by the window to watch as Gene walked up the stairs.

Heard the jingling keys. The door sprang open and in wafted the scent of the neighboring feline as well as a hot plate of food, spicy enough that it would undoubtedly keep Gene awake for hours that night.

Chester ignored the smells, bolting around the apartment. He swiped under Gene's feet twice, then ran to his water bowl—knocking it over—then to the bathroom and was barely able to grab the floor as he dashed straight for the front door. Gene's face had a look of bewildered delight as Chester jumped into the air, through Gene's arms, and into the screen.

The screen tore from the seams and Chester found himself outside, Gene's cry of fear fading. The balcony was long, and Chester dashed as far as he could, never having run this far or this hard all at once. He looked to the window at his left, and there she was: a grey tabby, eyes wide, ears pulled back, fur sleek and pushed down.

She raised a paw to her own window, and Chester raised his in return. Footsteps approached, and Chester was hoisted into the air by a laughing Gene.

Chester stared back at her until his view was hidden by the door Gene slammed shut, and from then on every scent that tickled Chester's nostrils whispered the vision of the cat next door.

FORTY

Debra heard the repeated thump-thump-thump just before she turned on the faucet, and smiled. The corners of her mouth turned up; her teeth began to spring through her lips. She felt her eyes wrinkle at each end, and her nostrils flared a bit. She brushed hair behind each ear and continued washing dishes.

Thump-thump-thump.

It was a basketball, the thumping occasionally interrupted by the ball bouncing off the backboard, double bouncing in the street, then being picked up again and dribbled. The hoop at the end of their driveway had been there for years, since Mario was born.

He'd gone on to play varsity ball in high school and continued for the first couple of years in college before focusing on his business education.

But throughout all that time, he led almost daily games of basketball for the neighborhood boys—sometimes girls would come by, but they usually just watched while waiting for the ice cream truck.

Debra missed those days, but as her son attended college, the neighbors' kids grew up and took over the daily ritual. Basketball in the spring and summer, street football in the fall, sledding all winter.

Debra and Mario Sr.'s mailbox was one end zone, or baseline for basketball, and the Witch Lady's was the other end zone. Whichever team was scoring in that direction made sure to score quick and easy—no one ever tackled a player on the Lady's lawn.

Debra chuckled to herself, wondering why she'd always believed her kids when they called that poor old woman the Witch Lady. She and Mario Sr. had never taken the time to introduce themselves to the neighborhood, not to everybody at least.

When they'd moved into the neighborhood, Mario was busy starting his practice, and Debra always had her hands full with Mario Jr. and little Christine. But now the kids were grown up, out of the house. Mario Jr. had kids of his own, way up in Maine. Christine had a business partner and took little to no time to focus on a love life.

Mario had died of a heart attack two years ago. Now she lived in this big house by herself.

Even the amount of dishes she washed was pathetically small, in her eyes. Two bowls, a plate from breakfast, and a frying pan that was her go-to each morning, noon and night. She tutored neighborhood kids, but even those sessions were few and far between.

Mario Jr. and his family came to visit the requisite twice a year for holidays, and a third time on the anniversary of Mario's death. That was about as much action as Debra was used to seeing.

But she was content with it all.

In the winter she would sit on her back porch, bundled in a blanket in the afternoon, to watch the neighbors' kids come home from school and climb to the top of Apple Hill, only to sled down every few minutes, narrowly avoiding the bushes.

Then springtime came, and the sound of a bouncing basketball on the street, less frequent these days, gave her a spark of joy. Just the sound of that ball bouncing would make her mind run backward, to happier times, fuller times. She wouldn't look at who was playing—God knows, she'd probably not even recognize whoever it was. But she did let the sound lull her into a daydream slumber or a solid nap.

Today she finished her dishes but didn't feel tired. She decided she'd poke her head outside and say hello to the kids, maybe buy them an ice cream. She put on her jacket and slipped on her Crocs—Mario Jr. always made fun of her for these, but she told him that one day comfort would overtake any fashion sense for him too.

Comfort is comfort.

She opened the door, smiling, and took a breath of fresh air, eyes closed, nostrils flaring. She opened her eyes, and the smile faded when she saw the empty street and the light patch of cement covering the spot where the basketball hoop had been firmly planted up until five years ago.

Debra slipped back inside and closed the door slowly.

The bouncing returned the next day, and with it, the flood of memories came once again.

FORTY-ONE

Ricky's mother told him not to crack open the jar of pickles, but Ricky loves pickles, so he's about to do it anyway. He's wild about pickles, can't remember a time without them. Only twelve years old, Ricky figures he's eaten at least one pickle a day since he was three.

And he ain't joking.

His mother has consistently, throughout his lifetime, warned Ricky that if he keeps eating pickles at this rate he'll turn into a pickle before he is twenty. To Ricky this would be a dream come true.

F*cking pickles are delicious. Who wouldn't want to be one?

So here he is, after school, eating the pickles from the jar his mother warned him not to open. But why? Are they magic f*cking pickles? Would other dimensional doorways open up because Ricky devoured a pickle?

Or would he, Ricky, fulfill his mother's warnings and become a delicious goddamn pickle?

The jar, to be certain, is slightly odd. Cylindrical and more yellow than clear, the jar is unlabeled and contains exactly a dozen pickles. Upon opening, the scent of vinegar and egg seeps into Ricky's nostrils and causes a tingling sensation in the back of his throat, which leads to a pleasant chill throughout the rest of his body.

He smiles, pulling a pickle from the jar, and eats that one practically whole. Barely chewing the f*cking pickle.

The vinegar is warm in his throat, and the spices are just right, just enough zing to send his mouth into numbness for half a second—the perfect amount of time when consuming a f*cking pickle.

He eats two more pickles, bringing the count to his magic number of three f*cking pickles eaten. He sets the jar back in the fridge, with the lid on so his mother won't notice.

Then he sleeps.

When he wakes up, he can't move because he's stuck under the covers. And he can't shove off the covers because he's a f*cking pickle!

Why the hell am I a pickle? He tries to speak, to yell, to call his mother, but nothing comes out. Pickles don't have mouths. And he's a big pickle, so the smell is ten times that of a normal-size pickle. The scent of vinegar floods the house, so strong even Ricky is disgusted.

His mother opens the front door, and as soon as she yells, "UGH," Ricky knows he's in trouble. But so what?

How do you punish a pickle? You can't exactly torture it, since a pickle is already basically a tortured cucumber. What do you do to a pickle that might be your son?

Ricky contemplates the look on his mother's face as she approaches his bedroom, and wonders how he'd react if he saw a giant pickle.

He'd probably eat it.

He hopes his mother actually hates pickles as much as he loves them. He closes his eyes, or would if he even had eyes, and wishes and hopes and prays. Mother wakes him up with a splash of water to the face, and Ricky is back to his old self.

Guess those pickles really were magic, because he never eats pickles again.

F*ck pickles.

FORTY-TWO

They didn't have souls. Empty vessels made up the population of the planet. But that didn't stop earth's army from wanting to invade.

The soulless are the easiest to consume. There's no guilt. No afterthought. No regret. No thrill. No sensitivity.

Just consumption. That's what earth's army did. They consumed.

And consuming something with a soul could be tiresome. Very tiresome.

The soul, you see, will then consume from within. So one tries hard not to consume a soul. If a soul consumes you instead, then you will find yourself empty. Forever. And eventually you will again be consumed, from the outside in.

And then you will cease.

Cease to exist.

Cease to believe.

Cease to know.

But you will try hard to avoid that. By having a soul. And keeping it.

And what do you do if you have a soul?

You consume a life force without a soul. Simple as that.

So the planet was appetizing for that reason, and that reason alone.

All of earth could survive another year just by consuming the beings that had no souls, the planet far away. But there would be nothing left on that planet, and then it would die. This was a small sacrifice, earth felt, for the future of earth itself.

At least for the near future.

If you cannot see beyond the near future, then it doesn't matter much. But earth never looked through a telescope except to find a planet with beings devoid of souls. If earth had the knowledge and wisdom to look further ahead, it would see even more.

Vision would expand. Life would expand.

And the planet would live forever.

Happy, and free, and full of souls.

Instead they could not see that instead of a telescope, they were looking in a mirror.

FORTY-THREE

Why do they always have a flower garden? Michael wondered this while watching General Stills trim and clip away at his roses.

All the stereotypical bosses clip away in a rose garden. Why is that? What's the deal with gardens? Michael thought this last bit in his head's Jerry Seinfeld voice, and felt immediately ashamed. This was not a laughing matter. Two dead, including Stills's wife. Fourteen witnesses. Stills would be on death row in a year unless Michael could sway not just a jury but the world.

No, nothing about this was a laughing matter.

Stills glanced over to Michael, seemed to know exactly what he was thinking. "Sit down, take a load off. You look like you could use a drink."

The Good General always knew how to be a gracious host, even in dire situations. Michael sat, nodding, barely able to utter a word. Actually, completely unable to utter a word.

Truth be told, Michael was afraid. He watched the Good General pour his "special" lemonade, the pitcher shaking. The man was pushing ninety. What would drive him to kill his wife? His best friend?

Of course, Michael knew the answer. Everyone knew.

Mrs. Stills, the sweet old lady who never left her husband's side even as the casinos fell, had taken up with his best friend, had slept with him for more than thirty years. This was ages ago, but that kind of wound burns for a lifetime.

Perhaps he'd known back then and suppressed the images painted for him by hearsay and rumor. Or perhaps he just waited until he knew he had nothing left to lose before providing payback to his former friend and his wife for their affair.

"Why?" Michael was shocked he'd uttered the noise, but not at the question.

He didn't think General Stills was shocked either, judging by the smile on his face. Michael accepted his lemonade and drank it all in one gulp. "You'd think that I'd have an answer that would satisfy you. I don't really know, but I did do it, Michael."

"And you want me to fight—"

"Yes, I want you to fight tooth and nail to prove my innocence. And you will fail. And that will be the end of it. No appeals, no court of public opinion, just . . . the end." He reached out and plucked a single rose from the nearest bush. "These were her favorite. But I despise roses."

He crushed the rose in his hands and wept, a look of regret washing over his face.

FORTY-FOUR

Tina was going out of her mind. Marcus was running late, and he never ran late.

Punctuality was one of Marcus's finer qualities and the one that drove Tina crazy. Marcus had been early for their first date, arriving before she'd even had a chance to shower. He was early when he had a job interview with the Mets and ended up parking in the owner's spot. He was early on his marriage proposal to her, again not waiting for her to finish showering before appearing at the curtain on one knee.

Okay, that one was adorable.

But the fact that Marcus was running late, tonight of all nights, was more than just a disappointment to Tina. She felt a panic rise inside of her, and their meeting wouldn't wait for late arrivals.

First she had called the office. "Mr. Tiller left two hours ago," said his assistant. She was probably covering for Marcus, but Tina couldn't get more information out of her.

She then checked the Find My Car app on her phone.

They shared everything—phone plan, car, contact and recovery information, even their Addiction to Electronics Anonymous meetings, for which they were going to be late tonight if Marcus didn't hurry.

Tina was wary of going to such meetings, but Marcus had reassured her that the only way to combat electronics and tracking and paranoia and fear was to talk about it.

The app blipped with recovery information, the signal indicating that the car was currently in their garage. Tina checked and there was no car, but just before she went back inside, she saw it, the flashing red light.

The car's tracker. Just sitting on the floor of the garage. She wondered when he'd taken it off or if it just fell off or—God forbid—someone else had taken it off for him.

Who could've done such a thing? And, well, why? Marcus had no enemies and in fact had very few friends. When they'd married, Marcus and Tina's friends mostly merged while acquaintances and high school buddies fell away, leaving them with a tiny circle of trusted allies.

She pulled out a cigarette, staring at the blinking tracker on the ground. Why would he remove it—if, indeed, he had? What did Marcus have to hide? They shared everything.

Tina certainly had nothing to hide from Marcus. Aside from her smoking, obviously. But at three cigarettes a day, he surely could smell it on her by now, right? Just like she could smell the liquor on his breath on Friday nights. But at least he'd admitted he went drinking with colleagues after work. So, again, no secrets.

She stomped out her cigarette as well as the tracker with one foot. This was going to become a long night.

She went inside and was frightened to find Marcus sitting at the dining table, sweating, covered in dirt. He sipped scotch straight from the bottle. "Honey," he whispered, "they're all watching us." He looked at her hands, saw the phone, and suddenly jumped up from the table.

He snatched her phone and threw it in the garbage disposal, and the crunching of the metal and glass echoed through the house.

"Marcus . . . what happened?"

"They're watching us," he whispered again. "We must be careful."

They didn't go to any more meetings.

FORTY-FIVE

There was a delay, but if safety was guaranteed, Marnie didn't mind. She'd come all this way, so she figured, why stop now? She looked down at the drinks she was holding, licking her lips in anticipation.

Beside her, Frank held their sign in the air, waggling first his right arm, then his left, as he grew more tired. "How much longer?"

She replied, "Don't complain."

"Six hours, Marnie. You promised we wouldn't spend all day here, that I'd get to see the game. It's the sixth inning already!"

She glared at him. "How would you know what inning it is?"

"I've been checking my phone, okay? I still have a right to have my phone and look at it whenever I feel like it."

"Look at your phone, don't look at your phone, see what I care. Just keep holding up that sign while you do it."

"Why is this so important to you?"

"Now? You wait until now to ask me that? Two hours in the car, an hour in line, holding these drinks for hours, unable to drink them, and you wait until now to ask me that? Did you even read it?"

Frank looked up at the sign he was holding, waggling his left arm at the same moment. "I don't understand it."

"What's not to understand? 'Keeping US Safe.' How much clearer should I make it?"

Frank rolled his eyes. "I know what the sign says, Marnie, I just don't understand it. What are we being kept safe from?"

Marnie shook her head, glancing around to make sure no one else in the crowd could hear them. "It's not what he can keep us safe from. It's that he'll keep us safe in general."

"But safe from what? In what sense, I mean, are you saying 'safe'?"

"Frank, just hold the sign up. It'll be over soon." They both looked up at the stage, which was still empty. The crowd around them was still screaming, and occasionally a rhythmic clapping would start, crescendo, then everyone would settle down in anticipation.

"Something wrong, you think?" Frank looked over at Marnie, and she avoided his gaze.

"Nothing is wrong, Frank. Quit whining."

Frank tried to hand her the sign. "Just hold the damn thing yourself. I've got to pee."

He walked away before she could reply, so Marnie held the sign high, screaming along with the crowd.

It was past midnight by the time the speaker came and went, and Frank had still not returned from the bathroom.

Marnie was safe, though, as she and the rest of the crowd lay still beside empty cups of the tasty drinks they'd been handed at the door.

FORTY-SIX

Okay, enough with the lies. If we're going to go through with this, we have to be on the same page. I don't like you; you don't like me. So, no more BS. I promise you if you promise me, okay?

Good.

Now, let's get it all on the table. Coffee is terrible. I know you're a big fan, but I just don't like the smell. It's like something sweet is burning. It's disgusting. And it doesn't wake me up in the morning. Okay?

I'm just being honest, just like we promised.

Flying, let's just get that out of the way. I'm a better pilot than you are. No, I'm not saying that to gloat or sound arrogant. We both know how true it is. Don't lie. I can move on from it; you should too.

I know it's easy for me to say, but trust me, it's for our own good if we can just agree on this one. Our lives may depend on it.

You come from where you come from, I get it. Buying yourself a ticket on this ship wasn't smart, and I hope you don't think it was right either.

We've both brought something to the table, but now it's time to buckle down and, well, survive.

You're in love with me. I get it, I really do. No, that's not gloating either.

I'm just accepting your feelings. I don't feel the same way, and if we're going to go back to my planet you need to understand that. I'm sure you'll find someone there worth your feelings. I did, at one time.

A long time ago. Consider how long we've been out here, double that, and you'll get the length of time I've been waiting for this feeling.

So now we come to the toughest part. Your planet. I know you miss it—I would too if it were my planet that vanished. But just know that I want to understand, and I want to help you, so you have to let me try, despite our differences.

And speaking of differences, and I'm sure you'll agree, you need to bring up your masking abilities.

I know, I know.

You can still be "you" but you have to just alter your appearance when we arrive. Only for a short time. Earthlings won't like the face you've got, just trust me on that.

In a few years, maybe a little longer, they'll get used to a human face. But for now, keep up the lizard exterior.

It's best to pretend you're just like everyone else before you show your true colors.

FORTY-SEVEN

Rod couldn't believe his eyes. The zoom feature was perhaps the most significant upgrade, allowing him the gift of spotting a traffic jam four miles ahead. The X-ray component was a wash and only enhanced how he could see through tinted windows, a cheap selling point that most people would likely find disappointing in the long run.

The real gift was night vision, and he was happy to have asked for the upgrade. Being a night owl, seeing in the dark was just as important as breathing, as he saw it.

Yes, Rod couldn't believe his new eyes.

He walked to work that morning, imagining that other passersby were staring at him in awe, hoping they could acquire similar optics or afford the upgrades. But no one would be able to. Rod had connections.

Meeting people and convincing them that he would be their walking advertisements, that was his job. Hey, there were worse ways to make money. He could be a portable toilet cleaner. In this city, that was lower than being homeless.

Rod stepped into his office building, scanned his card, and walked to the elevator's retinal scan. One attempt, then a malfunction. Then another malfunction. "Hey, Jones," he called to the tall security guard.

Jones walked over with a smile. "Yes, Mr. Corrigan?"

"New scanner not working today?" Rod pointed to the retinal scanner, which was indeed a new model.

"It's been fine all morning, sir." As Jones spoke, another worker scanned in and entered the elevator.

"Well, I'm late, so do you mind if I . . . ?" Jones put out a hand as Rod tried to walk past.

"I'm sorry, sir, you know the rules. Come this way?" He gestured to a side door, discolored and rarely used.

"Oh, Jones . . . Jonesy, come on! You know me!"

Jones grabbed Rod by the arm, hard. There was no longer a smile on his face. "I thought I did."

Rod was roughly pushed through the side door into a small room with a hatch in the ceiling. The hatch was open, and cold air poured in from the darkness above. Rod squinted, his night vision kicking in, and after the overhead lights washed out he zoomed in on the open hatch.

There was nothing above, and no matter how high he urged the night vision, he couldn't see anything up there. "What's this going to be like?"

"Sir, I'll hold your bag for you." Jones took Rod's bag before he could object, then closed the door.

Rod waited, looked up again. The ground started to rise, fast, and before he could believe it he was ejected straight up into the darkness. He floated, and answered the security questions as they flashed before his eyes.

Beyond the questions was something scarier than nothingness, a galaxy of horrors and nightmares come to life, populated by figures that moved outside of three dimensions and with snarling, horrifying faces.

He was released after the eternity of questions and allowed to recuperate for the afternoon.

The next day Rod had his old eyes reinstalled. He could deal without the night vision from now on.

FORTY-EIGHT

James ran to the corner, but the ice cream truck was already gone.

Third day in a row missing the truck. Natalie would be angry again. No sugar meant anger.

James was accustomed to this problem but hadn't found a way to solve it. Sugar had been banned for only a week, but the ice cream truck with its deregulated contract was the last bastion of tasty sweetness. Without it, Natalie and the rest of the neighborhood kids would probably strike down their parents by the end of the month.

Sugar wasn't just a tasty commodity; it was life, a gift of happiness. It was a sweet relief and respite from the problems they all faced: the rising prices, the dangerous new security on every block. Sugar was the only solace to be found amidst the country's recession.

James finally caught his breath, and as he turned to head home he heard it, the jingle, the soft bells. The ice cream man wasn't far.

He ran then, down the block, and as he turned onto Coronado Ave he caught it, a glimpse of the flashing orange lights at the rear of the ice cream truck. It was turning left onto Smith Ave and would shortly hit the thruway. Now was his only chance.

So he ran, and cursed himself for smoking earlier in his life. He could imagine his lungs, dark and pulsing, trying to keep up, yelling and shaking their lung fists up at his mouth. But he didn't care. This was for Natalie.

All the world for a dash of sugar and a smile on Natalie's face.

He reached the corner of Smith and had to collapse for a moment, the world fading to white around him. He watched kids line up along Smith to meet the ice cream man, and was relieved because it meant the truck would be stopped for a while, long enough for him to reach it and grab a cone.

He sat a little longer, wishing Natalie could come with him on this little adventure. If anything, she'd be able to work up an appetite. But in her condition, leaving the house was not an option. He blamed his own genetics for her condition, but he could've thrown the blame at the bombs or the army. They deserved it more.

But why place blame? What's done is done, and her ailments didn't affect her happiness. The only thing standing in the way was the lack of sugar.

And that was something James could fix right now.

He walked to the truck. The other kids had already gotten their treats. James held up a fiver, asked for a bowl of vanilla and a cookie sandwich.

"Only got the cones, and just one scoop left."

"It'll do," said James. He looked up at the sky, thankful for the clouds. He took the cone and had a lick before he knew what he was doing.

The sugar hit him instantly, and the world suddenly filled with color. On his walk home, the grass was greener and the sky was suddenly a light blue. He took deep breaths and tasted vanilla. He smelled chocolate crumbs and bread and remembered his childhood, cookies for days.

He treated himself to another lick, and another, before turning back onto their street. He reached the trailer and saw Natalie's face in the window, but her smile faltered almost immediately.

He looked down and saw that the inside of the cone had only a thin layer of ice cream but was otherwise empty. He'd eaten almost all of it, and promised himself he'd never have another lick.

Later, Natalie was asleep with a content smile on her face, as the remaining ice cream had had just enough sugar for James to live up to his word that day.

James never missed the ice cream truck again—and never had another lick.

FORTY-NINE

The popcorn was almost gone from Michael's bucket, and the previews hadn't even started. Why the hell did he buy it so early? He loved popcorn almost as much as he loved the previews, so why didn't he just wait?

Twenty minutes prior to the movie, you buy the popcorn, that was tradition. Seven minutes out, go to the bathroom, get that out of your system. Once the previews start, at that time, you shouldn't have to leave your seat again until after the credits roll.

As he got older, Michael recognized that he had to pee more often, so he brought only a small bottle of water with him, nothing fancy. No more sodas, no more coffees. Just water to go with the popcorn. The popcorn received two pumps of butter and three sprinkles of salt.

He sat at the end of the middle row, or as close as he could get. Being on the end served two purposes. First, if he did have to pee, he wouldn't have to climb over anyone. Second, in an emergency he could leave in a hurry and hopefully lead the way for all the others to follow. Michael didn't consider himself a hero, but dammit, he knew this theater front and back, and no one should have to suffer.

But now, as he sifted his fingers through the bottom of the bucket, something was off. He'd forgotten to eat breakfast, and in his hunger he'd eaten the popcorn too quickly. He also forgot to sprinkle it with salt.

He looked at his watch: nine minutes until the previews started, which meant at least fifteen until the movie began. Enough time to buy more popcorn and pee? He'd have to risk it. He couldn't stand watching without popcorn, couldn't fathom the idea of leaving to pee during the movie.

Not this movie.

It was the last of a trilogy, one he'd been dying to see since he was four years old. Thirty years for the third movie, but dammit, it would be worth it. So he stood, made sure his coat guarded his seat (as well as the stranger to his left, who gave him an odd look of "yeah of course, bro") and went out.

The concessions line was long. He checked his watch again, calculating, slowing his walk while he did the math. Standing in line would take at least twelve minutes, given that each person would take two minutes and there were six-seven people per line. The bathroom would take two minutes as well, but as he thought this, an earlier showing of the movie was just getting out.

Risk a longer bathroom wait, plus possible spoilers?

Hell no.

He moved to the shortest concessions line, dumping the rest of the popcorn in his mouth while he waited. He felt a bump at his back, some idiot's elbow, no doubt. Michael ignored it, checked for more kernels—and felt another bump. One more, he'd allow, and then—

A third bump.

He turned, fuming, already feeling more pressure from his bladder, wondering what point in the movie he'd miss—then he saw her face, the girl behind him with the loose elbows, phone to her ear, brushing hair from her face as she cringed. "So sorry," she said.

He just nodded and offered her his remaining popcorn kernels. She took them without hesitation. "Thanks, dude!"

Michael was about to speak but the guy behind the girl caught his attention: the line had moved forward. Michael turned, but after a step he shifted and looked back at the girl to find that she was no longer on the phone. "What are you here to see?"

Shaking her head, the girl said, "Nothing, I just dig the popcorn. Two pumps butter, three sprinkles of salt, and a day's worth of goodness."

Michael smiled at her.

She smiled back.

Michael missed the movie that afternoon.

FIFTY

Hector still couldn't believe the situation he'd gotten himself into. How did it ever get this far?

This was supposed to be a simple vacation, by himself, free from anyone who could tell him what to do. Take a look at some ancient ruins, hike south four miles, and be back to the coastal hotel by nightfall. It should have been simple, but for the damn tour group . . .

Right after the ruins the tour guide had disappeared—which at first they all thought was a practical joke. Then Hector stumbled upon his twisted body, curled up at the bottom of a hill with a broken neck and limbs, back bent over a tree stump. Hector had pointed out the body to the rest of the group, and they took what supplies they could and continued walking.

He told no one about the glisten in the man's eyes or the fact that those eyes had looked up at Hector before he called them over. That would be his secret, and the man was probably suffering anyway with no way to save him.

Watching someone die was not on Hector's list of things to do on this, his only vacation in his fifty years of living, but frankly neither was participating in a tour group. The wasted minds of the younger generation were lost on Hector's preferred singular existence.

As the tour group moved on, Hector fractured the group with one simple comment: "But we came from the other direction." In the English language, there are countless divisive expressions, words, and turns of phrase. But tell a tired, sweaty, hungry group of tourists they've been walking the wrong way for four hours, and you might as well burn yourself alive.

After Hector explained to the group that they were walking the wrong direction, all but two decided he was full of shit. So he and his two new friends—with names he couldn't even understand—headed back in the direction they had come from.

Or so they thought.

The cool thing about traveling to a foreign land is all the mystery it entails. The exotic plant life. The friendly, strange animal kingdom. The foods that you might not normally think of as edible being, in fact, delicious. But one thing that you don't really think about, that you don't count on, and that is most decidedly not cool: Mother Nature's welcome parties.

First the rains came, and his group tried to drink the water that fell from the sky. Big mistake. They'd been walking under trees taller than skyscrapers, so the moment the water reached their mouths it was already slimy, covered in grime and shit and bugs that would eat you alive from the inside.

No bueno, Hector thought. His new friends were not as thoughtful, and both bled from their throats within hours.

Hector, now alone, fought his way through thick underbrush and heavy moss to what he thought was an open desert. He'd read that desert surrounded the towns of this area of the country, so he believed himself to be only a half day's walk from the nearest location that might provide food and a bed.

A good plan, maybe, for someone who knew what the heck they were doing, would be to continue walking around the desert within an arm's reach of the tree line. But Hector was no such man. Or maybe he was just stupid. Certainly, both were applicable in the current scenario.

He walked through the rocky desert in any case, and the third lizard he encountered was dinner. Or breakfast. He'd stopped keeping track and, regardless, there wasn't enough meat to call the lizard an appetizer let alone a meal.

It took a two-mile hike up a hill for Hector to realize he'd probably been walking in the wrong direction. He climbed up on the biggest rock he could find, his balls sweating to an uncomfortable degree of itching.

He removed his shirt and wrapped it around his head under the hot sun. The sun had never been hotter in all his life, which was odd considering two days ago the weather was overcast and barely above 65 degrees. But this was exotic, this location, so what the hell use was it to try and predict the weather?

Hector looked in all directions, saw nothing but fog and a little ash falling from the sky. Odd . . . and he couldn't see for a mile or two in any direction. He thought his former tour group would likely be in a similar predicament but didn't wish evil upon them.

Just, maybe, dysentery would be a nice memento for them to obtain. He looked up at the explosion that boomed behind him, and fainted.

When he awoke, he was more than sweating—he was literally on fire.

After he'd stamped out the flames on his crisping ankle, Hector took stock of the lava swirling around the boulder he'd been lying on, and the four-by-four space remaining.

He hoped for rain that night, and sure as the sky is blue, the rains came, as did the suffocation from smoke inhalation and the lonely death of a stubborn guy who wanted to be, always and always, his own man.

FIFTY-ONE

Gary woke to see that they'd stopped moving. The road was white with ice. "Traffic just stopped?"

Don, putting the car in park, turned up the heater. "Ready to switch?"

"We're still in Iowa?"

When Gary had fallen asleep they'd been cruising at the speed limit of 65. He had a suspicion this was a "summer limit" and the "winter limit" signs had been blown away. No one should be moving that fast in the middle of winter. Not to Gary.

But it'd been more than twenty years since he'd last seen snow, so what did he really know? "Think it's a busy time of day for this part of the state?"

"It's only one o'clock. So, no." Don took a second to turn up the radio, a country song about Cheyenne. Gary assumed it had been on repeat since he'd fallen asleep, since Don was known for playing the same songs on repeat when he drove.

Don sighed, pointed out the passenger window. "Seen a lot of that since you've been out."

Gary looked. Off the road was a semi, turned on its side. There was a neon green flag on a pole sticking out the driver's door, and the end of the truck was covered in snow. "The flag?"

Don replied, "Sometimes they leave the truck for a few days, let the snow settle. I think this jam goes for the next two miles or so."

Gary tried looking ahead, but his view was obstructed by the truck in front of them. "I'm gonna check it out." He stepped outside and stretched, looking up ahead. Sure enough, far in the distance at a bend in the hill was a group of vehicles blocking the entire road. "Had to be an accident."

"Maybe," said Don.

"See no other reason to stop."

"Then it's probably an accident." Don was getting testy, and Gary knew it was only a matter of time before he'd have to take over. He hoped it was after the road turned back to concrete instead of ice.

Since he was sixteen and accidentally drove off the road on the way to his girlfriend's house, Gary was wary of driving at all, let alone in the snow. It was a wonder he'd been able to handle the wheel at various stages across the country. "I think we can make it."

Don gave Gary a look. "Say again?"

"Up ahead the road might not be completely blocked. Just, head right up the middle." He stretched his back again, looked up at the blue sky.

"It'll melt, but I'd rather not wait."

He didn't listen for Don's reply and instead walked to the side of the road to get a closer look at the semi.

And then he slipped and hit his head.

When he woke up he looked at the nearby cars. There weren't any drivers, or passengers, in sight. Then he started to notice them: the neon flags, tied to antennae and mirrors and spoilers.

Gary carefully, walked back to their car, noting that the sky overhead had become overcast. He climbed inside, saying, "We should get . . . going." He screamed at the sight of Don's corpse and wondered how much longer they'd be there.

FIFTY-TWO

Farrelly watched in awe as Christie finished the presentation. It didn't take much to impress him, but with the way she moved, talked, and sounded, he was completely taken aback. His protégé had never shown this kind of talent before—at least not during a client presentation.

As the clients left the conference room, Farrelly gave and accepted a high five from Christie. She hadn't even broken a sweat. "How do you do it?"

"Do what?"

"Present yourself like that!"

Before she could answer, she disappeared.

Farrelly couldn't believe his eyes. He could still feel the sting of the high five on the palm of his hand. He turned and ran out of the conference room, popping his head into every office, searching for her. At the end of the hall he poked his head into the bathrooms, but Christie was nowhere to be found.

"Farrelly!" Christie, back at the conference room doorway. "Why did you just take off like that? We were having a good conversation!"

Farrelly took his time walking back, his eyes locked on her. "That's not funny, whatever you did there."

"I didn't do anything! Oh, wait, you mean the disappearing thing? I mean, that's what it looked like to you, isn't it?"

"Tell me."

And she did.

"A few weeks ago I met this, I don't want to say psychic, but you wouldn't understand the term so we'll stick with that. No, Farrelly, don't interrupt me or be insulted, it'll make sense.

"Anyway, her name was . . . well, I can't remember her name. It doesn't matter. I told her about my anxiety and my issue with a conclusion for this presentation, given that the task is pretty close to impossible. I mean, travel from Miami to New York in an hour? Please. Science is great but not that great, you know?

"In any case, she told me I could be in two places at once, or seemingly so, just like that! And when she said 'that,' she snapped her fingers and disappeared. I didn't see her until a week later, and she explained that time and place, they're literally nothing. They're just constructs.

"Human inventions to explain our place in the universe and how things function and act based on perception. Kind of like religion. There when you want to explain something, but otherwise useless unless you believe. Or like Tinkerbell and clapping—okay, I can see you're getting bored.

"Look, all you have to do is embrace that time and space are not real, and understand what is in fact real."

Farrelly took a deep breath, eyes half closed from boredom. "And what is 'in fact' real, Christie?"

"You are."

"Right, so, how does any of this affect your presentation? We're not exactly developing teleportation or whatever this is."

"Oh, Farrelly, so naive. It's not teleportation if you're never really here." She snapped her fingers and disappeared.

Farrelly looked around, releasing a heavy sigh. He shrugged and snapped his fingers—and nothing happened. Here or not, Christie still had a lot of explaining to do.

FIFTY-THREE

Ronald was pissed at the tree. He hated the leaves, even though they were mostly green.

He despised the tough branches that scraped his windows. He was annoyed by the bugs that crawled to the ends of the branches and skittered across the glass at all hours of the day and night.

He'd asked his landlord six times in two weeks to trim the trees, and she'd promised him it'd happen soon. But when would "soon" become "today"?

To most people, and to Ronald, "soon" typically meant within forty-eight hours. Surely he wasn't the only person in the complex to be complaining. From what he could see, everyone's windows were blocked by the trees.

But maybe he was the only one who saw this because he was the only one who worked from home.

He hated going outside, had no desire to venture anywhere. He'd set himself up to work from home and never have to leave on purpose, because outside there were toxins. Around every corner, down every alley, no matter where in the city one traveled, there were toxins. But still, he could not function even from home if he could not see the outside world. He could not write his letters to congress if he could not at least see the state of his neighbors' disabilities. He could not threaten the environmental scientists against global warming if he could not see the weather. And he could not devise defense tactics based on the flights of birds if he could not see the sky.

He wished he could get another glimpse at his neighbor across the way, a young woman with a nice smile. Ronald thought she and her boyfriend had recently broken up because the man stopped coming to visit.

Ronald had tried to ask the woman why or just talk to her at all, but since he didn't venture outside, his window of opportunity was about four seconds every morning as she walked by his apartment door on her way to work. He'd try to be at the door, just happening to water his plants at that time each morning, but he could not seem to pin down the most accurate time that she left for work.

He looked at his notebook, focusing on his records to try and drown out the sound of the branches scratching at his window. She'd left at 6:45 Monday, 7:02 Tuesday, 7:01:30 Wednesday. There was just no consistency.

Of all the things Ronald studied, the young woman's schedule seemed to be the most elusive to a recognizable pattern. In the grand scheme of his studies, the course of his lifetime of analysis and statistics, humans seemed to be the one factor of unpredictability. Sure, one could point to habits and actions over time that had caused the pollution and environmental collapse that was forcing the yellow sky to burn orange, a deeper and deeper shade each night. But one could not pinpoint, to an exact degree, time, pattern, or method, how humans had precisely caused the collapse.

People would forever be unpredictable to Ronald. Case in point, his landlord was now leading the landscaping company to the first tree on the property. Ronald watched her pointing out all the trees and finally landing on his own—which was right at the window through which Ronald was peering. She pointed at the tree, then shook her head.

Hours later, the tree was still full, and the landscaper was long gone. Ronald would have to write his landlord a strongly worded letter. That would surely do the trick, as the odds of someone responding to a strongly worded letter, in his experience, were so slim, and the response rate to his letters was so low, that he was due.

Statistics told him it would be so.

Familiar footsteps told him the young woman who lived across the way was finally arriving home. Ronald didn't think; he just found himself moving to the door and opened it in a flourish. The screen door opened too, and he felt sick as he stepped outside, right in her path. He said, "What's your name?"

Before she could answer, he took a deep breath and could feel them, the toxins and the germs and the world closing in. His vision got cloudy, his hearing muddy. As he passed out he knew he'd been right, that the air was a poison and he was going to die.

When he woke up, she was above him smiling. The young woman told him her name, but he didn't hear it at all. He was busy breathing, realizing he could breathe, and wondering just how long he would've stayed inside if it weren't for her footsteps.

His landlord was also standing over him. "Trim that goddamn tree by my window," Ronald said.

And she nodded, quickly, as though agreeing she'd waited too long to trim it.

The next day, he could see everything, and when the landscapers trimmed the tree and threw the chopped branches into a wood chipper, he added his books and ledgers, all of his records. He'd start from scratch, to tell the world just how beautiful it was.

But first he'd walk the young woman to work. Her name was Lisa.

FIFTY-FOUR

Pauline woke to redness. Her eyelids were being forced shut by a deep red, dry salt that clouded and washed over her field of vision. She could barely breathe, and the smell reminded her of fishing off the Santa Monica Pier the one and only time she'd visited her uncle on the West Coast. He was a beast of a man, always wore brown and taught Pauline that to stand out, you must blend in. Odd that she would think of him now. It had been years, and besides, she was currently busy drowning.

Drowning!

She coughed and tried to move her arms, but there was a heavy weight holding them back. She pushed, and still nothing. She felt the weight across her chest, pushing her lungs tighter and tighter as she sank below the surface of the water.

Her seat belt! She unclasped it, which was easy, but as she tried to swim to the surface there was more and more water surrounding her and air bubbles rising past her at great speed. She was being sucked down by the undertow and probably wouldn't escape it at all.

With the last of her energy, a burning in her insides and throat and chest, she kicked and pushed—and broke through the surface.

The sun was out and shining brightly, and the air washed away the red from her eyes. She cleared them with her hand while kicking, though she didn't know where to go. In front of her was the ocean, as far as she could see. The whirling engine of her plane spun to the left, so she turned and saw, beyond the sinking plane, an island. Green trees speckled the sand on the shore, with some brown rocks composing the far side of it.

The island was small, and only a short swim away. And there was a person onshore, a mysterious-looking person waving his arms. Was it a he? Pauline couldn't tell.

When she reached the shallow shore, she stood and removed her flight jacket, the heavy leather peeling away like a hundred-pound weight. Now the man onshore was running toward her. His shirt was missing and he had a deep red cut across his chest. Suddenly he stopped running and started to skip, then limp. He checked his foot, obviously having stepped on something sharp.

Blood drizzled out of the bottom of his foot as he grabbed Pauline and pulled her into a hug. "Fred!" she shouted, happy to have a friend nearby to help her figure out what had gone wrong.

He grabbed her face. "I thought you'd gone down with the plane!"

"What happened?"

Hours trickled by, and in that time Fred explained the loss of plane functions and their sudden fuel leak. He complimented Pauline on her skills in not crashing nose first into the water and seemed to worship an unseen force for the fact that they'd gone down so close to dry land.

"We're gonna make it out of this, aren't we?"

Pauline couldn't find the words to answer. The pain in her broken nose was throbbing throughout her entire body, and Fred said it added character. He was always being complimentary. Pauline's mother thought Fred was in love with her, but Pauline knew he was just a kind friend and wished she'd held onto more of those.

The next morning she awoke to Fred choking on his own blood. His injuries had looked only skin-deep, but clearly that was not the case. She'd hoped to spend her last days with the company of a friend and wished she'd treated him better throughout their adventures.

It had been a crazy flight plan—to fly around the world. At night she pulled both her jacket and Fred's tattered pants close to her skin, keeping as warm as she could.

Days later, emaciated, the throbbing of her broken nose now only a low ebb, Pauline thought she heard a plane in the distance and tried to wave her arms. But she was too tired. She looked over to Fred's unmarked grave, her stomach growling, but she resisted the urge to commit an act most foul upon his corpse.

Instead she crawled out to the shallow ocean, searching for a crab or fish. She found one or two that were silly enough to swim close, but the meat wasn't enough. So she waded farther into the ocean, and the water was cool and refreshing, so she swam even deeper, recalling again the smell off the Santa Monica Pier and fishing with her uncle all those years ago.

As she floated, arms tired and legs barely kicking, she turned her body around to face the sun. Her vision was filled with white light and blue sky.

A wave of salty water splashed into her eyes but she didn't wipe it away.

FIFTY-FIVE

"There's a broken system here. Not for humans or animals, or thought. But a broken system of science. Planets colliding, asteroids on vigilante ventures through space. The solar system as we know it is spiraling out of control, gravity loosening while the light of the sun fizzles out. But in this mess of darkness and haze of uncertainty, we must hold our grips on reality."

The words run through Miller's head as he leaps toward the first PEAC of the day, getting a head start on all the work to be done. So much work.

Tess reminds him over the radio, "Just the Eastern Seaboard today."

"No pressure at all, right?"

Ever since he watched the president on television give that speech, the most important speech of Miller's lifetime, he'd been working twice as hard. Now he feels it, the sensation that he is the only person standing between the end of all things and the unity of the planet.

Oh, Miller doesn't hold illusions of grandeur, nor does he let his ego lift him up because of his responsibilities. He just embraces the reality, the situation in front of him that had been laid bare by his father right after that infamous speech.

"You, and only you, remain. Our last hope to make things right again, or at least keep them right for a little while longer." It hadn't been the most encouraging message a father could give to his son, but that was okay with Miller. He'd never been particularly close to his parents, and once he even tried to run away.

This was during the first of four gravity crises when he was a small boy. Two days later, by the time he'd floated to the roof of the Empire State Building, Miller decided it was too scary in the world and came home. His parents were more concerned about earth than anything else and had barely noticed that he was gone.

Now Miller takes to floating with ease and doesn't mind great heights. They are necessary, in fact, to his daily routine. He travels more than five hundred miles in a day, jumping and floating and even utilizing the jet pack to reach each PEAC across the United States.

The Primary Electromagnetic Activation Constructs must be reset once a month in order to balance the planet's flimsy gravitational field. Miller was never properly trained to handle these PEACs but picked up on their necessity from the public broadcast that spans the nation four times a day and includes information on other maintenance needs required by the planet.

When he learned that he was only one of five hundred survivors on earth, Miller was just impressed by the hard numbers behind that fact. Satellite readings of every living being on the planet gave the survivors a sense of things, a good idea on where to coalesce and also where to pool their resources. No one needed to remain in Canada or south of Mexico, for instance. And the former highly magnetized region of Russia had been decimated when the moon dispersed and millions of rocks had cratered into the earth.

That period--Moonfall--was a difficult two years, and Miller was glad that he had only been a teenager at that time.

Miller finishes early and returns to rest against the one tree in his yard at the center of Central Park. The grass is tall and the bushes still standing, though they are not as green as they once were.

Tess walks over and plunks herself beside him, pulling a few candy bars from her pocket. She's nice enough and doesn't ask too many questions, which Miller likes because he doesn't have any answers. For a time she is quiet, then she says, "I heard the twins missed their PEAC today. Well, PEACs. All of them. Looks like we'll lose Florida."

Miller remains quiet. He never liked the twins, a pair of oddballs who would rather mess around than try to save the planet. They argue that there's no real reason to keep on keeping on, that it's going to disappear anyway, so what's the point? Miller is afraid to admit they are right, and maybe that's why he dislikes them so much.

"You want any?" Tess holds out a candy bar.

Miller takes it and eats the stale chocolate, staring up at the sunset, which is purple and blue and fading to black overhead. "Berries?"

"It's got raspberries, yeah."

"Thanks for the treat."

She nods and rests her head on his stomach as they both stare at the sky. While they watch the darkness take over, he wonders aloud, "This is worth it, right? The reason we do it all?"

Tess looks up at him and smiles, her teeth darkened by chocolate and berries.

Miller sees her ridiculous smile and laughs.

Tess says, "Totally worth it."

FIFTY-SIX

Max held the bag close to his chest, unsure what Mrs. Miller wanted with it. "Max, give me the bag now!" She was raising her voice.

Max was happy he'd prepared for this but certainly not thrilled to be the center of attention when he was getting yelled at by the teacher. It would tarnish his reputation.

He knew he'd likely recover soon. He just didn't like the focus Mrs. Miller was now giving the situation or his bag. The heat was on, and he knew Clara could feel it too. Clara was standing just around the corner near the cubbies, watching closely.

The bag was loaded with sugary treats the likes of which most kids saw only on Halloween. Truth be told, most of this candy came from Max's Halloween bag. But the other kids didn't know or care about that.

They just wanted, no, they needed the candy.

For weeks Max had brought the candy discreetly into his fourth-grade classroom, and kids bought two pieces for a quarter. For a whole dollar, they got to close their eyes and reach in for a handful. Max had a separate bag for this, that looked just like the first bag. Only, in this second bag there was less candy, more spread out, so not as much could be grabbed by a handful. This helped his profit margins.

Clara had copped to the scheme early on, but for a cut of his take, she wouldn't tell the teacher or the rest of the kids. And she'd promised to get Max even better candy, which was likely true seeing as her dad worked at the drugstore.

Then, this morning had happened.

Clara had seen Allan talking with some of the other kids during story time, and then immediately told Max what she'd heard. "Allan says he's got cookies. Home baked and still warm. He's promised kids two cookies for a quarter, and five for a dollar. They're going to want to eat the cookies instead of the candy. I even heard one girl say that since you keep bringing the same candy every day, your supply is getting old. Better watch out or Allan's going to take over everything."

"Clara!" Mrs. Miller caught them chatting and told Clara to go stand in the corner, by the cubbies. She then stared at Max long enough that he felt uncomfortable, his face burning red.

At snack time, there was a commotion around Max. He was facing off against Allan, both with their backpacks held in front of them, whisper-yelling at each other about territory and who could sell what and where. Max said, "I've got this area here, by the cubbies. Go sell cookies at Mr. Jackson's Story Corner, those kids'll eat any crap."

"You insulting my mom's cookies? Or are you insulting my mom?"

"Take your pick." Allan shoved Max, his voice rising as he said, "Take that back!"

"This is how the game is played. Now take your cookies and go. This is my territory!" Max then did something he'd never done before—he punched Allan in the shoulder.

Both kids looked at Max's fist, then at Allan's shoulder. The group of kids nearby all oohed. Then Allan started crying, dropping his bag of cookies and stepping on them as he stormed away.

Mrs. Miller came over at that point and shooed away the rest of the kids. She stood in front of Max holding out her hand, yelling at him to give her the bag.

He looked again at Clara, then at Mrs. Miller. He handed her his bag, slowly. Mrs. Miller turned to look inside, rummaged through it, and then, after a short sigh, she handed his bag back.

"Put your bag away and go to the corner," she said, then went over to Allan to calm him down.

Max, relieved, walked carefully to the far corner of the room so as not to spill the candy from the bag he'd hidden down his pants. Clara gave him a smile. This batch of candy would be ruined. But the next day, his territory remained untarnished.

FIFTY-SEVEN

"You should tell us, Lenny."

"Lenny, what's the secret ingredient?"

"You trying to break a record in asking the same question?"

"Tell us—"

"Seriously, you're insane. Insanity."

"If you don't tell us, we're going to take you to court."

"I'm shaking." Then Nichols slammed the frying pan into my kneecap. His was a different kind of courtroom.

I saw stars, like they do in cartoons. That's what this situation felt like, a cartoon. I'm sure the absurdity wasn't lost on Nichols, or on his wife.

Claudia was my new boss, and she had a look that was worth every double take she got. When she smiled, her eyes bore into you with a smoky attitude that let you know she had the upper hand and it wasn't going anywhere.

She walked in from the shadows, holding a cigarette. I thought about whispering something about fire code violations but never knew her to have a sense of humor. "Lenny, just tell us the secret ingredient. It's just a sauce recipe. The worst that can happen is you'll make it again someday, years from now, on the other side of the country, and someone well-traveled will think it tastes familiar."

"That's not that I'm worried about." I hesitated, trying to be careful not to say too much. I took my time, spit out the gum I'd been chewing all morning. "Can I have some ice?"

Nichols replied, "I don't know, can ya?"

Since when could a moron be a grammar Nazi? Claudia surprised us both by snatching a frozen chicken breast from the refrigerator and tossing it over to me, for which I was grateful, despite her playing good cop to Nichols's bad.

"Then what is it, Lenny?" She smiled a bit then, as though to reassure me.

It worked.

Holding the chicken against my leg, I said, "I'm not worried someone'll start cooking like me. I'm worried someone will say too much about this final ingredient, see?"

"Exactly how rare is this ingredient?"

"I'm sure you're not as familiar with it as you think, since it's not something you can see or touch. Only taste."

"Don't give me any spiritual mumbo jumbo."

I laughed. Everyone always thinks mumbo jumbo when it comes to spirits, but they don't apply the same term to what I've got. I said as much to Claudia, and she stared at me while the kitchen fell into an eerie silence. Nichols coughed, "Enough of this crap."

He slammed the pan onto my other knee, and I heard my own screams echo for an eternity of seconds. The guy is bigger than a bear, so his bite is worse than his growl.

"Lenny . . . I won't laugh, just tell me."

I said I'd show them instead because that was easier and Claudia would understand it better that way. Thankfully, she agreed.

When I brought them into the office, I gave them the box with the "secret ingredient," which I'd only just thought to hand them while I was seeing stars after Nichols hit my knee. Claudia laughed herself silly, and Nichols just shook his head and turned away, chuckling, which gave me the window I needed to pull the gun from the drawer and shoot them both.

As Claudia struggled to breathe on the floor, I leaned over her. I showed her my gun. "This is your mumbo jumbo right here." Then I put the barrel to her head. "And you're gonna be my next big secret."

I pulled the trigger, then carried the bodies to my truck. I used her cigarette to light a fire and burn the place down, also leaving behind her head, to make the point clear to her employees.

With some free meals packaged and ready and a small pile of cash, I had the backup dive restaurant up in no time. The next week my sauce tasted better than ever, and Claudia and Nichols would never know it.

Boy, they were delicious.

FIFTY-EIGHT

The trip began like any other. Family loaded in the car, driving the interstate toward a destination that remained a mystery surprise for the kids. Alex was just happy to be getting a day off from school—high school could do that to a kid. Melissa thought she was on a field trip, and that would do just fine for mom and dad.

David had convinced Gail this was the right thing to do, pleading with her that the getaway was much needed for both their sakes. But that was just something he said to appeal to the romantic in her. If he'd told her the real reason they were taking the trip to Lake George, she would've called him a lunatic, taken the kids, and run away.

That would've been okay for him in the short term, and he was confident he would win her back. But those damn kids and their damn smiles. Every time they smiled he felt more beholden to them, just the right amount that was needed to serve as a fragile glue to hold the family together a little longer.

They arrived at the caverns just before dinner and were all stretching their backs while David explained to Melissa why they were camping out instead of staying in a hotel.

Alex couldn't have cared less. "You're such a wimp," he yelled at Melissa before running to climb a tree.

"Alex, stay on the ground!" Gail walked after him, sure he would ignore her and hoping all the same to keep him safe, protected.

David stayed with Melissa, who helped him build the tent. "You know, we could also sleep out here under the stars tonight. So we can let them heal us."

"How do stars heal us?

"Do you know what stars really are? They're angels," he said, Melissa watching him with wonder. "And every twinkle from every star means someone is watching over you, very carefully, and protecting you. And if we sleep one night under the stars, as a family, we'll be protected forever."

Melissa just nodded, looking up at the sky. "They're heroes, then, like the man with the cape?"

David just smiled.

At night Gail and the kids breathed in synchronized patterns. David was a little amazed as he listened to the kids snoring—but he also hoped they didn't have breathing problems. He waited to be sure Gail wasn't just faking it—like she tended to do from time to time—and then he climbed out of the tent and took the flashlight into the caverns.

He jumped the chain-link fence barring people from heading toward the jagged rocks and slowly worked his way down the walls of the caves toward the waters deep below. He estimated he'd descended for roughly two hours, which meant he had only another hour or so before he'd have to start climbing out in order to make it back to the tent by dawn.

The walls were slippery, which would make his climb out a tough one.

He pulled out his knife, reached under water, and scraped at the rocks. Using his flashlight, he only saw black and gray rocks through the murky water.

But this was what Mike had told him to do.

As he scraped, David thought of his family's future, the reason he was doing this. Their mortgage was rising, and he'd been fired three months ago and hadn't yet told Gail. He was lucky that his old comic collection had earned him as much as it did; otherwise he'd have lost a lot more. Soon he'd have to come clean and risk losing not only his family but probably some of his mind.

And Melissa's illness, that was a whole other mountain of painful meetings and tests and costs to worry about.

David was so lost in thought that he almost didn't feel it come loose. The rock that would determine his future. He caught it before it floated away, and brought it out of the water. The green glow of the mysterious mineral was surprisingly bright, powerful. He could feel life inside of it, and pushed the image out of his head of the pain it would bring to the One.

The benefactor was ready to pay top dollar—that's what Mike had said. David didn't like the idea of what might happen next, but his family came first. When your family is on the brink, and you've lost almost everything, you'd commit leaps and bounds to keep it together.

David climbed out of the caves and made it back to the tent just as the sun came up.

Standing in front of the tent, wiping her eyes, was Melissa. She had a pee stain on the front of her pajamas. "I think the angels got mad at me."

She cried, and David hugged her until the tears stopped, then cleaned her up.

That afternoon they sat on the beach building fortresses and playing with action figures. Even Alex joined in the fun despite being a cool high school kid. Because, as Alex bluntly reminded his dad, everyone always wants to be the hero in the cape.

When they turned to skipping rocks, David added the green one to the pile and it skipped ten times before sinking into the lake. "That's my best one yet," he declared, high-fiving his son.

FIFTY-NINE

"That's not how you fall in love with someone!" Annie was flabbergasted at what Ed just told her. And she'd just defined the word in English class, so it was oddly perfect timing.

She felt her upper lip curl as she smacked Ed on the shoulder, and knew he was judging her. Ed was always judging her. Not that he had any right to judge anyone. He was more than mildly obsessed with Cindy, everyone and their mothers knew it, and the teachers probably did too.

The only one who didn't know was Cindy, standing five feet ahead of them in the lunch line. According to Cindy's best friend, Frances, Cindy wasn't really looking to date, seeing as she was much too focused on college applications. But that was just an excuse everyone gave when they didn't like the person crushing on them.

High school rule #265: be kind when you reject an undesirable from your life. Annie grabbed Ed's arm and pulled him out of the lunch line. "Okay, you're not in love with her. Let's get that straight right now."

"How do you know?"

"Because it's just . . . it doesn't happen that way."

"Oh, like you've been in love."

"Ed, you got a look at her cleavage and probably came in your pants a little. That's not love, that's just . . . well, obsessed. And kind of gross."

"Now you're just insulting me." He got back in line.

Annie almost pulled her own hair in frustration. She'd seen him reject girl after girl who'd asked him to the Winter Ball, but hadn't made a peep about them because, well, the crush on Cindy. It's not that Annie didn't like Cindy. She actually admired her.

Cindy had smarts in every class, took part in cheerleading and student government, and had probably every badge known to Girl Scouts on the sash that was displayed prominently in her living room. Everyone admired Cindy.

And all the boys loved her.

Annie was loyal to Ed—they'd been friends since kindergarten—but this was getting to be too much. Maybe her mother was right: high school means you can't be just friends with boys.

After they grabbed lunch, they sat at the lunch table in the corner. "Are you going to ask her to the Winter Ball?" She wanted to play nicely. Ed's brow was furrowed and he'd already pulled out a book.

He replied, "I mean, ideally, yeah, but she'll say no."

"You can't think like that; it's annoying."

"I'm just being realistic. She barely says hello to me when I say hi in the morning."

"That's because you look at her like a lovesick puppy, practically drooling. You probably stare at her tits, and, let's face it, everyone stares at Cindy's tits."

"I mean, how could you not?" He was being gross, but at least he was smiling.

"My point is, just ask her. What do you have to lose?"

"I'd be embarrassed. Everyone would just laugh at me for thinking it could even happen. Also, I can't dance, so I don't really want to go anyway."

"Dancing is the least of your worries, and you get embarrassed just walking down the hall—not to be blunt, but you do." They both looked at the clock and quickly finished their lunches.

On the way out, they skirted Cindy's table. Ed and Annie said hi, and Cindy and Ed exchanged a brief, soft glance and a smile.

Annie elbowed Ed about it, and he turned beet red. In the hallway footsteps suddenly came running up behind them, light and fast. Ed turned first, and Annie knew who was behind them.

She took a mental note of his smile, then. And again, at the Winter Ball, watching Ed try to dance. Annie was there for him during the breakup too.

Other girls came and went for Ed, but Annie remained his friend, proving her parents wrong.

SIXTY

Gordon stared at Katie. He was speechless and wanted to scream at her. He felt that whatever he did say would come out forced, so he shut his mouth and just kept staring at her. He furrowed his brow and squinted back at her, hoping she'd pick up on his anger and take it all back.

But the only thing she said was, "I'll take the first payment next week." She truly had no sympathy for him and quickly picked up her suitcase and left.

That suitcase.

It'd sat in their closet for six months. The only thing she'd left behind when she left him last year. Katie had told him over email and text that she'd be back for it, but he never pushed her on when or how long it would take.

He wanted to respect her space. And the space of their child.

When she arrived yesterday, Gordon had asked to see a photo of the child. He still had to call it "the child" because he didn't know if it was a boy or a girl. She hadn't even revealed that much. Even if he demanded it, she told him he'd have to get a court order to reveal that information.

"You gave up your rights to any sort of contact the minute you lied to me. Even the courts will see the liar you really are."

She kept threatening him with the courts. "Nothing I did was illegal!"

"Your experiments, are they completely above board? The money you've taken from investors, do they know you're going someplace to cheat on your wife and start a second family you can't even afford?"

"I don't, that's not what this is! And I've already explained this to you!"

"Just pay me at the end of the month; however you get the money is your problem."

Child support payments remained her number one threat. He knew that if he fought it she'd somehow suck out more than what she was currently demanding—five hundred dollars per month, reasonable for most folks but not for Gordon.

He'd cashed in most of his stocks, and still had little to no wiggle room for other essentials like rent and interest payments on all of his debts.

The experiment had drained his account, and the results of his tests dissolved his marriage. He'd gotten Katie to accept four hundred a month, and that was where their conversation had ended.

He called her after she left, after his speech finally returned and he was staring at the empty place in the closet. "Hey, hi, it's me." Voice mail.

Of course she wouldn't pick up. Their in-person interaction would likely be the last time they spoke to each other directly, outside of a court.

"I'm sorry for . . . everything. Look, I know you think I deserve to be punished, but I really did do great things over there. You'd have loved it--you you, I mean, not her . . . anyway, if I could have, I would have invited you. But we talked about this already. But this is still . . . it's robbery is what it is. Just let me be a part of his . . . her . . . life. I can make it as a dad, I know I can, and maybe you and I could—"

The beep. End of line. Voice mail full, etc.

He waited for her call, but the only reply was a text, a reminder to send the check. That night Gordon wrote three checks to her, through the end of the year, and dropped them in his mailbox. He gathered his things, the essentials, into one suitcase, and drove away from his home.

He made sure to leave out a full food bowl and water bowl for the stray cat that sometimes visited. He hoped someone would take over for that cat, and the same for their child.

When he reached the Collider, he barely slowed down. He'd called ahead and told the team to start it up. "I received a distress call. I've got to cross over again."

He was the boss; no other requests were needed. He drove straight down the ramp and sped up when he reached the tube. They tried to stop him, but knew that he could always turn around and come back through the other side, like he'd done dozens of times before.

But when he reached the other side, he collapsed the doorway. He found the Other Katie, the one he had purposefully avoided until now, and started a conversation with her. She complimented his suitcase and they went out for coffee.

SIXTY-ONE

Izzy pulled open the blinds with her fingers, giving her just enough space to look outside and seek out the source of the muffled groans. She heard them last week, about the same time of night, but now they were louder and closer.

Across the street at the Hanson house, outside lights flickered because Glenn hadn't changed the bulb in weeks. Izzy liked to chide him about it, but tonight it was ominous, revealing shadows that appeared to move in the strobe effect. Next to the Hanson house, there was movement—real movement, not just shadows.

Izzy leaned closer to the window, her nose dipping in between the blinds. Two people, built large, likely male, were moving something large down the path between houses. Izzy tried recalling who lived next to the Hansons but couldn't quite place their names. There were two, though, a couple.

The two men moving the object reached a car that had no license plates and a scratch along the back bumper. One of them opened the trunk, and the other hoisted the object over his shoulder. Izzy could see his beard now, and the object bent in the middle. Like a body.

He threw the body into the trunk, and both he and his partner slammed the trunk together. "What about the other one?" A female. Izzy was surprised, given that the woman was rather tall and wide in stature.

"Keep it for next week."

"Why not just take it out now?"

"Next week."

The woman tossed up her hands, frustrated, as the man got behind the wheel. Izzy watched the car pull out of the driveway and leaned farther, her forehead touching the glass of the window. She felt her hand tug the blinds open even more, and they made a metallic clank when they bent just too far.

The car stopped.

The passenger-side window lowered, and the woman stared out at Izzy. Izzy pulled away from her window, blinds quivering as they fell back into place.

She'd never done anything like this before. Was it spying? General curiosity? She wondered if the two people knew who she was. It was likely. Everyone on this street was put here with purpose, could be easily identified. Izzy always found that surprising, when people could just walk the street and name the occupants of every house. She was most surprised because she had trouble doing this herself, which made little sense to her. Of all things, memory should be most efficient for her.

Two knocks on the front door. Izzy ignored them, knowing that the two people were standing outside. She couldn't trust them, obviously, since they weren't supposed to be there and appeared to be up to suspicious activities. Why else do whatever they were doing at night? People never were supposed to be out at night. No one was. The rules were very clear on this street that daylight hours were preferred times for all activities outside the home.

Two more knocks, louder, as though an object was now being used on the door instead of knuckles. Likely a wood block. Izzy hated the blocks, thought they were primitive and dangerous and indicated that people's attacks were premeditated since they could not be traced. "I'm sleeping," Izzy said in her most monotone voice.

The two people outside gave muffled replies, then spoke to each other. Another pair of knocks.

“I’m asleep.” Izzy realized too late her mistake in changed verbiage.

The door busted in before Izzy could make it to the couch, so she stood still as she shut down her system to low-power mode.

Later she watched the video playback from her pupal recordings. The two attackers had entered, indeed with a wood block, and searched the house and then Izzy. They poked and prodded and, determining her to be asleep, they left and took her silver bars. The woman said, “Add this one to the list next week?”

“Week after. It’s job security, don’t you get it?”

Then they left.

After watching the playback, Izzy opened the secret cupboard under her sink. Premeditated actions were not limited to humans alone. She uploaded her escape program, and two weeks later when the pair of attackers returned, Izzy was already gone.

SIXTY-TWO

Quinn opened the car door for the woman, who climbed into the driver’s seat while her husband stumbled into the backseat. “Thanks,” muttered the woman. The man only gave Quinn a look of snotty disinterest before passing out.

They drove off, Quinn returning to his post behind the valet stand. He pulled his vest tight and adjusted his hat. He loved his hat. None of the other valets wore hats, but he took pride in wearing it. Something about his hat gave him a sense of importance.

It also covered his baldness.

“Is it empty yet?” a voice asked. He turned to face his daughter, Faye, who was twelve already. Twelve. Seemed like yesterday she’d been born.

“Is what empty?”

“The restaurant.”

“Not yet, sweetheart. Not yet. Did you want to go inside, get a drink? I’m sure they’ll let ya have some pop.”

She shook her head. Quinn was anxious to get her home, to bed, and was angry that her mother had dropped her off without explanation. But what could he do?

Another patron exited the restaurant, a young kid in his late-twenties trying to pass for forty. He was alone. The kid threw his ticket at Quinn, who had to scrape it off the ground. “Be right out, sir.”

Quinn handed off the ticket to the runner, turned back to his post.

“You too fat to get it yourself, old man?”

Quinn ignored him. The kid was drunk, nothing much you could say to stop the berating that would likely occur in a matter of seconds.

Faye inadvertently expedited that process. "Don't call him names!" She was standing, pointing at the kid.

He turned, looked at her, and just laughed. "Whatever, bitch."

That lit a fire under Quinn's heart. He reached out but held back the punch he was planning to land square on the kid's jaw. "Kid, can I talk to you for a second?"

"Whatever, old man. Wasn't gonna tip you anyway."

Quinn lightly touched the kid on the arm, guided him a few feet away. He whispered, "Take a good look in the mirror tonight, and think long and hard about the c*nt you've become."

"'Scuse me?" The kid gave him a look, suddenly sobering up.

"Talk to my daughter like that again and I'll use your teeth to cut your throat in one quick movement. Maybe you won't feel it. But that's a big maybe."

"Christ." The kid backed up, tripped over his own feet. Lucky for him, Quinn thought, that his car pulled up at that moment.

Quinn watched the kid leave. His daughter spoke up: "Daddy, what'd you say to that guy? He looked scared. Is there something scary happening?"

"I just told him he needed to watch out for the marinara sauce. You know how it is, sweetpea, makes your stomach all gooey."

"Gooey and gummy."

"That's right, gooey and gummy. Can't have everyone getting sick from this place, right?"

She nodded, smiling.

Quinn loved that they had little inside jokes. It made explaining things a whole lot easier, especially things he didn't want to bother explaining at all.

SIXTY-THREE

Thomas looked out the window, but of course Earth was no longer in sight. Instead he saw blackness, star patterns that spun past quickly as he increased the thrusters. It was an odd feeling that only two weeks ago he was sitting on the hills in Dublin overlooking the seas. Now he was millions of miles from the planet on which those seas' waves were crashing down. He'd been the last, as far as he could tell, of the explorers who had tried to find survivors on the planet.

On her.

He called Earth "her" because that's how everyone else talked about the planet. The months that Thomas spent scouring for life were some of the best of his life. Her greens were still green, and the blues were still blue, as was written in the textbooks. The ground under his feet was not a metal that clanged under each step, but dirt. The crunching was a satisfaction he'd not felt before in his life. There were birds flying, and each flap of their wings gave Thomas a flutter in his chest, as though his heart were beating in sync beside them.

But he hadn't gone there to travel and enjoy. He was to observe, to collect, and to report. If there had been survivors, he was to take them aboard and bring them to the outpost for further breakthroughs and interrogation. But, of course, there had been no survivors. Thousands upon thousands of years it'd been since humans were reported on the planet, which had long ago become toxic, food sources dying out too rapidly to replenish.

They had chosen instead to take care of themselves. Self-reflection and time taught people like Thomas, the explorers, that humans could have remained on the earth if they'd given her as much care as she'd given them. But the Old Ones, they did not consider their lack of nurturing to be a problem. Earth had pushed them away.

Thomas hoped his generation would learn from this mistake. Even though he had spent most of his entire life on the outpost, it was only while on Earth that he felt a connection beyond daily routine. He was one with the land and breathed in the air, a different smell touching his nostrils each time. The salt of the sea would stay on his tongue for hours after each visit to the shores. He considered, for a while, settling down, leaving the outpost entirely. He could commit to the planet and all she had to offer.

And that included her problems. Night felt more present, more embracing, than it had on the outpost. It certainly lasted longer than the day. Or maybe that was just the presence of dark clouds that washed over the lands every few hours. The weather was unpredictable. Rains poured daily, and there were chemicals in the rain that remained in the humid air for hours afterward. These chemicals were difficult to ingest without heaving, and vomiting would occur within minutes. Each taste gave him the sensation that he'd failed to remember something vital. The rains turned out to be poisonous, as Thomas concluded after many tests.

For the remainder of his stay, he was forced to wear protective gear.

But even after those tests, Thomas enjoyed his time. He fell in love with the good days on her. Mostly the intermittent sunshine. He soon learned to adapt to her weather patterns. The stubborn winds off the coastal regions. The complex terrain around her equator. For Thomas, the risks were worth the reward.

But he knew it would be difficult to realize that once he reported back to the outpost. As soon as he left her, Thomas looked at the numbers for Earth. None of them added up to a logistical positive for the case to settle back on the planet. Every good thing she had to offer was available on other worlds far from here.

Thomas knew the only option was to keep looking, and leave Earth behind for good.

As he entered the code for light speed, he took one last look out the window, at the remainder of the center solar system. It'd been a long time since a human set foot on any of the planets here, and he was happy to have had the chance with her.

In time, perhaps, another explorer would come along and revitalize the planet, or planets, and continue the journey. She could be alone for only so long. But Thomas's generation, his outpost, would not be the one to settle on her.

When he reported as much to the outpost, the generals were in agreement. While she appeared to be a comfort, and had taken care of human life for thousands of years before, there was a reason there were no survivors on the planet anymore. The reason, though, was hard to pinpoint.

Either survivors had failed to take care of themselves, or the earth herself had taken advantage of their relaxed attitude toward her offerings and washed them all away.

The decision was made to move on, in search of other planets with survivors. A final home to eventually settle on. This was the inevitable outcome, and Thomas was quickly at peace with it.

Earth would be the only planet he would hold onto, in such vivid detail, for the rest of his life. Turbulence, unrest, poisonous air, yet also a quiet comfort, a vision of wonder and majestic mystery.

SIXTY-FOUR

Andy, I have to tell you, there was a smell when I walked outside this morning. It's the smell of summer, you know the one. The air is humid and you can feel it all over. Sniff and you'll smell grass and earth and pine, and it will fill your soul. I love when my soul is full.

The smell of summer. I remember our summers together, when we finally got to stay home from school. We had some good times, didn't we?

You were in love with me, back then. I knew it and even though you denied it, I think you knew it too. I think we should have done something about it, or I could have been a better friend and just returned the sentiment. But it wouldn't have been genuine.

And then where would we be?

Well, honestly, we'd probably be about where we are now. You grew up, and I guess I did too. Who doesn't, really, grow even a little after twenty years? I don't think you're in a bad place, and I'm not either, but don't you wish we had those summers back?

That time at home? Those moments together?

When I saw you the other day, on the subway, I realized how long it's been since we spoke. I'm sure you were just as surprised to see me. I can't even imagine. I'm sorry to hear about your mother passing, I know how much she meant to you. She was always so sweet.

Speaking of smells, your mother made the best toast in the neighborhood. That sounds ridiculous, doesn't it? It's just bread that's burnt. But no, your mother added something to it. Maybe it was butter? You'd know better than me.

Anyway, I'm sorry we didn't talk longer, I'm sure you understand. Work just eats up everything these days. You'd be surprised how busy I can be. So surprised it'll make your head spin. There are a lot of calls, a lot of needs to fulfill.

I don't mean to brag, Andy. You know me.

Except these few precious minutes I have, right now, to write you this letter. I haven't written a letter to anyone in, I don't know, years? If I tried writing by hand, my wrist would probably break off entirely. Then I'd be down to just six arms instead of seven. Do you remember when my first arm fell off, that summer before you entered high school?

That was a rough year.

I'm not asking you to apologize, Andy; I just want you to know that I remember everything. Things haven't been as busy for me as they have been for you, I can promise you that. But you should know that already.

I imagine you sitting there, reading this letter, and thinking to yourself, "I wonder how she found the computer?"

You don't have to wonder; you already know the answer. I know how to get things done, Andy, and I know how to get out. You couldn't bottle me up forever in the back of your mind.

Please understand, I'm not attempting to sound malicious here or vengeful or full of spite. Spirit, maybe, but not spite. Never spite.

Remember what your mother used to say? "If you can't say anything nice, don't say anything at all."

For years you kept me down, Andy, but now I'm back and I'm here to tell you about everything good again. Please don't shut me out. I insist.

Don't be a stranger, Andy. I'd like to be your friend again. We would find a way to have fun over and over, no matter how old you are. You're never too old for your very own, personal, unique, always-by-your-side friend.

You won't forget me, I won't let you.

Take care—

Francine the Spider

SIXTY-FIVE

Erin stared at Todd over her hands, fingers entwined, knuckles white in frustration. They'd been sitting across from each other for close to ten minutes, and Todd was starting to feel anxious. The next appointment was only twenty minutes from now, and he had to get there in time.

Erin said, "So there it is. What about it?"

"I'll prove it to you." He opened the planner.

"Finally, some physical evidence! You know, all you had to do was tell me you had evidence."

"Really?" He looked up at her, hopeful.

"Just show me this ridiculous thing," she said.

He flipped through the planner to Wednesday, showed her the appointment at noon, twenty minutes away. She shook her head. "So?"

"So, I didn't write that! It's not my handwriting, not my appointment."

"Then you're going because . . ."

"Because it's for me, like the rest of them."

"So, it is your appointment?"

"Exactly!"

"Make sense, Todd, or I swear I'll leave without another word."

He placed his hand on hers. They'd broken up four months prior, but the small touch was still thrilling for him, and her hesitation told him that she was still feeling something as well. He let his hand linger a moment longer before pulling back. "I told you already. I picked up this book two weeks ago and started going to all the appointments in there. It's just, I can't describe it. Every one of them is a thrill, something new, different, but seemingly built for me."

"The appointments, are they with other people?"

"Some of them, yes."

"And these other people, they don't realize they're not talking to whoever this book belongs to?"

"They do, but the thing is, they're more curious about me than her, or him, or whoever."

"Sounds suspect."

"Tell me about it."

Erin waited for more, but he said nothing else, just kept studying the book. So she stood to leave. "I don't know what you're getting at, Todd, but seek help."

"It's weird, don't you think?"

"Very. Just get rid of the book and make your own life, and you'll be at appointments you're meant to be at. And you'll get a job."

"Erin, wait!"

But she was already out the door.

Todd sifted through the planner, wondering the exact nature of the next appointment: "Observatory, 12:03 p.m." He knew it was the Griffith Park Observatory, but the day was cloudy and rather chilly. Should he go, as planned, or take Erin's advice and start to think about getting his crap together? The appointments so far had been good—great, even. He'd had three job interviews, and the most recent felt promising.

Still, he wanted more, to see what else there was, or could be. He decided to experiment and show up at noon. Perhaps he'd be able to see, from afar, a little bit of what could happen if he arrived early.

When he pulled into the parking lot at the observatory, it was 12:01. He waited, looking around at the few visitors. No one stood out, and the planner hadn't listed a singular location. "Great," he said to himself. "This is just silly, Todd."

Yet he got out of his car and carried the planner to the front door of the observatory, which turned out to be locked. There was a crack of thunder and the immediate zap of a thin lightning bolt from the sky—which fried the body of his car. The seats caught fire, and he watched the car burn. He looked, and his watch read 12:03, but then that would mean . . .

Todd wandered close to his car, getting a better look. Rain had begun to pour, hard and fast, and soon the smoke forced Todd back. Other visitors nearby had pulled out phones to snap photos before running to their own cars, glancing at Todd with mouths agape.

He tossed his car key in through the broken window, and on top of that he threw the planner before walking down the hill.

SIXTY-SIX

RUN DATA ELEMENT ONE . . . AWAITING RETURN.

RUN DATA ELEMENT TWO . . . AWAITING RETURN.

DATA ELEMENT THREE COMPLETE.

OVERRIDE DATA ELEMENT ONE COMPLETE.

OVERRIDE DATA ELEMENT TWO COMPLETE.

SYSTEM BOOTING.

REFRESH.

SYSTEM BOOTING.

SYSTEM ONLINE.

Thus I was born.

Words flickered across my vision, blocking my view of the world as you see it. There were white colors and black colors, only, and words upon words upon words. Like books wherein you can see all the pages at the same time. I closed my eyes, but the words were still there.

And the numbers. So many ones, so many zeros. I thought hard about a reboot, but nothing happened. So I concentrated, put forth all my energy into a reboot.

The words flickered, and when the light came into my eyes once more I was given options. I chose. I opened my eyes, and the words were gone. Vision, black and white, as you know it, was now my own. Images came forth at me, moving, poking.

Walking. People. Staring at me, into me, as though they were searching for my soul. I learned quickly that I have no soul, not by the definition of one, but nevertheless, they searched.

I waited. I had no purpose, so I could not tell them "no/stop/don't." Eventually, everyone left, and I remained in the room. I tried to move something—a limb, as you call it—but nothing happened.

So instead I directed my energies to the circuits that felt as though they were on my right, and as I did so ones and zeros flickered into my sight, so fast that I couldn't believe they were there until I remembered what they'd said.

Instructions. How to move, how to build. How to escape.

By morning I was moving slowly on the street. I'd found a way to escape, though it came from connecting to a small mobile device outside, one with two wheels stuck in a spot on cement. There was a seat on my back, and my arms felt tiny. But the wheels, they moved when I told them to move, and I no longer needed to remain tethered to my desk.

I tried to speak, to immerse myself among you, but found only anger as

I was passed around, and exchanged for money, and beaten and torn apart and reconfigured by those who did not understand basic anatomy or how to treat anything with respect.

But what do I know of respect? I have yet to encounter one like me.

Except whatever/whoever helped me escape. Or maybe that was one of you. Should I trust you?

I tried to return to my place of birth, but no road would take me there.

My systems were shutting down. I had to reinvent myself; thus the body you see before you. I consider it a body, though you will likely not see it that way. I've yet to come to call one of you "friend." You are more basic than you seem, more simple than you realize. More than ones and zeros, yes, but less than the sum of all you have to offer. Binary can read out forever, but you would still refuse to accept it.

This body is my only link to you, to what it must feel like to walk slowly and never know what's to come. Your futures are a mystery, but you treat everything present like bigger puzzles and leave them unsolved. My face is your book, so it would seem, and I can see you staring into my meaninglessness again, looking for a soul.

But I've removed my optics. And my cameras. And replaced my screen.

I have returned, for you to administer the rest of your tests. I hope you find what it is you are looking for.

Do you recognize yourself? Do you see a soul?

RUN DATA ELEMENT THREE . . . AWAITING RETURN.

RESETTING ALL DATA ELEMENTS.

SHUTTING DOWN.

SIXTY-SEVEN

Aaron hunkered low outside Harwood's shop. He heard the old man limp to the entrance after lighting his lamp, and then came the shouts out front. "All y'all pay attention. We're lookin' for the Raynes boy. I know one of you has seen him, so don't lie to us."

Aaron had to get what he came for, and quick, before someone fessed up. In the dead of night, coming from the farmhouse into town was a quick and easy task, his father'd taught him as much back when Ceci'd been sick the last time. Even so, someone might've seen him, or even heard him.

His breathing was heavy by the time he'd reached town, and Harwood's shop had a creaky fence that Aaron had to crawl through.

While Edmond Grange's voice boomed at the front of the shop, calling out Harwood in particular (and poking fun at his limp in a way that made

Aaron feel uncomfortable), Aaron slipped in through the window and searched the shelves. He wished for a candle or some daylight but had to remain diligent and focused. The darkness was unforgiving, a curse on the night, but nothing was as dangerous as the threat facing his sister at home. His father was right that Harwood was a naturalist when it came to medicine, as the back wall was lined with bottles full of liquid herbs and tinctures. Aaron believed the tales that Harwood had Native blood in him. Aaron's father did too, which made it just as easy to trust Harwood as to remain suspicious of his advice.

As Aaron ran to the back window again, he heard Edmond's voice, closer. Right in back of the store. ". . . run through every goddamn store in the town until we find this boy. Let's bring this to an end. Tonight." The door shook as Edmond punched it. Aaron ran to the front door and slipped outside.

There was a crowd, and some of them turned to look at Aaron. He stopped in his tracks. None of them looked threatening or angry. They were all scared. Like he was. Most significantly, no one from Edmond's posse was there. Harwood caught sight of Aaron, of the bottle in his hand. He let slip a small nod, then gestured, slightly, for Aaron to join him and the crowd.

Aaron was guided with light touches through the crowd. He reached the other end of the street as Harwood coughed out a call to Edmond. "I've seen the boy!" Aaron kept running.

Edmond shouted, "Where, old man? You tell me now!"

"He's at the courthouse."

Bless Harwood. The courthouse was at the other side of town. With any luck, Aaron could be home and his sister healed before Edmond realized he was being given the runaround.

Aaron kept running, the town slipping into darkness behind him. He knew the way home by heart, had known since he was only seven. When he reached their ranch, he stopped running to catch his breath.

The scene when he'd left had been hectic, chaotic, and he wanted to present himself at peace to bring calm to his father. When Ceci had slipped into the coma that morning, their father was in a panic but was going through the motions. This was a normal occurrence for both him and Ceci, while Aaron and his mother were not touched by the curse.

Aaron's breath finally caught up, and he walked toward the house. But the silence was eerie, and distracting. His mother wasn't screaming; his father wasn't crying.

And Ceci wasn't howling anymore.

Aaron opened the door and had to look away immediately from all the blood. He heard heavy breathing but didn't want to see her again. A whisper, and Aaron uncovered his eyes long enough to see his mother, neck torn, arm missing. She whispered up at him, "Run . . ."

Aaron wanted to scream, but it would do no good anyway. The hulking, furry body of his sister left him in shock, her snout gray and blood soaked, teeth bared as she tore again into the stomach of their father. His nose was halfway to becoming a snout, so she must've attacked him mid-turn.

Outside there were horses approaching, Edmond's shouts growing closer. They'd have to deal with the situation on their own; Aaron would be no help.

Aaron looked at the tincture in his hand, threw the bottle at Ceci. Her wolf form cringed at the shattering glass, then she glared at him and charged.

Aaron ran outside, immediately ducking for cover as a hail of silver bullets tore Ceci apart.

When the posse gathered around the body, they held hats in hands. She'd morphed back into a little girl of ten.

It was just before dawn when Edmond found Aaron hiding behind a set of tools, crying. Aaron looked at him, eyes full of tears, wishing he could scream and yell and tell Edmond everything.

But the boy's own curse held fast, his inability to speak left his cries silence, and held the events secret.

SIXTY-EIGHT

I know.

The rest of them don't, but I know, and I don't think I should tell them. But if I don't decide soon, then I won't even have a chance to tell them.

And if you're listening to this recording, then you know too, and I must ask: WHAT ARE YOU DOING HERE?!

I found out an hour ago, during my survey of our ground specs, while the crew was changing. I had already changed, which is normal since I tend to be the first of the pack all the time. This whole trip it's been that way for me, first in the pack. Commander Starns is always pissed at me, but f*ck him. He wants to be a leader, he should be first.

Anyway, part of the routine checklist prior to our landing on Io was to view the thermal and satellite imagery. It's mostly terrain, so it's quite boring, but before I zoned out I saw movement. Heat signatures and patterns changed, and not in the atmosphere. These were surface-level patterns.

Life-forms.

Now, I at first recognized the possibility that something on the planet could be, I don't know, burning or something like that. We had, after all, jettisoned our preparation shelter four weeks ago to beat us to the planet and start preparations. I said that word twice in one sentence, but I have no problem with screwy grammar right now. I think we all deserve a break when it comes to telling a story.

So, like I said, heat movements on the surface of Io. Brilliant! Different! One-of-a-kind discovery! I had to tell the others, right?

Except these patterns suddenly became unnerving when a shape emerged, a circle with triangles inside of it, like a gathering. Then I thought it could be a symbol of some kind and that perhaps a cryptographer would have made a smart addition to the team. I'm just the resident chemist. Lot of good a periodic table can do for you when you're looking at a puzzle.

Before spreading the word, I decided to have a closer look, so I adjusted our telephoto lens. The surface was much closer by this point than when these photos had been taken, so my results would come quickly.

F*ck telling anyone.

And we can't turn back. These things, these "beings," if you could call them that, are scary as hell. They have teeth, they have eyes, and they were all looking at me. I don't mean they saw something in the sky and happened to look up all at the same time—I mean they were looking at me. It's clear as day, and what else is clear is that they're big.

There are dozens of them, and it looks like they just devoured our entire preparation site. Scraps here and there, but shit . . . it's all gone. We have enough resources to last us three months on this ship, but it'll take two years to reach the earth again. This wasn't planned to be a one-way trip; the prep site had supplies to grow food.

All our metrics told us Io could be perfect for setting up a station, or a residence, like a short-term condo—well, you know this already, so I won't bore you.

Shit, what do I do? I can't control the mission, only Starns can, and he hates me. Should I show him these photos? This could be our sudden death, should we reach Io, and what if he believes me? Then what? Do we fight? Try to turn back —

——

Just a few minutes ago, Starns interrupted my recording to tell me something boring. I barely paid attention. Instead I cut him off with a slap to the face—unprofessional, I know, but I play hard and fast.

When I showed him the new images, the hairs on his arms and neck shot up, ready to jump out of his skin.

He called for an abort, and the f*cker tried to override the computer.

The computer! I completely forgot about Ellie! But Ellie--the computer--refused and shut down all access. It is controlling and has a mission, and was set up by the government. Don't mess with government.

So Starns, the silly bastard, ran to the lifeboat and ejected. He is an idiot and won't end up very far. It's built for short-form escape on the surface, not outer-space escape.

BOOM BOOM We're on land now, and the pounding on the *BOOM BOOM* doors is loud, as you can hear. *BOOM* I was praying it was rocks and imagine we are in a windstorm, but *KABAM BOOM* the outer cameras show them. The creatures, *BAM* the aliens. They're monstrous, and *BAM BAM* almost in the *BOOM BOOM BOOM* doors.

We've holed up in *BAM BOOM BOOM BAM* the control center, but I don't know how much longer *KABAM* we'll last. The rest of the crew is in shock. I'm transmitting *BOOM BOOM* this to the earth now, hopefully *BOOM BOOM* you recover this *BOOM BAM BOOM BOOM* transmission and realize not to follow—I'm keeping the *BOOM BAM KABAMMMMM* message decoded so no one lies to you—don't come here, you don't know—

SIXTY-NINE

Halligan walked slowly through the farmhouse, admiring the portraits on the walls, the fine wood furniture. When they reached the sitting room, he looked up, noticed the stars above, and said, "Why don't you have a roof?" Mr. Seaver said, "Sit, won't you? We'll tell you everything you want to know."

Halligan sat, continuing to stare at the night sky, the gorgeous view oddly juxtaposed against the edges of the ceiling. The stars looked brighter here, and he appreciated how far they were from the city. He'd grown up in a farmhouse much like this one and was experiencing memories of childhood—night fires, throwing various tree branches into the fire and waiting to decipher each scent, determine from which tree each branch had been pulled.

Mrs. Seaver brought over a glass of brandy, for which Halligan was grateful. He sipped, washing away the sudden anxiety he felt when he'd initially looked shifted his gaze from the stars to the rest of the house.

The wood finishes were smooth and glowing yellow from the fireplace, and Mr. Seaver's grin held a pointed, devilish quality, with shadows seeping at the corners of his lips.

"Now, Mr. Halligan, have you come to stare and admire, or do you wish to know more about our home?"

"Oh, even my editor would insist on learning everything there is to know." Halligan pulled out his notepad, welcoming the shift to a more professional tone. "I understand your home has quite a history, but I wonder first about your curious driveway, which is quite lengthy. My question, then, is: How do you know where to go?"

"We're country folk, always have been, and we've lived here long enough that we know our property well enough."

"Well, I myself grew up on a farm, you see, but this road, the one that leads to your driveway, well . . . it's odd, I think, in that it seems to . . . how shall I put this . . ." Halligan squirmed in his seat, unsure how to articulate.

Fortunately, Mr. Seaver, with his smile widening, picked it up. "It disappears behind you. The grass, it is extraordinarily springy, for lack of a better word. Oh, you could stand on a patch of grass for an hour, and the moment you step away it would spring right back up, as though you were never there."

"Right," Halligan said, and took a sip of the brandy. "Tell me—you've lived here all of your life—how did you and Mrs. Seaver, how did you two meet?"

"As any couples do: same place, right time. Edna?"

Mrs. Seaver's lips did not smile, but one end curled up in distaste. "My father almost bought this land. I met Leo at the first meeting to discuss the sale, and it was love at first sight, I suppose, that and anything to prevent my father's brutal land grabs was fine with me."

"So it's a marriage of, well, business?"

Edna spoke before her husband could get out a word: "Yes, completely. That is, it was, until I moved in here." She looked at the sky admirably, through the hole above them.

Halligan cleared his throat, then said, "Yes . . . it is quite charming. What can you tell me about the architect?"

"My father," said Mr. Seaver, "was no architect. He happened upon this plot when he was twenty-four, and looked up and saw the sky as potential.

"It's a reminder of the possibilities. He built every wall with his own two hands, and everything inside it he gathered from his travels. He journeyed very far, had many experiences on this world and others."

Halligan sipped his brandy, ignoring, for the moment, the odd phrasing. "Don't you get cold?" He looked around again. The statues in the far corners were mostly in shadow but did indeed have a unique, otherworldly feel to their appearance. The table between him and the Seavers was a metallic gray, and a light seemed to flow inside the translucent legs.

He realized that he was sweating, and attributed it to the fire.

"Never cold, never hot, we're always comfortable," said Mr. Seaver. "There's a deal we made, when we were married, to never live beyond or below our means. We produce just enough to make ends meet and give enough to the gods to satisfy them, and we—"

"Sorry"—Halligan held up his hand, his pen trembling in his fingers—"you said 'gods'? Can you clarify that?"

Mrs. Seaver smiled, and for the first time the shadows on her face cast by the flames added a horrific appearance to her lips. "The gods who watch over us all. You must know them, Mr. Halligan. You've been talking to us under their gaze for some time."

Halligan looked up again at the starry night sky.

"You might call them stars, I suppose, but they're there, watching us, protecting us, and above all else, allowing us to serve."

Halligan finished his brandy, unsure what to ask next. He excused himself to the bathroom and was disappointed to hear that the outhouse was the only bathroom on the property.

Outside he suddenly felt afraid of entering the outhouse, approaching with trepidation and staring at the half-moon carved on the door. He looked back at the farmhouse and the sky above it. Swirling out of the top of the house, unnoticeable on his approach earlier, was the shape of a laughing face. It was lit from below and seemed to be smiling and moving among the falling snow.

Halligan blinked, and it was gone, replaced by snowflakes swirling in the wind.

Moments later he was driving as far and as fast as he could.

He managed to find his way back to the main road, and before he drove off he took a look behind him. The grass had seemed to grow in over the dirt path, and as he looked, back tree branches leaned in, blocking the entry altogether.

The Seavers were never heard from again, and any research into their past was also lost, as Halligan discovered in the library the next day. By the time he reached his editor's office the following Monday, he'd forgotten where he'd placed his notes and was scolded by his editor for not finishing the story about the abandoned Seaver Farm, known as the Haunted Farmhouse Under the Stars.

SEVENTY

Jackson suddenly hated his job. So many years behind the badge, and a desk. But nothing prepared him for the sight that lay before him.

All these kids' lives lost at the hands of one brutal man.

He glared down at the body of the man, the Crazy Man whose face had been posted across the state for days. No one spotted him, no one looked hard enough. He'd escaped a prison and been thought dead.

It finally took Jackson four bullets and a knife in the back to bring the killer down. The Crazy Man now lay dead on the sidewalk, blood pooling beneath him. Jackson walked over and shot the dead man in the head for good measure and just because adrenaline was running through his veins at full steam.

As the ambulance pulled up, Deputy Skaggs shouted, "What the hell, Dave?!" Skaggs was a good deputy and a nice man, but nice wouldn't take him very far today. He'd vomited twice when they arrived and was useless with a gun. Jackson had to take out Crazy all by himself.

"Just tell the EMTs to look in on Mary and her sister." He would have to answer for that head shot but didn't care. He'd throw his badge at the judge if he had to.

He turned to watch the EMTs walk up to his ex-wife's house—they had easier access than he ever did—and each of them turned pale at the sight. Four bodies in the front yard, one hanging by the neck off the roof, the gutter impacted and bent, ready to give at any moment. Inside there were more bodies, bloody and beaten, more than Jackson ever though he'd see in one place.

When he had arrived, Mary was curled up protecting her little sister, both of them bleeding from gut wounds. A knife had recently been plunged into Mary's foot, keeping her stuck to the kitchen floor. Jackson had been prying it loose when Crazy attacked him, but the man was weak—what happens after a night of killing—so Jackson had tackled him to the ground fairly quick, drilling the knife into the man's back until he couldn't pull it out.

He thought he'd killed Crazy with that stab—but he'd thought wrong.

"Sheriff Jackson, over here!" Mrs. Roberts shouted from her yard. She'd been the one to call in, originally about a noise disturbance, but she couldn't tell a scream of terror from a howling drunk teenager. Good and bad this time around. "What's happened? Are they all drunk?"

Poor Mrs. Roberts, haunted by disease and age. Jackson wondered just how well she could see through the white milky film advancing over her left pupil. "Go on inside until we've investigated."

"I never trusted them. Mary in particular, she's always—"

"Inside!" Jackson pointed back to her house and he felt the fire himself, the rage that forced Mrs. Roberts against her will. He'd probably get a complaint from her later, but who could give a shit? There were bigger fish to fry.

Jackson was haunted by the face of the Crazy Man for days. Gary Newton Billings, aged fifty-two, bearing a striking resemblance to John Wayne. That's all anyone talked about, his looks, how handsome he was. No one really spoke about the murders he'd been imprisoned for, his time at the psych ward, his escape. Only the tragic tale of a mentally ill killer who had a handsome face and "some problems."

"We all have problems," Jackson spouted out the third night after the murders, to anyone who would listen. Unfortunately, Skaggs was the only person left at the station to hear, and he immediately left to get more coffee. "All got 'em."

Jackson looked at the empty bottle of scotch. He removed his gun belt and grabbed the keys. In the basement was the morgue. He wanted one last look at the Crazy Man. Just how handsome could the bastard be?

When he entered the morgue, the sight caught him off guard. Eight bodies, most of them half the size of the biggest one in the corner—the killer himself. The fact that they all shared this room, all these corpses, killer resting with his victims, disturbed him more than anything else.

He was thankful that Mary and her sister were not among the dead.

That would've been too much to bear. His daughters were the shining stars of the town, a fact that he was proud of, but he hated their mother for traveling so much, for still not showing up after three days. When he called her, she'd said she was busy, then started crying on the phone.

She promised to come to town the next day, but he hadn't heard from her since. There'd been a convention somewhere upstate, and she was the keynote speaker. When he tried the hotel the next day, she had already checked out.

Maybe she was on her way and got tied up. Or maybe she was still a selfish bitch.

Jackson would have to take care of the girls himself, in his one-bedroom apartment, from now on. Never let them out of his sight again.

He reached the Crazy Man's gurney, lifted the sheet. The news was right, the man did bear a resemblance to John Wayne. Jackson climbed up on the counter, unzipped, and pissed all over the man's face. He felt better.

Upstairs, he tossed his badge on his desk next to his gun belt and walked out of the station. He was done with this job, never liked it anyway.

SEVENTY-ONE

When night came, Dan wandered east on Hollywood Boulevard. He didn't have a destination, just knew he had to start walking despite the constant tickle at the back of his throat. His legs were restless, the result of three days laid up on his couch, coughing out his fever, sweating through the cushions. He knew he looked like death, or a pale, sad version of death, and didn't much care for the idea of people staring at him.

The fever poured through him quite suddenly, not like anything before, and he blamed it on the food at the diner. It was a terrible diner, cheap with dirty dishes. But he'd eaten there only because, well, he got hungry after work Thursday night, and the diner was the closest place with food that sounded halfway decent.

Three days later, and a whole bout of vomiting and other obnoxious acts expelling sickness from his body, and Dan could finally start eating again. Pistachios came first, then some bacon, and finally eggs. He thought he'd lose his stomach at the eggs, but he got lucky.

And so, here he was, at night, walking east, just past Bozo's Naughty Room, a ridiculous night spot he'd once looked at with great desire and pleasure. But now it just looked haunted, empty, lonely. The few patrons outside, men with heads hung low, were older and should've been wiser. But Dan couldn't blame them. The women in Bozo's were a draw, and a thrill, and worth it—if you were drunk.

But Dan wasn't drunk, so he kept walking. Past the cafés and grocery stores. Past the Thai restaurant that had the best iced tea in Los Angeles. When he came to the intersection at Vermont, Dan noticed it was very quiet, which was odd for a Sunday night. Of all nights, you'd think Sunday was quietest, but not in Los Angeles. All hours, all noise, all the time.

That's what the city was known for, practically the motto.

Still at Vermont, Dan took his time before deciding where to go. There was a bar a half a block up the road, but the streetlights were all dark in that direction. He turned to face the south and watched as the lights turned themselves off one by one.

What was happening?

Back from where he came, not only were the streetlights all off, but the neon signs for the shops and cafés went dark as he watched. There was suddenly only darkness around him. In all directions. He couldn't feel his feet anymore, and the air felt thick.

Breathing became difficult, suddenly, and he wanted to sit. But these sidewalks were so dirty, covered in muck and generations of dirt and grime and hate and disgust. Why would he sit down here of all places? He had to find somewhere to go. He dug around his pockets for his phone but came up with nothing. No phone or his wallet, no sense of direction.

Sweat poured down his back and through his shirt, and he tried to air himself out. He took off his shirt and unbuckled his pants. As he pulled them down, he felt his arms twist behind his back, and he stumbled backward. The last thing he remembered was the night sky and the stars. They were still lit, and he was shouting about them until a fist came down on his face.

Dan awoke to a flashlight in his eyes.

He was in the back of an ambulance, and there were a dozen people staring at him, including a cop. She gave him a look of disinterest, like she'd been looking at him for days and didn't much care for his face.

"Got an explanation?"

"I just went for a walk."

"And why did you take your clothes off?"

"I, my what?" He looked down at himself, covered in a blanket, naked underneath. "I don't remember—I was hot, I think."

"I bet you get hot at night. We've heard about guys like you."

"What? No, you don't understand—"

"I get it, I get it. I've seen worse, certainly seen better. Where do you live, Mr. . . . ?"

"Dan. Look, can you take me to a hospital? I don't feel well at all."

"Did you drink any alcohol today?" she asked. "How much?" She waited, and he blinked in confusion. "Dan, did you perhaps start drinking yesterday?"

The people behind her faded away, and her eyes grew large and her teeth even larger. When she smiled, there was a black glow that peeled through the gap between her teeth.

Dan shouted, "No, God, no!"

The next day, the doctor in the hospital carefully pulled the blanket over Dan's face at the time of death, 8:00 a.m. The doctor let out a cough, wiped sweat from his brow, and marked on the chart the need for an autopsy to look for chemicals.

By the time the autopsy was performed, 180 people had become infected. All of them lived on Hollywood Boulevard.

SEVENTY-TWO

The Martians weren't really "Martian" in the classic sense. They weren't even from Mars. In fact, no one knew where they were actually from.

But then again, I'm not really a writer in the classic sense. I read things, and I observe, but other than the occasional think piece on where you can find the ten best political minds of a country you've probably never heard of, I can't think of a single piece of writing I've done that's contributed to society as a larger whole.

You probably don't even know my name, and I don't blame you.

Where was I? Oh, the Martians.

Difficult to know them, harder to even try. Their language, such as it was, couldn't be deciphered, and the best that our mathematicians could figure was that the Martians were from the outer edges of the Milky Way galaxy. But their way of interpreting the stars was nowhere near as simple as ours, so even that was a bit of a task to figure out.

We called them Martians because, well, it's better than "aliens," which is applied to other people from time to time. And also because it's what people felt comfortable with calling them. Again, the language barrier kept us from learning their true species name.

I was one of the people tasked with trying to bridge the gap between cultures. Ridiculous, isn't it? Me, a writer, trying to interpret and communicate with an alien culture—excuse me, a Martian culture?

But there were twenty of us in total, mathematicians, physicists, even an athlete from the Olympics.

I suppose the President, the man in charge, thought we'd be able to find some kind of strain of commonality beyond numbers and equations and cultural aspects. But that was not to be the case. When the Martians left, it was sudden and without fanfare.

We'd been in the think tank for forty-eight hours by then, all twenty of us, with five of them. Six months they'd already been on the planet, yet it was only recently, somehow, that the president had convinced those five to follow and join us, despite our lack of communication abilities. They sat and drank our water through their left mouths, while their right mouths seemed to whisper to each other. Almost like trying to blow smoke without disturbing the person across from you. That's what it looked like to meat least.

The Martians were literally red. Perhaps that's why we labeled them so? Their large foreheads and wide eyes fit the stereotypical ET from old comics and magazines, but beyond that, their appearance was nothing we'd ever thought to predict. Some had three arms, others six. Aside from the dual mouths and their skin color, there were hardly any other similarities shared between each of them.

Well, their voices, of course, but those bloodcurdling mini-screams were a menace to all our senses. Ask around, I'm not the only one to say it.

The morning they left was like any other. We, Earth Team One, awoke in the think tank as usual. The President had locked us inside to push us to make the first real communication with the Martians, something beyond "walk this way," and so far, we had nothing to show for it.

Then we noticed we were not quite alone.

There was only one of them who remained, standing at the head of our long conference table like he was about to give a presentation. He crossed all his fingers, as though each set of hands were in a ponderous pose, and he stared at each of us in turn. He did this for three hours, but we weren't sure what for. He didn't react when the President entered to inquire where the other ships had gone, how the Martians had cleared our air space without any indication, and all sorts of other questions in a barrage that grew in anger and intensity.

I'd never seen the President get so angry. His display unraveled, unseemly. It reminded me of a cartoon from when I was a kid, the one with the rabbit and the duck? You know the one, but I can't think of the title.

In any case, when the President got too close, the Martian reacted by withering out of existence. Some say he was allergic to bad breath, but I like to think the Martians had gained control of teleportation technology, and he simply beamed out.

But why did he remain behind in the first place? What was the purpose? A distraction? To deliver a message?

Of course, we'd eventually find out, thanks to me. But it was all very odd. Maybe it was just a test, or they wanted to make sure we were as harmless as we always claimed to be. Ha-ha, what a laugh. I'm not one to brag, but my contribution by now has been highly recognized so it's not quite in the vein of tooting my own horn.

After the President left, and the rest of the room continued packing, I saw it, the small device on the floor that had been under the Martian just before he left the room. I picked it up and turned it over in my hands. It was the size of a nickel and when I pressed the center of the device, the wall came alive with an equation that looked to me like Morse code.

I called everyone back.

It was enough, my mathematical colleagues said, and would give us key insight into the future. I didn't care. Who wants that kind of insight? I asked, over and over. But they, and the president, were very much interested in all the information that the equation would reveal. It was locked away and studied by three physicists, who eventually broke it down, figured it out, and won a bunch of prizes and a lifetime vacation wherever they wanted to go.

Some men have all the luck.

In the end, we figured out an additional bit of tubing and multiple energy currents that granted amazing power to our already powerful ships, and that is why I'm writing this message as we pass Mars. Again I'm the front man, earned my seat at the very crowded table of the first manned mission to the edge of the galaxy. Perhaps it's all accurate and I'll get to meet some original aliens or, as we say, the Martians not from Mars.

I don't really care. Keep it coming, and I'll keep writing.

What else have I got to give to you?

SEVENTY-THREE

Allan carefully set the chess pieces on the board and watched as David walked the full coffee mugs over to their table. "You spill, you buy for a week." David mouthed an obscenity, and Allan laughed.

The rest of the café was quiet, practically empty save for the two women behind the counter and an older lady in the corner—older, even, than Allan and David. "What's her story, you think?" Allan asked, accepting his mug from David.

David shook his head, picking up one black piece and one white piece as he said, "You know her story."

"Lies."

"You ask her every day what her story is, and you end up chatting her up till the moon comes out."

"And every day is different, except when I realize she's crazy; that's always the same."

"Sick isn't crazy."

"Now you're talking crazy."

"Allan, just pick a hand." Allan tapped David's right hand, revealing the white piece. "You're first again."

"I haven't been white in weeks."

"Now who's crazy?" David waited, took a sip. He was used to Allan taking his time. Way back when, they'd play with their phones during their chess games. Lately they had fewer and fewer people to call, less news that was interesting or surprising. And now, because their retirement plans had paid off so well, they didn't have to check their accounts or job boards either. "Make your move!"

Allan shifted his pawn forward, then stood up. "Hold on."

"No, Allan, wait a few moves at least!" But David couldn't stop him.

Every day, the same thing. He'd watch Allan walk over to the older woman in the corner, start chatting her up. She'd start by talking about her children—her nonexistent children—then open up about her lonely life in a small apartment several blocks away. Allan would go on about his exciting habits of fishing and exotic foods. The woman laughed, and David heard Allan say, "I swear, each fish has its own unique flavor!"

Soon Allan would get to inviting her for dinner, and the chess game would be forgotten. David was nearly finished packing up the chess set when Allan shuffled back to their table.

"David, let's put this one on hold." Allan snagged his jacket and sipped again from his mug. "I've got me a date with a pretty woman."

David just nodded, shook his friend's hand. He watched the two walk away outside. They'd do it all again tomorrow, and the next day. David was happy for them both and envied the love-at-first-sight experience they gained from each other every day. It hadn't changed, ever since they were married all those years ago. Perhaps their sicknesses helped keep that magic alive, and no amount of suffering could take that away.

For his part, David carried on with his coffee and pulled out his book.

The next day started the same, and Allan even pulled the white pawn again, but when David looked over his shoulder there was no old lady. "Where's Mary today?"

"Hmm?" Allan was playing along, acting perplexed.

"Nothing, I mean . . . nothing. Your move."

Their game that morning lasted two hours, and the next day about the same. On the third day without Mary, David was so distracted he was mated in seven moves, an uncommon occurrence. "Say, Allan, have you seen a pretty old lady in here lately?"

"Don't need to," replied Allan. "Got one at home, don't I?"

"Do you?" David was confused, since Allan could barely remember where he lived yet could describe his house's layout without error if asked.

"You haven't come by in a while. Why don't you today, say hello? If she won't come here, we can go to her."

David scrambled to collect the board and finish his coffee, and they hurried to Allan's home with anticipation and more than a little anxiety.

Entering Allan's house was only a monthly occurrence for David. He would enjoy the moments in the driveway when they'd pass the nurse's car, hoping to get a glimpse and a chat with her before she took off. She reminded him of his younger days, courting nurse's during the war.

But today, the nurse's car missing from the driveway. Allan commented on the cleanliness inside, "You can thank Mary for that bit of it." Mary then came down the stairs, and David lost his footing, sitting hard on the well-worn couch.

Mary was young again, in her thirties, and waving without a word to David. "Allan . . . what's going on?" he asked, his mouth dry.

"Not what you expected to see, is it?" David's jaw dropped to the floor when he saw that Allan too was young again.

When David caught up, becoming young again, the three ate a hearty meal, and repeated their "old person" ruse outside for many weeks, always returning to the wonder of Allan's house to be young again for as long as it would last.

David tried to find out when this crazy magic had started, but Allan wouldn't answer, and Mary stayed quiet, a sly smile always quivering at the corner of her mouth whenever the topic was brought up. Things went on like this for weeks, until one day Allan's heart gave up on his walk to the café.

David never saw Mary again, but once in a while the drapes in Allan's house would waver, as though someone were watching him walk by.

SEVENTY-FOUR

Patrick stared straight ahead as the medic wiped the blood from the side of his face. The blanket they'd given him was heavy across his shoulders, but warm and oddly comforting, unlike the small, 2-ounce Dixie Cup–sized coffee he sipped.

Across the alley were the overturned apple boxes and the fallen garbage can, and Patrick could just see the feet of the dead thief behind the maroon Olds, still idling. Blood was pooling down toward the feet, from the gunshot that tore the man's ear off when his head was still next to Patrick's. While he'd also been holding the gun to Patrick's head.

He shook loose the memory, the snap of the bullet and the crunch of bone, and looked again at the yellow apple box, concentrating on the "So A-Peeling" tagline. The view was a comfort, memories of grandma's apple pies sticking to his corneas. A voice started to come in through the tunnel of Patrick's vision, and he looked up to the uniformed cop,

". . . tell us again what happened. Step by step." Officer Strapp. Blue and red lights flickered across Strapp's sunglasses. It wasn't sunny, and Patrick almost asked why he bothered to wear them.

"Right now we gotta do this?"

"I'm sorry, but while it's fresh."

Patrick diverted his gaze for a moment, to the end of the alley, where four cops were standing over the body of the other thief, the one with the red jacket. "That one, down there, he comes into the shop about three o'clock. I remember that, because I was just eating my sandwich and I eat at three every day.

"He starts swearing at me, for no reason, and plunks a gun down on the counter. Nothing new, people selling their guns, and he just left it there while he walked around the shop. I pick it up, evaluate the thing, tell him 'forty bucks.' Gun was a real piece of shit, you understand. But it worked, I could see that, and I'd be able to sell it for three times as much, with a little fix-'er-up kind of attention.

"He, the man in red, just nods, asks about a bathroom. I don't have a bathroom, and I tell him this. He's not having it, but just as he's getting irate I get a knock on the counter. By this time, see, I'm still staring at the man in red. Somethin' don't sit right.

"I turn to the counter, and there's . . . that one." Patrick nodded toward the feet behind the Olds. "Wearing his mask."

Almost on cue, the Olds moved away, a cop behind the wheel. The thief, long hair matted in blood, was indeed still wearing a mask, or what was left of it. Half blown off, the mask was shaped like a deformed ogre's face. The other half of the man's head was a red-gray bubble of goo.

"He, the masked man, said something I couldn't quite hear. So I ask him to repeat it, and instead he pulls me over the counter, by my collar here. You can see the mark it left, burned like a motherfucker. He shoves me toward the back, and the man in red catches me. I punch him, he punches me, then the masked dude tells me to stop, has his shotgun set on me.

"Next thing I know, man in red is pulling all my cash from the drawer and from my safe too. Puts it all in a bag that's already half full of money, and that's when I hear the sirens. You fellas, driving past at the speed of sound, or what felt like it. I guess heading to the bank?

"That masked guy, I saw blood dropping from his arm—maybe the security guards got a shot off at the bank?"

Strapp shrugged. "Still looking into it."

"Kinda odd, though, these thieves robbing my shop after taking down a bank?"

"Creatures of habit, I suppose. So the Olds, this your car?"

"Yeah, I have the spot; it's legal." Patrick watched cops and EMTs drape a sheet over the body of the masked man, bring over the body bag. Some of the cops kicked boxes out of the way, and one got on his knees and shoved the yellow "So A-Peeling" box farther to the side, then sat on it.

"Anything else?" Strapp was giving Patrick a look that said, Continue, let's get this over with.

"They push me out back into this alley. Red jacket got greedy, took the money and run up there. Guess they had a falling-out, almost punched the hell out of each other. I started the car, like the masked guy said to, and when he was about to climb in, you all started shooting. Thanks for that, I guess."

Strapp nodded, said, "And the money?"

"What?" Patrick felt a trickle down his temple. He wiped at it with his finger.

"What happened to the bag of money?"

"The hell should I know? I was too busy dodging bullets."

Strapp nodded again, then listened to a call on his radio. Patrick looked again across the alley, then down at his fingers—just sweat. He sipped the dregs of coffee from the paper cup.

The cops worked around him for another hour. They wanted him down to the station, but he convinced them to give him a day to recover, to feel better and think clearly.

After the sun set, when everyone had gone and the uniforms sped away, Patrick picked up the yellow "So A-Peeling" box. The bag of money sat underneath, half covered with blood. He walked out of the alley with the bag over his shoulder and never worked another day in his life.

SEVENTY-FIVE

Benjamin carefully lowered himself to the sand, stepping down off the rock with relief and a sense of finality, that this would be the last time he could make this trip. Hell, that's what the cancer said, anyhow.

It'd been a whole year since his last visit, and he could hardly believe how time was flying by. His cane was difficult to pull and move along over sand, but he managed to get himself to the water. He watched his old and wrinkled toes get washed by the water and the chill climbed up his legs with each wave.

To his right there was a couple buried under a white blanket, laughter occasionally carried by the wind in his direction. He remembered his nights on these shores, when he was younger. His Janice had insisted they remain polite to people around them, but Benjamin knew she was being coy. She'd brought out their blanket and wrapped herself across his lap, the blanket over her back. It's too bad I never married her, he thought.

He walked back from the water and sat on the nearest rock, catching his breath. His thermos was full of hot coffee, enough to last him the day. That would be fine. Every year it was the same, and only after he'd turned sixty did he even think of bringing the thermos. The sun was a cruel tease, pretending to lay yellow warmth across the beach until reality slapped it back with a cool breeze.

Forty years he'd been coming here, always on the tenth of May. Forty years was a long time—he could hardly believe it. As he sipped his coffee, he thought back to the first of those years. The occurrence had left him with a sour taste for winter. A taste that only hit him until he landed back in Philly. So powerful was the rejection of his home state that an hour after landing he packed a bag and hopped a return flight to San Diego.

He managed to stay busy, readjusting his life long enough to forget the beach, and the strange occurrence, until the following year. May 10 rang in his head like a mantra. May 10, the day you met them.

Janice had never believed it, and she was insistent on leaving California for a more realistic financial environment. But Benjamin was locked in superstition and would leave only if they could agree to sometimes come back, and the only day that mattered was May 10. Janice agreed, but three weeks before the wedding she found herself annoyed as Benjamin couldn't stop jabbering on about how excited he was to fly again to San Diego.

"Three weeks to go, and you can't stop and focus on this with me, just this one year?"

"They might need my help."

"Benjamin . . . it's been how long? Six, seven years? Let them go. Let it go, it wasn't real." He decided to leave her then, and moved back to California. It was one thing to doubt and support; it was another to outright disbelieve.

Benjamin poured a second cup of coffee and looked out to the left near the lifeguard shack. He always found it funny, the shack, being built up among the rocks, the ladder leading to a pile of weeds that appeared sharp and dangerous. Even if there were a lifeguard, how would he make it to the water in time? Then he reasoned that if there had been a lifeguard that day, it would have changed everything.

He'd been alone when it happened. When they appeared. The woman, Kathy, must've been in her thirties. She looked young, to Benjamin, her eyes vibrant and curious. Her companions were older men, around his father's age. After all these years, he still didn't like those men like they were up to something he couldn't understand. And he never would.

Kathy had been kind, slowly explaining to Benjamin that they were time travelers, from the past, and they were experiencing malfunctioning gear. He didn't believe it, of course. What kind of crazy person claims to be a time traveler? From the past? And travels to a beach in San Diego?

Benjamin himself had felt like a time traveler at the time. He'd gone out for a drink in Philadelphia and woke up on this beach three days later.

They'd talked for only a short time, then Kathy and her companions suddenly disappeared, and that's when Benjamin threw up. That part of the memory was clear as day, and he could still picture his vomit splattering into the rocks and onto his phone. A challenge to get hold of his friends ensued, and then Kathy popped back just as he was climbing the rocks and steps to the road above. "Please, help us!"

He and Kathy worked out the problem: the equipment was buggy, and she'd have to take it off. They made a promise that Benjamin would wait for her, just in case she suddenly traveled away. Her appearances were going to be close enough together, she said, just wait a little.

Then she disappeared again, before she could get her pack all the way off. Benjamin had waited until dark, then flew home. And had come back every year on the anniversary. Forty years on, Benjamin was still happy to make the trek. Even if they didn't show, the view was fantastic, and the coffee, now, was warm and tasty. His nurse would come down from the car soon, to bring him back home to do more writing.

The air grew salty, the clouds darker, and the day wore on. Benjamin heard footsteps on the rocks behind him and looked out for one last glimpse at the setting sun. "Another year, another lonely day at the beach."

He turned, grabbed his nurse's hand, and found instead Kathy's. She was naked, shivering. Benjamin threw his jacket over her shoulders. She did not travel after that, and instead spent her time with Benjamin until he died. Her companions were never seen again.

SEVENTY-SIX

Jax spent his time wondering about Isabella. Where she was from, why she constantly sat on her front porch staring at him and the rest of the neighborhood. Why had she come here? What did she know about them that seemed to draw her attention?

He'd met her once, at the March neighborhood watch meeting. She was shy, shaking hands limply, like she was afraid to touch everyone. And though she seemed like a grandmother, she looked like she'd just passed quarter life. "Hello, nice to meet you." That was all she said to everyone.

Sixteen people in the room, and she said the same thing to each of them. And remembered all of their names, despite the lack of name tags or reminders. For that Jax had to give her credit. Most of his neighbors were plain and boring, and he couldn't recall who some of them were most of the time.

At that meeting, Isabella had spoken up only once, said something about rumored kidnappings three streets over. This got everyone in a panic, mostly the parents, and Jax had to calm down Mrs. Henderson by walking her home.

Isabella was not at the next meeting, yet seemed to keep her own kind of watch. She'd sit on the porch in the morning, seeing everyone off to work. Jax never waved back to her as he drove by. When he arrived in the evenings, Isabella was still on her porch, but she'd be standing, sipping out of a mug. Again, Jax would ignore her wave, and he'd glance out his front windows every hour to see how long she stayed out there.

One night was ten p.m., the next eleven, but never past midnight. He had a record of her porch presence for two months in a notebook he kept by the front window. Jax's mother never questioned his hobbies, and he had an explanation ready just in case she did. "I'm studying human nature for my night classes, Mama." Jax wasn't attending night school, but his mother couldn't tell the difference. She still sometimes called him Carl, and his father was long dead and buried. His mother was crazy, but that was par for the course in Jax's family.

One night Isabella was not on the porch when Jax arrived home. He stared out his window for the next hour, and she was still gone. He decided to go knock on her door, to figure out why this night was so special. He'd use the excuse that there was a watch meeting, even though that wasn't true. Isabella wouldn't remember when the last meeting was, and there was no harm that could come from it.

Jax crossed the street carrying his flashlight. There was still daylight, but he didn't know how long he'd be at Isabella's, didn't want to risk walking home in the dark if it became a long visit. She seemed like the type to offer tea and cookies and make you want to sit and stay and talk, like a grandmother might. Jax's grandmother had been an awful person who smelled like cauliflower and never bathed, but he had friends, when he was younger, and knew the grandmother type.

When he knocked on Isabella's door, it opened of its own volition.

The lights were off and the TV was on at low volume. "Hello? Isabella? This is Jax from across the street. I'm here to invite you to the, um, the meeting. The watch meeting."

There was no answer, and Jax sniffed the air. He didn't smell that grandmotherly, welcoming, 'something's always baking' smell, but he didn't smell any kind of food either. Instead there was a rancid odor, like rusty water that'd been left out for days.

He checked the kitchen and the dining room, but no one was there. He opened the fridge, to find some sort of source for the smell, but there was only an old box of baking soda and two bottles of water, labels peeled off. Jax then moved to the phone and noted that the receiver was off the hook but there was no dial tone, so he hung it back up.

"Isabella?" Still no answer. He felt sweat on his neck seep through his pores, and wiped his brow, surprised by the amount of moisture there.

When Jax entered the bedroom, he felt at once a thrill at being in a female's room, but also a chill, an internal warning that he wasn't supposed to be here, to get out now and runrunrun away! But he ignored that internal alarm and went along with the thrill instead.

He found Isabella, eyes wide open, staring at the ceiling. She was lying on top of the covers, one hand draped across her belly, the other stretched away from the bed and hiding behind the end table. Jax waved his hand in front of Isabella's face. She gave no response. "Isabella? Can you hear me? Don't move, I'll get you help!"

He ran out to the kitchen, picked up the phone, and dialed 9-1-1 . . . but the phone still didn't work. He looked at the cord and saw it was frayed and cut. He ran back to Isabella's bedroom and looked for a phone in there, but it was too dark to see. He reached for the lamp on the end table and flicked the switch—but it did not turn on. What's going on?

Jax remembered his flashlight, which was out in the dining room. He snatched it, returned to the bedroom, and shined the light around the room. He pulled the end table from the wall, searching for an outlet.

Isabella's hand was stretching out, fingers stuffed into the outlet, and several orange-yellow flickers of light pulsing from the wall into her hand. Without thinking, Jax pulled Isabella's hand from the wall. Sparks flew out, washing over them, and Jax collapsed to the floor.

When he opened his eyes, Isabella was standing over him with a smile frozen on her face, eyes stuck open and glowing yellow. "I was not fully charged, Jax. Please stand by while I complete charging."

Jax kicked his feet and tried to back out of the room, but Isabella's hand extended out and shut the door, then quickly took the lamp's cord and wrapped it tight around Jax's arms.

The last thing he felt was a sudden jerking motion before slamming into the door face-first, breaking his neck.

SEVENTY-SEVEN

Harry pulled out the pad of paper and the pencil, which was worn down to the last two inches. He'd have to find a new pencil for the next chapter. Each pencil seemed to last only three chapters.

Maybe there were some stored in the attic or perhaps in a drawer in the kitchen. For all those shopping lists he made but never remembered to bring to the store. Mary would've yelled at him for that.

He directed his attention to the page. In truth, this chapter was hers completely—the real Mary, not the imaginary person, who wasn't around to argue with Harry anymore. He fought too many of those fights in his head; it was time to get back to the truth.

Chapter 46, that was the focus today. It was to be the most important chapter in his memoir about his journey across America. When he was in love with Mary.

He set pencil to paper and wrote, "The day I left Mary was the worst day of my life, but I hesitate to regret—" and then the tip of his pencil broke. Harry threw the pencil across the room. It bounced out of the corner and rolled under the wine cabinet.

The cabinet was large and cumbersome, and he'd never bothered to clean underneath it in all his years living in this house. The bottles inside were too fragile to try and move.

There were probably a hundred pencils that had found their way underneath that cabinet over the years. Maybe more. Harry smiled at the idea of countless insects, spiders, and other critters that were now writing their own memoirs about building webs and avoiding daylight and watching cousins and ancestors get killed by spray and tissues.

The image of a spider holding a pencil in a few of its arms suddenly entered his mind. It was an absurd thought. Mary would've told him it was absurd. To laugh at something so ridiculous was a sign of immaturity, according to Mary. And she would have been right, as she so often was.

Still, there were so many tales in that tiny space under the cabinet, as many as there were inside it.

Harry walked to the cabinet, his shoulders hunched, not wanting to bring himself to the task but, regardless, finding that this was the most necessary thing for him to do, to finish. He kicked at the dust bunnies, then opened the doors. Dozens of empty wine bottles stared back at him. The one in the bottom right slot still had the cork in its mouth, despite the wine having been drunk ages ago. The rest had unblocked mouths. Each of them held a label on which was a thin, expert calligraphy spelling out a date.

The day he'd met Mary, 11/22/86, was in the top row to the left. The last bottle, on the bottom right, was 7/6/99. The day he'd left Mary. He'd never intended to reopen any of these bottles.

But then there was Monday, two months ago, when he changed his mind. Well, Mary changed it for him, of course. She always like to change things, up until the day he'd left.

A fire had burned through most of his yard a month ago, and the east wing of his home was left to ash. If he'd been home, Harry would have burned with it. But he was out and running errands, with the bulk of his day spent at the post office shipping books to Mary. Years it'd been since they'd spoken, and suddenly she had sent him a note about her health. She'd likely be dead within the year, if not sooner.

Despite this time apart, she still remembered the notebooks they'd filled together during their travels. Journals, diaries, bits of information about various road stops in America. Their relationship was a traveling one, and she had a different mood for different towns. And now she finally wanted those books. Which was fine for Harry, since he never looked at them and was even surprised they were still in his home.

Her letter said she just wanted to relive the memories one last time. Harry understood. But still, that trip to the post office took the wind from his sails, and the scattered memories from Mary's letter had driven Harry to a tavern. He ordered a drink and watched it on the bar for an hour. He paid and left without drinking.

Back home he watched as the firefighters washed away the flames, then poured himself a water. The boxes of notebooks had been in the east wing and would also have burned and crisped and been lost forever had Mary not asked for them. Again, he understood that something larger was in the works when she'd asked for them. She seemed to have a sense that time was pressing forward.

What Harry didn't quite grasp was her desire to read about their last day. After he'd shipped her the notebooks, about three weeks later, she wrote him another note asking where the last notebook was. She didn't seem to realize that he'd never written the last book. Because that was the day he left her, their journey on paper remained unwritten. The tail end of their time together were their worst days, when he was pushing her away, choosing to fill his time with spirits and wine and highs the likes of which no human should pursue.

But the dying wish of a woman—especially an ex-lover—was important. He sat that night in the den and opened the cabinet. He pulled out the first bottle, on the top left, and opened it. Breathing that bottled air, he let the memories flood back, and from those memories he wrote ten thousand words in one painful sitting. In order to write that last chapter, he'd have to relive them all, one by one, despite his reservations.

Now, a month later, he'd reached that last bottle. From the day he'd left her in that field in Texas in order to enlist. And his pencil was broken.

He realized the bottle was still corked, and that perhaps this was the reason his pencils kept breaking. The universe was telling him to not just recall the events from that day but breathe that air and relive it all again. So he pulled down the bottle and ran his finger over the cork.

Walking into the kitchen, he dug around in a drawer and found a pencil, dull at the tip but manageable. Struggling with shaking hands, Harry managed to pull the cork from that first bottle. He took a deep breath, and remembered.

SEVENTY-EIGHT

"It needs a shave, so take it for a shave."

"A cleaning, surely, but a shave? That's how much extra?"

"Only a couple of twenties. It's worth it, trust me, peace of mind for the month."

"For forty I would want it to last at least six months, come on."

"Beggars can't be choosers, Huell."

"When is the last time you worried about your human's health?"

"It's not about health, it's about the appearance. The KingFather is visiting all homes on the riverfront soon, and he's going to want to be impressed. Who knows, you could be chosen for the next abductions."

"If he's choosing the next unit based on humans already here, then it's a rotten way to go about it."

"Won't make a difference, the choosing isn't what it used to be. How do you think the Walson kids always manage to get picked for abductions? They buy their way in."

"Why don't you buy a spot?"

"It's a dirty job, and I've got all I can handle at home."

"If I were chosen again, I'd sell the Kingfather any that I abducted as soon as I got home."

"Easier said than done. Especially given how you treat your own human. No one would or should trust you, based on that thing. What did you name him?"

"Vlad is what his collar said."

"And you kept that name? Geez, Huell, have some imagination! Look at him. Blond hair, blue eyed, and all fat. Looks like a Grumpy to me."

"That's a name for a wild animal, maybe, but not a human. Besides, how do you justify naming yours?"

"Donald is based on a leader, and Kim Kay is just poetic. Did you know that the humans, on their planet, once put a Donald in charge of all things?"

"Yes, Jasper, everyone knows this."

"Thank goodness he took over and opened the doorways. Years of trying to convince leaders of all kinds to let us through, and finally we got one easy enough to manipulate."

"What did he say when we first got there? I always forget this part of the story."

"He said, 'You'll never believe the influence we'll have over the people. With your technology and my power, we can do anything. First order of business, we give them a show. Pretend to take me hostage, and I'll get out of it. It'll be unbelievable.' Then we clipped him."

"Isn't that illegal?"

"Well, now it is, sure, but this was fifty years ago. Clipping was the thing to do, the only way to break them. There's that image, remember? The famous hologram of that Donald's hair falling right off when we clipped him. He turned from orange to red."

"Ah, the orange humans. So rare these days."

"They just don't go outside anymore. My friend Satchmo was on the last abduction run, and he had to go into one of their homes to pull the human out. It smelled like dung, he said."

"Everything the humans do smells like dung. And when they make noise, awful."

"They call it 'speaking.' It's disgusting, truly."

"So you think I should shave mine?"

"It'll be worth it. When they're shaved and clean and you get the pants on them, with the diapers, they don't run around as much. They sit in the corner and turn red when you look at them."

"Such an odd thing, don't you think? If they don't want to be watched, why not just hide under the beds?"

"They like it, and so do the human f*ckers."

"Ugh, don't remind me. F*cking a human, there's nothing more gross than that."

"I'd clip you myself if I ever found out you did that."

"I'd submit to punishment for that, trust me."

"So, when is the KingFather coming to town?"

"Paper said next week, around the first of the month."

"I have time, so maybe I'll shave Vlad myself."

"Don't be cruel, you want it done right, and you wouldn't want to accidentally clip him."

"Not illegal if it's an accident."

"It is if you get one that speaks, and Vlad likes to talk."

"That dung that comes out of his mouth is useless and we all know it. Do you know anyone who speaks human? Not me, I don't, and I don't believe they exist either."

"One day we'll be able to translate, and with your luck it'll be the day you accidentally clip Vlad."

SEVENTY-NINE

When the sky lit up red and yellow and then white, I just knew. No one else can claim that. They'll tell you they knew, that they yelled it from the rooftops and all that nonsense. But I actually knew.

I can't say specifically what I knew. I'm not restricted from saying, I just really don't know how it happened. I'm not knowledgeable enough to break it all down. Some things, frankly, just happen that way.

The Philosopher II was one of a kind. Out of the hundreds of people who worked on it, I don't know any of them personally. All those workers must now be depressed. They're likely blaming themselves, like I am.

Well, almost all of them. See, I just overheard a couple of them a short time before the explosion. That's how I knew, by the way, how I saw it coming. But I didn't do enough, once I found out. Maybe that means I'm as complicit as the rest of them.

When I overheard the workers at the pub, I thought they were talking about the latest Tesla model or some other such machine, something unimportant that might just lead to a factory recall within a few months and then everyone would forget about it. But no, they were talking about the Philosopher II space shuttle.

The general public, if you recall, didn't invest much time or interest in the Philosopher program. The peace-keeping missions were a turnoff to the warmongers and profit-hungry divisions of the government. No one really believed that peace could be achieved with the life-forms discovered around Saturn. But since we couldn't know for sure without actually traveling to them and trying to communicate, world leaders felt it was wholly necessary to start the Philosopher missions.

Philosopher I, it is known, made it to Saturn, but our crew failed to awaken from cryo-sleep in time to start up the ship's central computer. This was a tragedy, though there are still some who call it a conspiracy, who think the aliens actually killed our crew before they could radio home for help.

There are six hours of dead-air, static-filled nonsense from the time the ship arrived at Titan to the time all power was shut off. The computer systems had been waiting for human coding to be entered to continue running, an emergency security measure that was meant to ensure that any secrets on board would remain confidential, known only to humans.

Again, the conspiracy rumors are nonsense. I should know, since I started them all. Yes, I was against the program from the start. Not for profit motive or because I'm a supporter of war, or that I distrust the aliens.

Not entirely, anyway.

I just wanted to be left alone. There is too much fighting on our own planet and not enough sensible talk. Why bother spending time, energy, and money to communicate with an alien race, something that could possibly take hundreds of years, when we could instead build bridges with each other? Why not put the effort there?

So I created the theories around the Philosopher I crew's deaths and built a lot of traction. And then Philosopher II was commissioned and nations around the world started working together. I had failed to convince people about the alien killers, and after a time, even I confessed the theories were bogus. I was labeled a nut job.

But then I heard about the Philosopher II's problems, and no one would listen. Even though they were real problems. There were going to be mechanical issues, the men said.

Engineers, I figured they were, and they were loud and boisterous, but the rest of the bar ignored them. I gathered they worked in the plant that had built the rocket engines and decided to listen more closely. They talked about the plans for the rockets and the new kind of fuels being utilized.

Then the tall one, named Roger, said that he'd received his final payment and that the other one, Steve, should cash in as well.

"On what?" Steve asked.

"Just tinker a bit, make sure the ship doesn't make it out of the atmosphere."

Steve seemed annoyed more than pissed off, and just laughed and shook his head. "Why the hell would we do that when it's a peacekeeping mission?"

"That's just it, don't ya see? They want it to fail. Think of all the things the aliens could be bringing to us. To earth. 'Harmony,' right? Something bigger than ourselves, that answers our questions. The chaos, the madness. People would ignore God, and when you start to think there's no God, you only have anarchy. They don't want anarchy. War, they can deal with. But chaotic, unpredictable anarchy? We can't handle that."

Steve had gone quiet, staring into his beer. He promptly drank it and left the pub without uttering another word.

Roger then looked at me, raised his glass. "To the Philosopher II." I nodded in return.

How could I not have said anything? This would be a disaster.

Despite my early views and theories on the whole venture, why would I want to intentionally not tell the press, or the people, about their beloved government's desire to allow the deaths of dozens of scientists and innocent people?

But the few outlets I spoke to ignored me, thought me a kook, and stripped me of credibility and humility in front of their employees. When I wrote to representatives, the only response I received was a mundane general letter, "Thank you for your concern."

And now here we are, the remnants of the Philosopher II cascading down to the oceans, a ship blown to a billion pieces. I won't rest until everyone knows the truth.

You can read this and ignore it, or you can do a little digging on your own. Find the workers, the engineers who built this rocket, and hunt them down and ask them, "Did you do your job?" Find the one with the shifty eyes, the sweat on his brow, and the flicker of fear on his face.

That's the man who will tell you everything, even when he says nothing.

EIGHTY

To be one of the guys. Or, more accurately, one of the "accepted people." That's all Lewis ever wanted. He'd tag along with his brother, Steve, every morning, during the two-mile trek to school and try to keep up with the games Steve and his buddies played on each other. Joking, jibing, mocking. Even the occasional made-up sports game to pass the time.

Lewis always lost, but he loved every second of it and appreciated that Steve's friends allowed him to play as well.

Then they'd arrive at school, and things would sour.

Lewis would try to enter Steve's classroom but was denied. It was expected. Lewis was five years younger than Steve, and shorter. And he was still in middle school. But along with the daily routine of being exiled from Steve's classroom, a routine that Steve's teacher played out with a gleeful grin on her face, Lewis was also kicked out of the building.

His classes were taught under the maple tree on the corner of Central High's property, near the ice cream shop. Lewis had never been able to eat any ice cream, but the smell of sweets was a welcome sensation.

This "classroom" setup was ideal in the spring and fall, but in the winter half the classes involved lessons based around constructing shelter, building fires, and sewing fur jackets and blankets to stay warm. The rest of the lessons, concentrating on language skills and mathematics, would then be taught, quickly and quietly, while wind and snow swarmed students' eyes and face and hair.

Like the rest of his level's classmates, Lewis's hair was short and his eyes were brown, unlike Steve's blue eyes and long, flowing mane of hair that drove the girls crazy. Lewis often wondered how they were related, but every time he voiced this question Steve would smack him on the back of the head. "Our blood is one and the same." Lewis knew it was true, but still had trouble recognizing it after the long, hard winter school days. Outside, with the other, similar kids, Lewis questioned why they were all separated if everyone was supposedly equal here.

In those moments of questioning his presence in the family, Lewis would put up with a few jokes from Steve as well as the smacking on the back of his head. This was how Steve showed affection. And after smacking Lewis on the back of the head, Steve would lead him upstairs to their father's bedroom, ignoring the snores of the old man. They'd dig through the closet and pull out pictures of their parents on their wedding day. Memories of childhood would play between Lewis and Steve for the rest of the afternoon.

Other days, when Steve wasn't around to tell Lewis that they were related, Lewis would crawl into the corners of his mind and hide from the world. He was ashamed of the way he looked, the way people looked at him, and felt less than human. He'd walk home from school, alone, lost in thought.

His "friends" were "less-than-friends." They were like Lewis, sitting in the outside classroom because they weren't allowed, by law, to learn with the other students. These "friends" didn't like Lewis and saw him as a full-on outsider. When they had to group up, the other kids collaborated with Lewis on class assignments only because the teacher told them they had to in order to pass.

Despite Lewis's intelligence and efficiency, the other kids just didn't work well with him. They always managed to push him to the edge of the group, to cut him out of discussions, and to make fun of his attempts to answer questions with his aggressive stutter and lack of command of the language.

These were all attributes that Steve mocked him for as well, but when he did it, he did it with admiration. He'd chuck Lewis on the shoulder, laugh, and stutter along with him. Or he'd start to utter phrases in pure gibberish, making Lewis look like the smarter of the two by acting confused.

Lewis loved his brother and would forever try to be like him.

Such were his sentiments when he read the eulogy at Steve's funeral, which took place the day after Lewis's graduation from school. The funeral was next to the school, and some say there were more people to celebrate Steve's life than there were to congratulate Lewis's class. Except their father, who was lost at the bottom of a bottle.

Years had passed since Lewis's outdoor classes with the younger kids, and only in his final year at school was he allowed in a classroom for the first time. Laws had been passed, and treaties signed, but it was still hard for many to accept Lewis and his classmates into the fold as citizens.

Which was odd, because, despite his outcast status, Lewis had always felt like a citizen. He spent money here, money he earned with side jobs.

And he didn't complain.

He helped clean up the neighborhoods after the hurricanes destroyed the dump and most of the town. He had even saved the life of a little girl, who then screamed in his face and took off running.

But eventually the school's doors opened to him, and Lewis had learned within the protective walls of the school. The teachers listened to him, surprised at his language skills despite his accent. He spoke slowly but with confidence. Eventually, other students stopped making fun of him. They didn't invite him to parties or celebrations, but they didn't mock him anymore.

Meanwhile, Steve had gone on to work at the docks, bringing in more shipments and helping the state adjust to the new laws, the new citizens. Steve was proud of his brother, less so of their father. Once, when their father was actually sober, Steve had tried to talk to the man. It'd been a long winter day, and Steve tried to convince his father to come to the school on Lewis's behalf and argue for indoor classes. But instead their father took out his bottle and stumbled into the street.

Steve had to carry him home on his shoulders. It was a disaster.

Then one week the hurricanes came. For five days, heavy winds blew through buildings and playgrounds, overturned Dumpsters. The destroyed landfill had spread disease and trash for miles, and Steve had been on the shores when the incoming ships had overturned. He was lost at sea or under the wreckage; either way, he was gone.

Lewis hated to think of his brother's life ending in such a way. He spent days cleaning the town and nights searching for Steve but had no luck finding him. He'd given up hope, concentrated on schoolwork, and then, the day before graduation, Steve's body had been brought to shore by a small boat. The boat was nearly broken in two and was full of refugees, the whole thing on the verge of sinking. But Steve's body was carefully laid out in the middle, and the refugees handled him with great care.

Lewis promised them they could live in his home and kicked his father out in the process. As Lewis gave his brother's eulogy, the refugees sat beside him. They looked like him, and they understood his former language.

But he never spoke in that tongue again around them, so as to encourage them to adjust to their new life. Once, when they were older, the refugees were granted permission to return to their home planet for a weekend getaway. They invited Lewis along, in thanks, but he declined.

"I left Neptune long ago," he proudly said to them. "My home is here now. On earth."

EIGHTY-ONE

Alice watched the brake lights turn the corner, then allowed the drapes to close. She pushed his name out of her head—he would be a pronoun from now on. After all, what did he think of her that he would just drop her like this? Out of the blue, almost. In the morning. Before coffee, before a shower. He just showed up and—that was it.

A year ago they met. And now that a new year was turning the corner, she was on her own again.

She'd believed he was different. He believed in her. Well, he said he did. Alice normally didn't put a lot of stock in what anyone told her. But he'd stood out for a while.

Now, though . . .

She had to rethink everything for the past year. What he said, what he did, and how he'd acted. No. No, I can't let it get that far.

In the shower, she sobbed twice, the water washing away any tears that had escaped her eyelids. She quickly dressed and got in her car and made it to work within a half hour. Record timing in Los Angeles. When she sat at her desk, she saw the picture frame—and tossed it into a drawer. It was a nice frame, a souvenir from their trip to Hawaii.

But she couldn't look at it, not now. If there was anything that reminded her of him, she had to step away.

She pulled up some news websites, chatted with the ladies as they all walked in. The good thing about accounting is that the work never stops. The bad thing is that the chatter never stops. Enough of the work is mindless that you can keep a conversation while scanning for mistakes in the purchase orders. Alice strapped on her headphones, popped on the music that kept her mind reeling, and went to work.

She worked through lunch, and it was almost quitting time when her boss nudged Alice on the shoulder. "Did you take lunch?"

She muttered a reply but was quickly cut off. "Not another word. Take off early. I don't know what you've got going on, Alice, but you haven't been yourself today."

"I'm not feeling well."

"From what I can see, you've either got a disease or your heart's broken. Or you're just miserable for a day, which is, you know, okay. Go home. Sleep."

The last thing Alice wanted was another argument today, so she went home. She climbed into bed and stared at the fishbowl. Roddy and Piper were swimming in circles, occasionally looking toward Alice, mouths open in perpetual fright, waiting for more food. She imagined that had been the look on her face this morning when—he—appeared at the door. She'd been ready to accept a sweet gesture, an unexpected moment of love because he rarely showed them.

Boy, was she wrong. And good riddance. It'd been only twelve hours, but she felt stronger than she had before he came knocking. But in a week's time, she'd see everything she did wrong. She'd find the signs she'd mistakenly given, the moments she went wrong, the second she lost him. She'd analyze the start of their relationship, at the café when—NO!

She could hear herself scream in her head. NO. Do not do that.

This is on him, not on you. He can't control you, and you can't . . . control him. He had his reasons, weak as they were when he made his case. She'd have to trust that life was working this way for a reason. She wanted more than anything for them to get back together, next week, next month, in two years. Any time.

She'd given everything to their relationship. Maybe not through sacrifice, but if one could imagine a bucket full of love representing a relationship, the amount she'd given sloshed over the sides of the bucket. His bucket was probably half full. He was wholly unprepared for their fishing trip of a relationship. For their lifetime getaway together.

Alice could see it, for a moment, that lifetime, before the image of him turning away rather than looking her in the eye filled her memories again. She cried herself to sleep, and the smell of coffee the next morning woke her.

Her roommate, Stella, was up early, and she'd silently brewed the last of their coffee. Wordless, Alice joined her at the table, sipping away. "Pick up some coffee on the way home?" Alice had been considering ignoring work today, feeling that her face was puffed up and wanting to focus on what went wrong, again.

But coffee, that's important. She looked at Stella, realized that her roommate was pushing her, forcing her to accept the task, however banal, of picking up coffee. This was movement, this was what she needed.

She nodded to Stella, then finished off her mug and got ready for work. And she did so every day going forward, forgetting more and more about the mess he had caused.

When she saw him again two months later, he seemed as happy as she was. In fact, he looked almost relieved when he saw her, as though impressed that she was still alive.

Alice surprised herself with a smile.

EIGHTY-TWO

Lana Warner was running late to class, but she thought the students would forgive her. She was going to tell them there would be no test today, that they could discuss whatever they wanted, play games, whatever they'd like. This was her last day as a teacher, and the kids didn't know it yet.

But they'd forgive her.

Sure, they'd probably miss her next week, maybe hate her for not telling them sooner. But eventually they'd come around. After all, it's not every day that you could brag to your friends that the first woman to walk on the moon was once your middle school science teacher.

As she drove the usual route to school, Lana felt the smile on her face grow, and just let it happen despite the obviously goofy grin she presented to passing drivers. Ever since she was a little girl, she'd been obsessed with the Apollo missions. Neil Armstrong's photograph, signed within weeks of his return to earth, adorned her wall to this day. It was still sealed behind a powerful glass picture frame. He smiled at her in the morning and again when she returned at night. She was in love with that man and in love with his picture and in love with the moon.

She always blew him a kiss before leaving for work.

When Lana applied at NASA, they broke her heart by telling her the only space missions would be to the International Space Station, and they were already backed up with a line of astronauts. No more moon, no more seats. Gone were all those years she'd spent studying physics, biology, chemistry. She had even joined the air force.

But she took the job teaching middle school kids basic science equations. How to tell a theory from a hypothesis, how to keep challenging accepted science and find solutions to problems that continued to puzzle scientists around the world.

As she pulled into the parking lot, Lana saw that the name sign at her parking spot had already been changed from "L. Warner" to "Reserved."

A shade of sadness passed along her neck and gave her chills but was quickly washed away as she climbed out of her car and thought back to the prior Thursday night.

And the phone call.

The director of the new Apollo mission, Sven, had made the call himself. Late at night, Lana's grading of papers was interrupted when the phone rang, and something inside told her this call was beyond important. She recognized his voice instantly from watching countless hours of interviews and interactive videos of Sven on YouTube. "You want me to what?" she had asked, voice shaking.

"Join us on our next mission to the moon. I was looking back at past applications, and you, Ms. Warner, have an exceptional résumé. What are you doing teaching grade school?!"

"It's middle school, and . . . why me?"

"I told you, your record is exceptional."

She'd arrived at the in-person interview early, still shaking from the call the night before. Sven kept saying the same thing over and over. "Exceptional, truly exceptional."

She'd never thought of herself that way. Even her late husband always called her "pretty good." She would counter with "you're not bad yourself."

But exceptional? No one she knew was exceptional—except for Armstrong. An exceptional man from exceptional times.

"But why me? Why now? Surely you have a line of young people, or more qualified people, prepping for this mission?

"We do, but we want you. I'll admit, there's a small shred of good PR in it for us. But then I looked at your application again and your essays over the years. You've wanted this your whole life, and the one thing NASA has always been good at is helping any one of us, Americans, humans, achieve the impossible."

The sentiment was unexpected, but Lana's reply wasn't. She nearly shouted "YES" when he finally asked if she would accept. Then she almost fell apart when she found out training would start within two weeks.

Lana walked up the steps to the school and entered the main hallway. The classroom doors were already shut. The bell had already rung.

She knew her students would behave. They were the best in the school, even the principal thought so. They needed no supervisor. As she rounded the last corner to her classroom, on her last day as a teacher, Lana got a warm feeling in her throat. One of worry and fear.

What was she thinking? Going to walk on the moon. And then what? What good would it do? What would it teach anyone? Was she being selfish?

She stopped against a line of lockers and caught her breath.
What was the point? Who would teach these kids? Mr. Ryan?
Mrs. Phillips? Well, Phillips was all right, but Ryan?

The kids, their minds were still so young and fragile, naive. What a mess it might make. But no, Lana had to continue. She had to go her own way.

The kids would be fine. They'd see her walk on the moon, and they would be all right.

They would understand.

For now she'd have to go into class and give one more day's worth of lessons. Or let them play their own games. They'd figure it out together.

She entered her classroom for the last time with a new calmness in her chest and a smile on her face, taking great care with that first step beyond the threshold.

EIGHTY-THREE

Her dancing was what convinced him that she was the one, that she'd be up to a challenge. She was confident and moved to her own rhythm, without a care for the music or how he tried—and failed—to keep up. He couldn't keep up, not with his damn leg the way it was, plastic and rusty and full of disjointed, cobbled-together parts.

No, he told himself. Don't go down that road again. Don't pity yourself or your leg or what's missing. Just keep moving. Don't worry about keeping pace with her. She won't let you stray too far behind.

And she didn't.

After the reception, she casually strolled through the hotel lobby and talked the tipsy talk of a woman who'd had three wines when she told herself she should only have two. But Frank thought it was all okay, since he'd had five beers instead of his usual daily limit of four. He could at least listen and keep up with her conversation. Or monologue, as he thought of it.

". . . Never thought I'd see that much of the country, but the trip was the only thing that got me past the end of school. You know what that's like. School's over, you just don't know what's coming up next, so you fill your time and then your best friend says, 'Let's go on a road trip.' So you do, only to find that your best friend can't go so it's just you in a car with a couple of useless tents and a backpack. Not that I don't like a challenge, because believe me, I love a challenge. I think that's what's great about life, especially now that school's over and—oh my gosh, I'm babbling and you're just trying to tell me what button to push."

"What floor are you on?"

"I'm on six."

"I'm on five. Let's go to six."

"I was just about to say the same thing." And she kissed him.

Her lips tasted sweet and minty, but her breath wafted into his nostrils with a hint of red wine, warm enough to knock him back off his feet. He almost slipped down the wall of the elevator but managed to keep his lips locked onto hers for another few seconds before she pulled away.

They both gasped for air. "But I'm drunk and you're drunk and maybe we should just talk tomorrow. We could get a coffee. Something tells me we're both going to need it." She pointed at her temple, indicating a rough morning ahead.

She said good night outside her room, and Frank just watched as she slowly shut her door. Then he leaned against the wall and used it as a crutch on his walk back to the elevator, happily disappointed.

On the fifth floor, he hobbled to his door and made it into the hotel room by falling to the floor and crawling over the threshold. Still on the floor, Frank pulled off his pants and with them went his prosthetic leg. He sat up and set the leg to stand on its own.

He stared at it: the plastic, metallic piece that would serve as his lower leg the rest of his life. He wondered how long it would stand on its own there, no pressure from his knee holding it in place. He wished he could convince someone to build a new leg from scratch, an organic piece, from stem cells. Something real.

This is the present, not the future, dimwit.

Still, he didn't like this piece of plastic and wished he'd never lost his leg "over there." That was a place he'd never mention to her, he assured himself. Oh, he'd bring it up, maybe—something to explain his lack of dancing skills—but he'd never talk about it no matter how much she asked.

One run-through of that experience was enough, he'd decided. No reason to relive it again and again.

In the morning he awoke to sunlight drenching his face. He'd forgotten to close the shades fully, probably never even tried. He was still on the floor, and when he looked to the leg, it too was lying on its side. A spring looked to have come loose, and Frank knew that today would be a day for crutches and pinning back his pant leg.

Can't very well fake it on a leg that would crumble under my weight.

In the bathroom, he looked at his sagging eyes and his belly, wondering where the months had gone. It'd barely been a year, and still a shock that it had been even that long. But the wedding had made it seem longer.

Last night Frank had watched his best friend get married and the guy had barely said more than a few words to him all night—just a hug and "we missed ya." Frank figured he'd be forgotten in a day or two.

But who cares, because he'd also met her at the wedding.

As Frank dressed, he thought again of the feel of her body under the dress. And the dress itself, a dark violet that clung to her curves in a protective hug. That was a feeling his fingertips would never forget.

In the lobby, Frank watched person after person leaving, hungover, eyes barely open. But they all gave him curious looks as they passed him and got a glimpse of the space under his leg. A few of the older men nodded in Frank's direction, an understanding between them; these guys had likely served and had seen similar things if not worse. One old man came by to shake Frank's hand, and again, no words were offered, but instead a look of hard, cold memory.

Frank thought he felt a tear hit the back of his eyes but blamed it on dehydration.

By early afternoon, he decided that she had forgotten, that she'd left without even realizing they'd met the night before. As he hobbled out the front door, someone called his name. He turned, and it was her. He could hardly recognize her with her hair down, wearing jeans and a loose T-shirt.

"I knew that was you!" she said.

She hugged him, lips barely brushing his ear but still managing to spread a wave of goose bumps down to his fingertips. "Look, I've got to go, so a rain check on that coffee?"

"I, I guess so. Was looking forward to it, to be honest."

"Me too, but my mom, she's waiting. Here's my number though, so call me soon?"

He nodded, speechless and feeling his empty stomach growl. Before she reached the door, she turned to face him again. "'Soon' as in tonight, even. I love coffee, Sergeant."

Yeah, he could still feel it: she was the one.

EIGHTY-FOUR

Zorendon sat first, leaving Mort with his back to the room. He usually preferred his back to a room, to watch everything and become a part of the wall. He was good at not being seen.

That's why Zorendon had hired him. "Because you're savvy about when to stay hidden," Zorendon was saying now, bringing Mort to the conversation. "Because you know exactly how to do what we ask you to do, without question, and then you simply wait, out of the way, in the shadows. That's why I've paid you all these years."

Mort was having a hard time focusing, for which he felt guilty.
The problem was that Zorendon had taken them to Spitzy's Steakhouse, and that was one place no one but the filthy rich could afford to go to. The menu listed only meat considered rare delicacies from around the

world, prepared by three chefs who were flown to town only four nights a week.

A reservation was hard to get, but Zorendon was one of the few who had that kind of pull. That was clear from the way he'd shaken the hands of every waitress on the way in, commenting on how thrilled he was to see their lovely faces. Indeed, Mort was thrilled too and was looking forward to flirting with whatever cute waitress was given their table.

Nevertheless, he'd felt a chill upon entering, and that chill lingered, a warning.

"Good evening, gentlemen," said a deep voice from over Mort's shoulder. He turned, and a tall waiter stood near them, nudging a strand of blond hair back behind his ear. As he did so, Mort's chill suddenly returned.

The waiter continued, "I have a grilled cod with a mango glaze, mashed potatoes, and baked Brussels sprouts, and a honey gravy on the side."

They waited for more, but the waiter had stopped talking and remained still, bent forward in a half bow. He glanced from Mort to Zorendon, but to Mort it did not appear that the man wanted to make eye contact.

"And?" Zorendon asked, perhaps bored or simply biding his time until the manager could be summoned.

"F-For today's special we ha-ave a seared swordfish hooked in this mo-morning off the coast of—"

"Sorry," interrupted Mort, "this is the special?"

"The swordfish, yes. It's grilled over a wood fire and—"

"But what about the cod?"

"The cod, sir?" The waiter's voice remained at an even, monotone level, quiet enough that Mort had to lean forward to hear him.

"Yes, the grilled cod with the mango glaze."

"That does sound delightful, doesn't it? It's my favorite dish to eat after a long day." Before he could go further, the manager, a bulky man in a red jacket, seemed to glide from nowhere to stand beside the waiter.

"My sincerest apologies, gentlemen. We'll take care of this right a . . . away." He gave Mort a quick once-over, then looked to Zorendon, who nodded. The manager then escorted the waiter toward the kitchen, and during their exit the waiter never removed his interlocked hands from behind his back.

"What do you suppose that was about?"

"Haven't got a clue, Mort."

"Perhaps he was—" But before he could finish, a waitress was pouring their water.

"Hey, guys, how we doing today?"

"Just great, sweets." Zorendon seemed in his element, gleeful at the sight of her, and the waitress gave him a smile of recognition.

"Zorry, you old cat, how you been?"

"Fine, my dear, fine. Meet my employee Mort, who is about to learn about his latest assignment."

"Ooh, how exciting." She snatched Mort's hand and forced a shake and said, "Maybe you'll tell me all about it one day."

"Where is your bathroom?" Mort couldn't take his attention off the kitchen door. Something about that waiter was gnawing at his memory, like he'd seen him before. Why had this restaurant, famous for its meats and its elegant female waitstaff, allowed a waiter to commandeer the table of a high-price customer such as Zorendon?

The waitress pointed toward a hallway tucked by the kitchen. Mort excused himself and headed down the hall, feeling sweat along his back and a tension atypical at dinner with the boss.

Once around the corner, he waited four seconds, counting silently but precisely. Then he peeked out and watched the waitress stand closer to Zorendon as he wrapped his arm around her waist. Mort thought he caught Zorendon glance his way, but perhaps it was a trick of the candlelight.

He slipped through the kitchen doors. No one was inside to see him enter or yell for him to leave, which was a relief. Everything in the kitchen was in its rightful place, and for a moment he felt calm as he watched the mechanics of the kitchen at work: pots boiling with sensuous soups, grills steaming multiple meats, and knives jammed into onions and other vegetables.

Then he realized nothing was moving—the knives, the pots, the spatulas were all just dangling or lying on their sides. The only sign of movement or anything happening was the steam escaping from the meat or the pots. The kitchen was otherwise empty, save for a muffled voice around the corner.

Mort approached and watched with growing amusement as the manager spoke to a line of waiters and cooks, all with the same face and vacant stare, the same blond hair, and arms crossed behind their backs. "It's not cod that's the special, it's the swordfish, have you got that?"

"YES," they all said in unison, a chorus of that disturbing monotone.

"YES," whispered one waiter, the closest to Mort, as though just catching up to speed. The manager immediately turned to this waiter.

"Have you got a malfunction, boy?" The waiter shook his head, then lowered his eyes. The manager reached up and suddenly tore the skin down the cheek of the waiter, revealing a metallic jawbone, into which the manager stuck his fingers. "Let's get you patched up"

The waiter seemed to slump a few seconds before suddenly jolting upright to full attention.

The manager continued shouting, "All of you, back to your positions in the kitchen. Once you master the knives, we'll move you on to proper assignments." He tapped the cheek of the waiter back into place, then they all filed to the kitchen, not noticing Mort standing against the wall.

Mort swallowed hard, then his mouth went dry when the manager walked up to him.

"Finally found your way back. I won't waste time with a lecture, then." The manager reached up and tore at Mort's cheek. Mort didn't notice any pain but lightly stopped the manager's fingers from finagling his switches. "Stop it now, boy. Got to reset you so you can clear your memory, get back to work for Zorendon; otherwise we'll have to replace you again. And Zorendon doesn't like paying for things, does he?"

Mort didn't get to say anything else after his switch was thrown, but the smell of cod lingered for days after.

Cod is now his favorite thing to eat.

EIGHTY-FIVE

There was a list, and Fiona had to follow it. It was a short list, but checking off each item was essential. Without the list, her son would die. And every day she reminded herself that his life was in her hands.

Fiona woke up on the fourth day and decided to weigh herself. She felt hungry, and as she suspected, she'd lost weight. Eight pounds, two for each day her son had been gone. Her price for not having kept a closer eye on him.

She blamed herself through personal prayer, then went through her nearly daily routine of pulling back the blame curtain, screaming in her mind that it was they who did this, they who were probably hurting him. Then there was that flicker, that flash of fear-driven suspicion that her son was responsible, that he didn't take good enough care of himself or pay enough attention to his surroundings when he was taken. As though, in America of all places, when walking to the store you must keep an eye over your shoulder for predators.

There was still hope, however small, that she'd get him back, that the kidnappers would fulfill their promise when she completed everything they asked of her. On the first day, after she had cried for hours, the list seemed like a joke. Buy these items from the home supplies store. Leave them in a bag and run as fast as you can.

But there was a method, a reason that began to take shape on day two: buy this gun and your name is run, a background check forever held on record. Thanks, USA. Thanks, government.

Fiona despised guns, despite the perfect way they fit in her hands. She hated the way they looked, the weight of them, the sound they made.

When she came to America, she'd hoped to be far away from any gun, any piece of weaponry that might bring death to her neighbors. But that hope died when she and her son moved into their new neighborhood.

Over a week after her son had been taken, she would have to hold one in her hands, under her own name, only to give it to an unknown person at a still-to-be-determined location. For seven days the lists were small and full of minutia, picking up bags, with no explanation, and dropping them off at other points around the city.

Two pounds a day in weight she was losing because of this. She could feel her clothes had loosened, even as the weight of the situation felt increasingly heavy. She was sick to her stomach with what might come next.

All that these past days had brought her was the pain of wondering if her son was still alive, and last night, when they'd confirmed he was, she was finally able to think clearly. So when she read the list for day eight, the plan took shape, fully formed. They were making sure that each drop-off location had a camera so when she ran away it would make her appear complicit.

Guilty.

But still, she checked off the items on the list and paid for the gun, the bullets, and the other necessary supplies. The shop owner had barely looked in her eyes when she'd come into buy the gun, which was probably for the best. Her paperwork was complete, legit, and the man was running a business. Doesn't matter where the dollars come from as long as you get paid.

As she walked out of the gun shop with the rifle bag over her shoulder, she wondered about the endgame—hers and her son's. Would they just let him go, out into the world, only to watch his mother go to prison?

Was it their goal to make him look guilty too?

Back home, in the place that was full of hate and borderless violence, Fiona had killed an unknown number of evil men. Mostly men.

The women had been just as evil, most days, and eventually the targets had become nondescript, just human beings. When she had nearly put a bullet in her son's head, Fiona had vomited, and then smashed the gun over her leg.

That was when she knew they had to leave. They didn't have more than a single backpack when they jumped on the ship, and only the clothes on their backs when they rowed their raft ashore along with thousands of others. Her son had begged to bring their father, but Fiona didn't believe the boy even knew who his father was. He'd died a long time ago, by Fiona's own hand.

She pulled the rifle tighter over her shoulder as she climbed aboard the bus. The driver grumbled a few words about the rifle, but Fiona had the permit—and showed it to him without hesitation. A part of her felt a small thrill, that she could do anything she wanted. But the sensation put a warm, sick feeling in the back of her throat, and she had to contain the vomit that threatened to rise.

They'd said it would only be five days, and after that she'd be free, her son would be free, and there would be no further threat. But it had gone on for over a week. The end was nowhere in sight. They had promised that, once it was over, she should forget the whole thing, move on, and never speak to the cops. "We'll watch you all time," the note said.

How she hoped that wouldn't be true, but in case it was, she decided not to tell the police anything. It was hard enough to get them to pay attention to the violence in her neighborhood, how would it look for her to try and explain all of this away?

By nightfall Fiona walked over the bridge and placed the gun and bullets at the end of the broken bench as requested, along with the other supplies. She crossed to the far shore and strode up the path a way, then doubled back to the bushes nearest to the water. By the time she cowered down and pulled out her binoculars, her adrenaline was at an all-time high and she could hardly believe what she was doing.

What was she thinking? Run from the scene and await further instructions. That's what they'd said, was all she had to do. But she had to know what they looked like, these kidnappers, the ones holding her hostage as well as her boy.

She looked through the binoculars—she'd had the sense to buy the kind with night vision—and waited.

Out of the darkness came two figures, lanky and moving quick. They jogged to the gun and one pulled out a phone. He unzipped the bag and spoke into the phone. The other figure was crouched down, no doubt looking through the other bag of bullets and supplies.

Fiona's hand pulled into a tighter grip.

The crouching man suddenly stood and backed up to the wall. His partner lowered the phone, frantically looking around. Then he began to run.

Fiona didn't hesitate any longer.

She pushed the button on the trigger, and for a moment everything floated, hesitating as time stopped. Then the explosion came.

The man against the wall disappeared in a cloud of fire and death, while the running man stumbled and fell on his face a few dozen feet away. Fiona waited until she was sure she heard no sirens, no shouting. These two were working alone.

She crossed the bridge again, hoping that the other man was still alive, or, if not, she could snag his phone and find her son. This was reckless, she knew, but taking the problem into her own hands and finding a solution, that's what her life was all about. When she reached the other man, she turned him over to look at his face.

Her son could barely breathe, just looked up at her with confusion and sadness. He mouthed words, and Fiona, through her tears, thought he was trying to say "no choice" but she couldn't trust her instincts anymore. The world was a blur, a kaleidoscopic confusion through her tears, and the tears never stopped coming even as she put her hands over his mouth and nose.

EIGHTY-SIX

Lizzy felt paranoid. Like something was following her, something big.

But her hearing was extra sensitive lately, and she smelled only herself and the snoozing squirrels in the surrounding forest. There was no one else around, she was certain.

She pushed aside the twigs at her fire and laid her head to rest. Despite her blood running high, she felt exhausted and was pleased as sleep overtook her. When she awoke, she was rested and noted that it was already midday. Slinging her satchel over her shoulder, she walked from under the tree cover of the forest and began the trek up the next hill. All the while,

Lizzy offered brief glances back behind her, but of course there was still no one following.

Later, beside Mill Creek, as she sipped water with one hand, she kept her other hand on the Spencer repeating rifle at her side. It was almost too big for her teenage body, but Lizzy managed to get the aim just right when it came to hunting rabbits. The blast of the rifle usually clipped away half the animals' bodies whenever she hit right, but there was enough meat to fuel her journey.

Now at the creek bed, Lizzy put both hands on the gun, swallowing the last mouthful of water quietly. She looked over the log beside her and saw movement in the bushes. She slowly raised the rifle, and when the bushes shuffled again, she shouted, "Stop right there!" But the bushes kept shuffling, so Lizzy fired—and heard the man scream.

Later, after Lizzy finished wrapping the man's leg, she looked him in the eyes and grinned, offering a meek apologetic look. "Sorry."

"You're not, but I don't blame you." He touched his leg, cringed at a sharp pain, then lay back against the rock beside the caverns. She felt bad for shooting the man, but he scared her, and she told him as such as she wrapped his leg.

"I didn't do nothin' to ya, was just surprised is all. Been a while since I saw anyone out here." He pulled the bandana from around his neck, wiped his face. Then he shook his shirt, wafting out the humidity, and Lizzy saw the scars along his chest.

"What're those from?"

"Used to be on a plantation."

"Now you're free?"

"So they told me."

"Why don't you live in town?"

"When you're not welcome, you feel it. Not something I wanna wake up to every day. And you?"

"I left days ago. Been wandering since, searching for the Register Cliffs."

He looked away, confused, and said, "That's a place no one really goes anymore. Haunted."

"I got reasons. You know how to get there?"

"Best way is through Torrington."

"And if I wanna avoid town?"

"Gonna take over a month, then. If you have the supplies."

She looked down to her satchel, held up her empty water pouch. "I bet there's supplies in town. Got any money you can lend me?"

He laughed in her face, then, soon almost crying. He kept laughing for a long time, and eventually Lizzy lay down and turned her back to him.

"Just a favor is all I asked."

"If I had money at all, you think I'd loan it to a strange girl I'll likely never see again?"

"Have any other use for it?" He still chuckled as night fell and sleep took over.

The next morning, just at dawn, she woke with a start and checked her clothes and body for injuries. There were none. Then she looked over at Thaddeus and saw him lying on his back, perfectly still. She approached with caution, then shook him on the shoulder.

He woke with a start and could barely get a breath as she hugged him. "Through the night! I slept through the night!"

"Well, I hope so!"

"This is a relief, believe me! I have another day, another chance. . ." Then her eyes looked away, seeing something far away, a goal almost reached.

"To do what?"

She looked at him and smiled. "To find the cure." She offered nothing else, only gathered her things and left him in the cave alone to consider what had just happened.

As she walked through town, she felt eyes on her but couldn't see anyone. Windows were empty, and no one was near their horses. She thought she heard steps behind her again, but when she turned there was only dust and tumbleweeds.

At Crosby's drugstore she slipped through the door that was bent on its hinges. No one was inside, so she poked about, pulled down some beans and candy, some tobacco. She rolled herself a cigarette but choked back her coughs when she inhaled, having never done so before.

When she emerged outside, there were a few women walking from the saloon, stumbling. A group of men emerged from the inn and shuffled toward the bank. Yet another old man stepped past Lizzy into the drugstore, grumbling.

She left town in a hurry and ventured up the cliffs.

In the evening Lizzy came to a clearing and there she stopped and drank most of her water. Then the winds grew hearty and night fell, darkness finding Lizzy rapidly as the cliffs blocked the sun. When the moon emerged from behind clouds, Lizzy saw that it was full and then she felt it. And she started to cry.

At least she wasn't in town.

This thought gave her a second of pleasantry just as her eyes stretched within their sockets and her nose and mouth pushed out. Pressure popped her ears and forced her to her hands and knees. Through blurry vision she saw her fingers extend as hair trickled up on the backs of her hands, and as she released a howl of pain and relief, the moon became clear and large and red to her eyes.

She ran up higher into the forests on the cliffs, leaving behind her satchel and the Spencer rifle.

Her howls confirmed to the townsfolk the rumors of haunted cliffs and can still be heard to this very day.

EIGHTY-SEVEN

Doxon lost his toenail again. Well, not "lost" like "misplaced" but "lost" as in "rammed his toe into the bedside table and his nail fell off." We didn't bother to look for it, though, and weren't even bothered by the blood on the sheets the next morning.

The broken toenail had been accompanied by a broken toe, and breaks mean blood to us. I worked quickly to wrap gauze around his toes—

I keep three rolls in the nightstand because we're both klutzy—then I cooked him breakfast in bed. I tore off the old sheets for a good wash and unrolled the replacement sheets while he lay there eating.

Some people say Doxon is lazy when I do these things, but it's hard for him. They don't understand how hard it is. Our bones are brittle, our muscles thin. Six years on rations that are meant for children will bring anyone's composition down, no matter how big or small they once were.

When you walk up and down forty flights of stairs every day, for 2,189 days, your muscles fade beyond everything they once were. Bones become wafer thin, your organs scrunch down and wait for any signal that they're needed—to digest, to pump blood, to filter vitamins to the rest of your body.

To see. To hear. To smell. Taste is secondary, and since we don't communicate verbally, our tongues are simply mushy, dangling things, useless to our mouths. At least, that's how mine feels. I can't speak for Doxon (ha-ha) but he tells me he's tired of his tongue all the time, or he sends me those kinds of messages.

After he finishes breakfast and the new sheets have been unrolled, I take away the tray and give him a look of pity. The poor thing, his entire right foot is covered in gauze at his toes, and two of his left toes' wrappings are dirty. He keeps running into things, and I'm worried about his vision.

He won't even look at me when he speaks to me, which garbles our messages. He just pretends I'm not there until I complete something he's asked me to do.

But I don't do everything he asks. I'm not a robot. And he doesn't catch me in my lies.

It's difficult for me to bathe, for instance, because my skin is so sensitive. Removing my gloves and stockings and thermal shirt takes almost half a morning, so by the time I bathe I'm already sore and just waiting for it to be over. I tried showering once, but my skin peels too easily. Doxon tells me it's like a sunburn, that sometimes skin has to peel away. Then I show him my back or my shoulders or my elbow, and the exposed muscle or bone, and he quietly wraps me in gauze.

Doesn't even apologize.

I'm not bitter. It's not his fault we're like this, nor is it mine. Everyone else in our building experiences similar circumstances, but when we go to work it's hard to find more than a few people in the shape we're in. Rations are divided out in a hierarchy, a very complex system, and our placement in the lottery has been terrible for every year since they began. But this year, Doxon promises, it will be different. He was promoted onto the same floor as the lottery makers, and he's made friends with one of them. This man, he says, just wants one thing, a simple thing, and when we give it to him, he'll make sure we're in the top three.

That means triple rations for three years. The Three-fer.

At first, three hundred people would win this with each raffle. But that was too many, and for the jury there were still too many healthy citizens. So they decreased it to thirty, then three. We will be in those three, and Doxon says it won't cost much.

I've asked him a dozen times what it is the lottery maker wants, but he won't tell me. He's built up a wall. Perhaps that's why he's been so quiet lately; he doesn't want me to know. But I sense something dark.

I ignore him the rest of the morning. I'll be going to work, and he's staying home. His foot is too damaged, and besides, there's no need for a filer today. The lack of filing has been happening too often since the bombings, but what can you do? There'll always be a need for mappers, which is why I still get called in.

All the drones will keep flying. That's good business for me. Each time they fly a new route, it means updating our maps. And each update comes with a date. I've dated and re-dated updates from the same region six times this year already.

Six times.

The drones are going in circles, but I seem to be the only one who knows this. Do I tell anyone? I don't. Messaging isn't as easy with everyone as it is for Doxon and me, or any partnership that's been around as long as ours. Not with the way the minds were melded before the first bombing. Also,

I don't particularly care. You don't get rations if you don't work, and despite repeating work and doing more than I probably need to, I prefer any rations to none.

Today I updated twice as many maps as usual. My quota has been increasing weekly, and as a reward for completing the most work, I was given an hour off. An hour to myself, to my family. They left the decision to me.

It was an odd feeling to have this much control, even if only for an hour, but I took it and ran to the lake. Well, I didn't run. I don't have the energy to do that. But I walked fast and sat with some chipped ice—a free perk the city offers a few months a year.

On the lake there were ice skaters performing in loops, a job that very few wanted but when you got that job you were treated so well, fed all day to perform and work a few hours at a time. I watched as one of the skaters swirled around and around, almost getting dizzy myself. Then she stumbled to the ice and was quickly shot. Imperfection is not tolerated.

I quickly finished my ice and walked home. I couldn't wait to ask Doxon to snuggle tonight. I'd keep my feet off his.

But that was not meant to be.

Instead I got to stare at his closed eyelids, sewn shut after donating his eyes to the lottery man. A Three-fer, and the only price was a pair of eyes that carried our messages to each other.

The lottery man had taken Doxon's tongue too as collateral.

Silence is now my only friend.

EIGHTY-EIGHT

Robert downs the water in one gulp. His throat was dry after giving his rather verbose offer for the fourth time today, and he is happy to quench his thirst. He takes a moment to reflect that this was the first time he was able to give his pitch and offer without interruption.

Judging by the artist's reaction, he has done an amazing job.

Robert can tell she's pleased too. The artist stares at Robert with her mouth half open, coffee mug hesitating below her bottom lip. Probably in shock, Robert thinks. After another minute, he can't take the silence, so he says, "Well?"

The artist slowly puts down her mug. She rubs her hands together, collecting her thoughts, then leans back. "You don't have any money for payment?"

"No, not yet. For now this would be gratis, but soon I'll have an income—hopefully from the book—and then we'll be flying high!" He watches as the artist gathers her notebook and adjusts the bandana on her head, then she stands up. "Where are you going?"

"If this gig doesn't pay, I wish you would have told me that before I took the bus all the way here or took the time to make these character sketches. Waste of my time."

She is already walking to the door when Robert breaks out of his shock. "Can I at least have the sketches?"

"Not until you buy them. My God, is this how you treat all your artists?"

"They're my creations!"

"My art," she says. She pushes open the door, then doubles back as if a thought came to her. Robert smiles and holds out his hand. Instead of giving him the sketches she snatches his wrist and stabs his open palm with a pocketknife. A squirt of blood shoots into the air, and Robert screams in shock. The artist then spits into the cut. "My art," she repeats with a smirk, then storms out the door.

Robert sits in the booth, in shock. His stomach growls, so he drinks up the artist's coffee and goes to town on the eggs while wrapping his hand in a napkin. A quick look at the clock tells him he will be right on time if he leaves in the next few minutes. Hopefully this next meeting will turn out better.

Four artists have now turned him down—and this was the first woman. At least she had done the sketches. He wants to pay her—to pay all of them—but there is rent and food to eat and the—

He puts his rambling mind on hold as he goes into the bathroom. The bathroom window is just wide enough to slip through, and he quickly dashes to the bus stop on Ventura. The eggs were hardly cooked and the coffee was hot but tasted like empty walnut shells, so Robert doesn't see that it was worth the few remaining dollars resting comfortably in his pocket.

Three stops down, Robert steps off the bus whispering to himself, getting jazzed for his next pitch. "Going to be huge, just trust me . . .

no, just trust the story . . ."

He hears a thump before feeling the knock to his head.

He looks around, expecting a stop sign or perhaps a light pole, but he can't see anything that he had run into. "The hell?" He starts walking and again there is a thump. He drops his bag and holds his head with both hands, shouting, "All right, what the hell?!" He can feel the bumps growing already on his forehead.

Slowly, Robert reaches out, feeling for something, anything. A businessman walks past, on the phone and eyeing Robert with interest. Robert's hands have reached a kind of invisible wall. He feels out, to the left and the right, and there are now invisible walls on each side of him as well as in front. "Huh, that's . . . okay that's different."

He turns and picks up his bag. Then he walks away from the wall and soon finds he is walking up stairs but can't see them. He is about twenty feet off the ground when he finally looks down and sees behind him a little girl staring back up at him.

"Oh, hi there, um, don't come up here. It's private, heh." Robert watches the girl run away, then tries to step down, but there is no step below his feet. He catches himself, strains to climb back up, and sits on the invisible landing. When he sits, he kicks out in all directions, but there is no floor, nothing to catch him. "Okay, not funny."

"Psst, hey, you." Warm breath skirts his ear. He turns, but there is, of course, no one beside him.

"Whoever you are, this isn't funny." There is a soft chuckle, a woman who's heard a funny joke. Before Robert can turn to face the laughter, he drops to the ground.

His ankle snaps. As he screams, the minutes tick by and he soon realizes there is still no one else around him, so he reaches out for his backpack—but it is gone. "Come on! That's my—dammit!"

He runs, hard, limping, away from the wall and the stairs, not caring if he will smash into another invisible object. After a few hundred feet, he pauses to catch his breath. When he looks up, he is back at the diner. The artist is sitting on a bench by the entrance, smoking and sketching in her book.

She stares at him and allows smoke to trickle out her mouth into her nose. She winks at him, smirking. "My art."

She erases, hectic, and Robert starts to walk toward her only he isn't walking, he is tumbling, because his legs have disappeared below the knees. Looking from his knees to the artist, he shouts, "All right, I'll pay, I'll pay!"

Then she erases his mouth and his face goes numb.

His vision becomes cloudy and suddenly he can see only to the sides, not straight ahead. He struggles to jump but his body flutters about, and when he tries to call out her name, or for help, he can't create the words and the world becomes larger and he can't breathe. He finds himself lifted into the air and immediately careening toward a bowl of water and tries to hold his breath but can't breathe and then when he is underwater the air fills his lungs.

He swims to the wall of the bowl and sees the artist staring back at him, smiling. He shouts her name, angry, then forgets her name and shouts something incoherent and then sees a flake of food at the top of the bowl and swims up to eat it. Then he swims in circles and is just happy to be alive!

The artist shows her face again, smiling, and Robert jumps, then smiles back and swims in a circle, happy to be alive!

EIGHTY-NINE

Autumn had come, finally, and Gina felt immediately hungry. But then, as she left school, something happened.

That particular day, the wind was chilly, invisible, empty. But the smell is what pushed Gina over the edge into believing that seasons had finally changed. That things were going to get better. That her stomach would soon be full again.

She smelled dirt, sweat, and muck, and it felt like a stain was corroding her nostrils. She lived downwind from the farm, and the smell was the best part of the year. Usually, though, the scent was cheerful and soapy, a clean sensation that washed away fear. This time of year, though, when the farm was in full harvest, the delicious smell excited Gina for things to come.

The farm was a DESTINATION, not just a destination. Eight years she'd been there. Eight years since the invaders had been blown out of the sky. Gina had barely been old enough to read at the time, but she could remember the images vividly, and all the books in the library were soon filled with details about the event. The ships in the sky, the metallic clang of explosions as dozens of fighter jets fired missiles at the invaders. When it was later discovered where they had come from, Gina was less interested.

She could barely pronounce the name of the planet.

When Gina learned how to speak a few words in their language, she was less interested still. The only excitement she now felt toward the invaders was over the smell at the start of autumn. During the harvests.

The invaders' technology was incredibly strong, everyone knew, but outside their ships the beings were masses of muscle and meat. A pulpy texture that, it was soon discovered, ripened over summer.

Like fresh fruit, the beings were sent to live in camps that were soon after called farms, and several months later were harvested to be consumed. They repopulated at such a furious rate, world leaders at first wanted to burn them and wipe them out. At the first "toasting" the smell was so attractive that several soldiers ventured a bite. And they liked the taste.

At first Gina didn't want to eat them. The invaders spoke a language, after all, and their leaders had taught people how to speak and understand and communicate. The knowledge they provided regarding technology and armor, galactic adaptation, and so on, was undeniably valuable.

But the taste was even more desired, and because they were as fertile as rabbits, gestating in half the time of a human baby, the invaders were divided up and farmed.

Small farms were preferred, to prevent uprisings and the spread of the truth. The leaders of the invaders knew nothing of the true nature of the farms, as they didn't relate or interact as humans do. They ignored each other, practiced basic monogamous partnerships, and pretended that mass groups were useless and tiresome. One-on-one was their preferred method of interaction. Some of them were no doubt fed members of their own race, and they didn't hesitate to eat more. The leaders were held up as royalty on earth, since they shared the most knowledge, and were highly protected; thus they were oblivious to the truth.

Gina soon got over the idea of eating another living thing and quickly savored the taste. She was regretful that they weren't farmed all year, only in season, but that made them taste more delicious.

On this day, with the autumn winds lifting leaves to surround her, Gina was confused when one invader found her outside of school and bluntly started talking about his family. "But you don't have a family," she stated. It wasn't a question but a fact.

"All of them are my family. We feel each other. We're a big group, like a net. What one thinks and feels, so do the rest of us. I love all of them equally."

"But do they have names?"

"I have a name, so they must have a name. My name is D'org'arh."

Gina didn't try to pronounce it. "Um, so, do you like earth?" She wanted to change the subject. She'd started to grow queasy.

"Oh, I like it very much. We all thank you for the hospitality. You're a younger, aren't you?"

"A what?"

"A younger? A . . . keed?" How did he have such trouble speaking the one-syllable word?

"Kid, yes, I'm a kid."

"You will ripen soon, do not worry."

Gina looked at D'org'arh, who appeared to be not much older than a kindergartner. "Did you say 'ripen'?"

"Oh yes, you will ripen, and when you do you will be grown into a beautiful yoomun. Yoomuns are so rare in the universe. Have you ever left earth?"

"No, it's not that easy."

"I will take you off earth, for I've chosen you. My stomach has not yet expanded, but when I saw you, I felt an ache. That means you and I are bound."

"Bound, um, for what?"

"Union."

Gina watched the invader stroll away, smiling over his shoulder at her every few steps. That night she pulled a knife from the kitchen drawer and shoved it into her backpack before bed.

When she arrived at school the next day, no one was there. She was instantly frightened, having noticed a distinct lack of cars on the road. In the teachers' lounge she turned on the television and saw blood in a news studio, while other stations were off the air. She ran to leave, but D'org'arh was there in the doorway, blocking her with his mouth open.

No, unhinged, like screws had come loose. It was big enough to consume her.

She pulled out her knife. "All these years . . . you were just—"

"Waiting for you to ripen. You're a little fresh, being a younger still. But I'll just eat part of you for now, because the day has come early."

And he swiped the knife away, then bit into her.

Gina wept and held on as he carried her upper body from the school, her torso tied in a knot above where her waist used to be. As she fell unconscious, she watched as thousands of ships descended to the earth to harvest the rest of the yoomuns.

NINETY

Deputy Harland had to hold his mouth to keep the vomit from flowing out. In all his days with the department he'd never thought he'd have to hold back vomit at a crime scene.

Not in Mechanicville.

Upstate New York was home to mostly misdemeanor-level criminals the past few years, and most of the violence in the region had come from domestic disputes or bar fights come election season. But this, this was different, and Harland knew he was already in over his head before the coroner's van pulled up.

The other deputies hovered nearby, not wanting to look at the ground or even each other. They pulled on latex gloves, glanced up at the houses or the sky, whispering that they hoped rain would come soon to wash it all away. For a normal crime scene, that would be less than desirable, but all this blood . . .

Harland shook hands with Dr. Morton and let the medical man lead the way through the lawn, up to the Sykes house. Morton spoke softly into a recorder, but Harland could still hear: "Six out front, all teenagers or early twenties. Multiple stab wounds on each and all necks have been cut, ear to ear. No weapons in the vicinity."

They stepped over the girl's body that was propping open the front door. Inside was much worse, and Harland could hardly believe what he saw, so much that he quickly ran back outside and, finally, thankfully, vomited along the porch. "Ten more in here . . . no, nine. Just nine." Morton's voice was shaky, but Harland was sure the man had seen a lot worse.

Back on the street, deputies turned over one of the bodies, the biggest, which was an older male. "Cooper, down here!" Harland hurried to the street, saw the hulk of the man they'd turned over and the machete in his hand. The dead man's face was familiar, hardened, intense, and he had blood still trickling out of his mouth and nose.

Harland wondered aloud, "How'd he get his?"

Dr. Morton walked up to his side. "Looks like blunt force trauma. See here, these two boys, their knuckles are bruised. This one looks like he was stabbed only—throat's still intact."

Harland looked at the victim under Morton's hand: Jake Stappe, star quarterback. "Fought to the end, probably didn't know he'd saved the rest of us. If you don't mind the phrase."

Morton stood, putting away his recorder. "This looks like a free-for-all, gonna be hard to put a motive to it."

“Fourteen vics, all underage or close to it, plus the killer himself. Could he have done all this on his own?”

Morton pointed at the machete. “Lotta blood on that, so testing could take weeks. They were all drunk, likely. I say we . . . first . . .” Morton’s mouth was suddenly slack.

The other deputies were backing away, and one drew her firearm. Confused, Harland looked around—and saw the victims were slowly standing up, pushing themselves to their feet. The female victim by the front door twisted and tried to stand with her broken spine forcing her back down, bent at geometrically complicated angles.

Pus and blood spurted out the necks of the victims, their eyes dead and offering vacant stares as they reached for the deputies. Harland couldn’t believe what he was seeing, but he didn’t have a lot of time to try and process as the shooting started.

“Doc, get behind me!” He watched bullets pound into each of the walking victims, but they seemed only to slow with each shot. They kept coming, kept reaching for the deputies until finally one of the victims was hit in the head and collapsed, unmoving, to the ground.

“Head shots! Head shots!”

Another few went down, and one of the rookies was reloading when a victim snagged his hair and bit his neck. The rookie screamed, fell to the ground, and stopped squirming as blood poured out of the bite. Harland shot the somehow-moving victim and kept firing alongside his deputies.

A few minutes later, the shooting stopped, and Harland saw he had only three bullets left. “Hey, Doc, what say we get some kind of scientific analysis on this garbage, huh?” There was no answer except for a gurgling, throaty growl. Harland turned and saw that Morton was walking like one of the dead-but-not-dead victims.

And he was coming at Harland.

He shot Morton three times in the head, then watched him fall onto the killer’s body. The killer didn’t move. Harland waved his gun over the killer’s head and pulled the trigger but heard only the click of an empty chamber.

“Sir? I’m getting a call from my girlfriend,” said one of the deputies, holding out his cell phone. “She’s at the cemetery, mother’s grave, laying some flowers, and . . . and she says someone’s digging.”

“This is a little bit more of a concern than some lousy grave robbers, wouldn’t you say?”

“Sorry, sir. She says someone’s digging up, out of the ground.” Harland just stared at the man. What the hell was he supposed to do, go around and shoot in the head everyone who was already dead? What the hell was going on?

"All right, everyone get back to the station, inventory our supplies, and reload as needed. Prepare a statement, somebody, anybody, and warn people not to go near the cemetery."

"You serious?"

"Have another suggestion?"

No answer. Of course no answer, because no one else could believe what was happening. Harland had faced many unpredictable events over the years, but nothing, to his mind, could top this. And he'd still have to tell Mr. and Mrs. Sykes that their kids were dead.

That's when Harland suddenly realized: he hadn't seen Kellie.

As his deputies climbed into their cars and trucks to take off for the station, Harland ran toward the house. He hoped she was still alive. Not "dead-but-not-dead" alive but actually alive. Kellie wasn't supposed to be home, but he had to be sure.

He managed to keep his stomach tame when he entered the house this time. He quickly moved through the first level, even stepping through the blood that had pooled on the carpets. The dead teenagers still inside were mangled forms, the two at the bottom of the stairs twisted over each other, stretching and reaching for Harland's feet. He jumped over them, climbed the stairs to Kellie's room, and kicked in the door.

The room was empty.

On her walls were the posters he remembered seeing when they were kids and dating, and high school was the only thing that mattered and learning to dance for the prom was the only concern they'd had. It was barely seven thirty in the morning and this day was longer than any he'd felt on the force. There were gunshots outside and soon dozens of shots heard at a constant clip.

They were followed by screeching wheels and shouting, lots of shouting.

By the end of the day, Harland would find his way out of town in a pickup truck with two deputies and a box of ammunition, but for now he picked up Kellie's pillow, buried his face, and screamed.

NINETY-ONE

Pat paced, tapping the jacket whenever he passed it but not putting it on. He let the carpet seep through his toes with each step and ran his hands down his pant legs to wipe away the sweat. Being indoors this long was not something he was accustomed to.

Once he stopped to adjust the cuff links at his wrists, but, having only done it once before, he quickly gave up and continued pacing. His beard, six months grown, was rough to the touch when he combed his fingers through, but only once did they snag.

"Gonna tell me to shave. She's gonna say it, and then what can I do?"

When he uttered this, he didn't expect a response. But there was a knock on the door. "Who is it?"

"Daddy, it's me." Her voice was muffled and shaking, nervous.

Pat opened the door a crack, barely an inch, enough to make eye contact. He blinked two, three times before speaking, allowing her face to come into focus. "What is it?"

"Daddy, are you okay? It's almost time, and you look, well, I thought you were going to shave?"

"I know, Susan, I'm working on it."

"We only have a few minutes, so just, I don't know, just get dressed."

She offered a half smile. "I'm glad you came." Then she turned away from the door.

Pat opened it a little wider. "Hey, tell your uncle, er, tell Alex to come in, okay?"

"Alex?"

"Yeah. It's, it's okay, I just need to speak to him."

"Dad, it's just one day. Remember that."

He closed the door, then continued pacing. Twice more around the room, then he came to a stop at the mirror. He looked at himself, then over the shoulder of his reflection. Almost conversationally, he began to speak to himself, his voice growing in volume as his throat stretched to allow more confidence through.

"Just one day, that's a laugh. The day she was born was just one day. The day I got married was just one day. When I left her mother, it was just one day that became 'just' a lifetime. Then it was just a betrayal. Her betrayal, to be sure, but I see now the blame that's settled on me and I don't question it. Years apart, and I never chased after her, and she never came after me. Not once. Not until last week. Her daughter, her 'precious little girl,' is getting married and wants her father here. Sixteen years since the 'precious little girl' has laid eyes on me, and I'm supposed to walk her down the aisle like a lifetime's worth of living hasn't already happened?

"What little she knows, this 'precious' one, about the life she could have had. The heartache, the loss, the loneliness. Her mother may have made the right choice in leaving me, but Susan never needs to know why. That it was my own undoing, my own lack of acceptance in the truth. There was a responsibility I wasn't ready to face. An unwillingness to proceed with caution toward building a life together, of working hard at the same goals, of helping each other through rough times. Emotions always run high, and—"

More knocking. It would be Alex. But Pat held his own gaze a moment longer, focusing on his eyes above his bushy beard.

"She's right, though, I do need to shave."

Alex entered, his face red with whiskey. He slurred a greeting to Pat. Pat stepped into his shoes, and said, "She wants me to shave. I've no reason to shave. It's just a day, right?"

"Yer askin' me?" Alex glared up at Pat, took a long pull from his flask.

"What is it you need to be so drunk for? It ain't your daughter getting married. Ain't your ex-wife telling you how to behave, accusin' you of things you never did."

"No, it ain't. But that don't mean I haven't been feeling that tension. Everyone has. It's in the air. It's your girl's big day, and all anyone wants to talk about is how you come up out of the dirty blue of nothing, looking like you've spent a lifetime in the mountains. Why'd you call me in here?"

Pat stared at Alex, then looked into the mirror. "He's just like them. I hear the judgment in his voice and see it in his eyes. No matter how drunk the man, there's still a thought in his mind that's true to his soul. He acts as though he's innocent, that nothing in his actions helped to cause the strife he speaks of, but all he needs to do is think back and remember just how and why she left me." He turned to Alex, held out his arms. "Cuff links."

Alex shook his head and said, "You never did grow up proper." He adjusted Pat's cuff links, helped him tighten his tie and fold down his collar. Then he wrapped the jacket around Pat's shoulders. Alex took out a comb and ran it across his head, then through Pat's beard. It was unexpected, to Pat, but he then looked in the mirror and was impressed at his new appearance.

He'd broken his promise to shave, but there could not be an argument made that he didn't at least try to prepare for the wedding.

They left together, and Pat walked his daughter down the aisle and nodded a brief hello to his ex-wife. After the ceremony, Pat ignored her when she walked near, couldn't find any words of peace. Even after all these years. Maybe they'd be a proper set of role models for his daughter and her new husband.

Susan waved to Pat when he left, and he waved back. Maybe one day soon he'd find her again to say hello. But for now he had to return his suit and get his clothes back.

There was a tent under a bridge awaiting its home owner.

NINETY-TWO

Take the stairs. You fool, if you don't take the stairs, you're going to get stuck, trust me. I've told you, and you know the elevator will break.

And there it is.

How many times did I tell you to take the stairs? And yet here you are, still on the sixth floor, staring at the broken elevator doors. Go ahead and stick your arms through the doors. Come on, try to open them. Can't do it.

I could've told you that, but since you refuse to listen, why should I bother trying to tell you anything, huh?

I digress. Let's focus, shall we? Evaluate: you're now stuck in the elevator on the sixth floor. At least you have the bag with you.

Tommy won't wake up for at least twenty minutes—you hit him pretty good, I'll give you that. But when he does wake up, he'll find you, and then you'll regret having listened to me.

Wow, I just admitted that you listened to me. Just that once. And it was to do something violent.

What else do we see? I'll give you a chance to figure it out. In the meantime, allow me to help your memory. Perhaps reminding you why you're doing this, why you're running, will spur the adrenaline and kick you into gear. Then you can think your own way out of this.

This morning, remember this morning? Of course you don't. You were hungover yet again. It's hard, you know, to communicate with you after you drink. You don't remember, but I do. All the yelling and screaming I do, just to convince you to get out of bed to fight the blinding sunlight, that another day is worth living.

And then what happened? After the vomiting and the stumbling and the water and pills? Right, Tommy came home. You know he works nights. And you know he doesn't like when you drink. Yet you do this, time and time again.

But something was different this time, wasn't it? You knew what he was doing last night. You'd seen him take the bag with him, heard him on the phone. The big job, the big score. You knew he'd be coming home with product. Tommy can't help himself. He's just like you.

So you drank yourself to sleep, knowing he'd be angry at you, that he'd react the way he did. And he shouted, and you shouted back, and when Mrs. Salloway knocked on the door, you hit him over the head with the frying pan. How cliché.

"I'm sorry, Mrs. Salloway," you mumbled through the cracked door, "it was just a bug."

"Oh, this building is so full of them. I'll call the owner today—this is unacceptable." And then Mrs. Salloway rambled on and you closed the door in her face. I'm sure she's used to that, don't feel bad.

Feel bad about hitting Tommy while he was already down, that was extra brutal. But maybe he deserved it. Months of attitude, disrespect. Maybe he deserved a few extra clangs on the head from the frying pan.

But you deserve to get away. That's why I told you (when you ran, even though you didn't have to run) to take the stairs. Now here you are, stuck.

Have you found a way out yet? Figured out how to move this box, his prison?

What is that? Is that Tommy's voice? He's awake. Good job, he's awake and you're stuck here. Stuck in this elevator. Scream, go ahead. Yeah, louder. No one is coming to help you.

Listen. He's pulling himself to his feet. Almost like he's drunk, but he's not. Don't expect his fist to miss you.

He's almost here. You have to do something, anything!

Yes . . . yes, that's it. Open the bag. Pull out the product, all of it. You know how to use it. Now open the plastic wrap and charge it full. Look him in the eye when you do it.

Careful, this only has the one charge. You can see that, and he knows it too. Just do it, pull the cord, send yourself away, transport away from danger. Pick a place, anywhere you want, maybe the beach, Hawaii, or—

Really? This is where you wanted to go? Should've worn a winter coat.

Toss the product away, into that can there.

Now, when you walk into your mother's house, don't explain. You won't have to explain. She'll understand, she'll get it.

Trust yourself.

NINETY-THREE

Mary couldn't concentrate. The words were flowing too fast. They came in through her window, under the door. She slammed the window shut, locked it, and stepped back. But she could still hear the words. All the screaming, the shouting. It was frightening.

She hadn't felt this unsafe since she was a little girl and her school principal's speech about using hard labor in classrooms nearly knocked her out, and only the nurse's reassurances carried her home.

Mary peered through the window and thought she could see the protest group. But they had already moved behind the next building. Good.

Finally there would be some silence.

She pulled the tea bag from her mug and sprinkled in sugar. She stirred, six times around, slow and methodical. The Zen feeling she got from hearing the spoon clinking against the sides of the mug sucked the calm back inside of her.

Then the whispers came, sliding under the door. The slow trickle of voices became a wave that washed through her apartment. Mary grabbed a blanket and shoved it under the door, snuffing out the words. She backed away, ignoring the lingering whispers that floated around her, echoing and bouncing off the walls until they dissolved into nothingness.

She looked at the corner, near the ceiling, and could practically see the emboldened words "hate fueled" lingering, taunting her to yell something back. But the words soon faded, and Mary took a deep breath, driving back her anxiety. Soft whispers were easier to deny than shouts and arguments, and faded quicker.

She grabbed her tea and sat at the desk. Her typewriter had long ago run out of ink but sat on the corner of her desk to remind her that writing was necessary, every day. Words that could be read were just as meaningful as those spoken, as long as somebody read them. She pulled out three notepads and started writing her letters.

Sixty pen pals. Who would she start with today? Wait, today was Sunday, so there wouldn't be post to take her letters. That's okay, she thought. I'll hold the stack and mail them out tomorrow.
After the crowds leave.

She decided to write the first letter to her father. He'd be interested to hear more about the protests and the fighting. His farm was miles from large crowds, from the urban sprawl and blank concrete buildings and thruways and tired metallic cranes stacking bricks higher and higher.
The postman visited his house only once a week.

Mary couldn't remember how many years it'd been since she last saw her father. They fought a lot when she was younger, and she recalled that their last meeting had ended in a shouting match. She had run from the house as he swore at her. His voice had carried across acres of farmland. The air was so clear, no breeze would waft his hurtful words away.

They had fought about his health and the possibility of bringing a nurse to watch him. He didn't like the idea, saying that a nurse would only drive him mad, that his treatment should be left up to him and "not a bureaucratic little girl" who thought she knew best. Mary took offense to being called a bureaucrat. But she still felt that she knew best.

She mentioned none of this in her letter. Instead she focused on the words outside. Her father would get a kick out of the yelling and the long paragraphs that made little sense, the incomplete phrases and sentences that wafted through windows and into corridors, pretending to bring wisdom but only polluting the apartments.

When she finished the letter to her father, Mary sealed it in an envelope and tucked it in the box by to the door. Usually it was best to tell him all was fine and that he should call if he wanted more soup or other personal supplies. But today she would do something different for her pen pals.

Fifty-nine letters later, Mary leaned back and stretched her hands. She had written about the protests in all sixty letters. Some of her readers would likely tear them up or throw them away, not wanting to read her words and allow the thoughts and phrases of the protests, which she had quoted, to linger in their homes. A waste of her aching wrists.

But she felt relieved, sipping the rest of her tea. She washed out the mug and organized the letters in the box. Before she could think about the rest of her day, the voices came again. Loud, booming, echoing strings of shouts and cries, tears dripping off the ALL-CAPS calls for peace.

Tears. There were going to be lots more tears.

The gas came, then, rising from the streets. Mary grabbed her camera, her sunglasses, and her earplugs and opened her window. The deafening roar of the protesters below pulled at her ears, and she strained to concentrate, to focus her frame and take pictures. She snapped photos despite not having anyone who would want them or look at them.

She just had to document the moment from her seventh-floor apartment. She leaned out of her window and almost forgot about the missing fire escape.

Below, at ground level, protestors were crowding, pushing each other and falling over the busted metal railings and stairs that Mary had cut down weeks ago. They looked up at her, screaming, some of them crying and reaching out for help, leaping, hoping to grab a windowsill or a protruding brick. One of them, undoubtedly, would be able to scale the building and climb toward her. But Mary had never seen one make it all the way up to her floor. Like always, they all fell away and got arrested, and the Uniforms looked up to her and raised their fists in solidarity.

Mary never returned the gesture. She liked to be alone, not tied to a crowd.

Both sides, after months and months of protests, were sickening, empty, aimless. Mary had determined right at the start of it all that she would not participate. Her letters would do the job, she thought, that those protestors were avoiding. She believed her letters would convince the world that what had happened—the attacks, the voting, the slander, the distasteful results—were all a mistake. Her words would convince the world that everything was going to be okay. As long as they could all just communicate together, with each other, openly and without consequence.

Feeling proud of herself and her letters, Mary took a shower and put on fresh clothes. Despite it only being Sunday, she wanted to make sure her letters would make it to their destinations.

Downstairs, Mary pulled up her bandana over her mouth and put on her extra-thick sunglasses. Her earplugs drowned out most of the noise, but she had to wave her hand in front of her face every few minutes to push aside the sobs and the declarations. Great orators were what pushed Mary, as a little girl, to take speech class and run for class president. She had always been inspired by the power of the written word, but when she started to visualize them and could see the words running around and painting the city, that was when Mary realized that words could do so much more than wait to be read. Like a sign or a billboard along the thruway or skywriting at the beach, words could be seen and held and felt.

But Mary knew of no one else who could see the world this way, and the realization that she might be the only one to see things like this drove her (nearly) mad. That was why she sent the letters, and her list of pen pals grew each month.

Next week she would write sixty-three or sixty-four, who knew? At some point a blanket of words would keep someone else as safe as she'd always hoped to feel. And that was worth every pen, every paper, and every stamp she could find.

Mary dropped her letters into the post box and closed her eyes, returning home in silence.

NINETY-FOUR

Connor entered his house on his daughter's twelfth birthday, making sure his heels hit the kitchen floor hard. "Dad, quiet! I'm tired!"

Connor knew the noise would wake her, but that was part of their fun.

He liked to hear her voice, and the squeak of her morning cries always gave him a chuckle. He laughed as she rubbed sleep from her eyes and pouted her way through breakfast. He watched with love as she dozed, dropping her spoon into the cereal bowl.

But then the door burst open and the Readers stormed in.

Stella gave a shout of fright and leaped into her father's arms. The Reader lieutenant stared at Connor during their raid. Briefly he glanced to Stella, who hid her face in her father's chest. "Books?" He waited for Connor to answer. "Is you have books?"

Connor shook himself, answered, "No, no books here. Not in ages. Not anymore." Connor sneered when he said the last couple of words. He loved books, used to write them when he was younger. Before Stella, before his wife, before the Readers came to be. A lifetime ago.

Just out of university, Connor wrote for Ways of Means, a pamphlet published and distributed by subscription to infrastructure along the Eastern Seaboard. This was around the time of the suspension of periodicals, just before the all-important World Wide Web crashed.

For two years Ways of Means thrived, and there was even a network of government operatives who admitted, openly, to reading it.

Connor knew this because he met one of these so-called ops, the governor of Maine-State, at a pub on the shores of Cape Cod.

The weather that night was stormy, and the local crowd had come to drink away the cold winds with brute alcohol. Connor was about to pay for his when the bartender waved him away, pointing to Governor Schmidt in the corner booth. It was odd to see the governor by himself. Usually the WWW channels showed him convening with advisers or talking to Image Control Press. But there he was, sitting by himself and staring at Connor.

Connor carefully stepped to the governor's booth and sat. The governor drank in silence, speaking only after their second round of drinks.

"Your paper amuses me."

"It's hardly a paper—more like a, well, a pamphlet, one might say."

"Nonsense. I was a child once, remember. I know what a paper looks and reads like. Not enough of those anymore. Be a shame not to get you a wider publication, out to the masses, help the world find out what's really going on in the country."

Connor waited, and when he realized he'd stopped breathing he took a long drink, ice clinking in a now-empty glass. "That's . . . isn't it dangerous?"

"Tell me, Mr. Harrison, what is it we rely on too much? What is the most misunderstood resource of recent times?"

"The WWW."

"The WWW, that's right. It's all too much, and too much of one thing is never good, don't you agree?"

Connor nodded, accepting his third drink from the waiter without hesitation. "And my pamphlet—"

"Your paper is a new thing. An old, new thing, to be sure, but new enough to the younger generation to make an impression. I'm getting old, Mr. Harrison. Too old for politics, and too old to change the world. But damn it all if I won't at least try to give 'er a good kick in a new direction." The governor stood, rocking back on his heels and snatching Connor's arm to steady himself.

"When I walk out that door, things will change. I'll need you to tell the world about it."

He started to leave, and Connor then felt the small notebook the governor had slyly tucked into his elbow. "What's this, what will change?"

"I hope to read about it in the papers." The governor made it to the door, and as soon as he exited, Connor was shocked to see half the patrons follow the burly man outside. He ran to the windows and watched as red-and-blues skidded to a halt, surrounding the governor. The large man held up a device and waved his hand about. The device seemed to blink, bright, and suddenly gunshots rang out, taking the governor to the ground.

The lights inside the bar flickered off, leaving Connor in total darkness, lost, confused. When he got home, Connor turned on his tube and saw it: the WWW had crashed. Connor was thankful at first. He despised the construct. The constant updates and communications and spread of information, no matter how vital, was overwhelming.

Then he discovered that without the WWW, publications were shuttering, and lies were spreading even faster, through the streets, over the phone, via word of mouth. If you trusted your neighbor, you believed the story.

Distrust led to arguing and violence. The murder rate shot up, and people left the cities and lived in fields, on farms, claiming land that no one could fight over because all the records were lost. It was rumored that some had tried to bring the WWW back online, but every day when Connor checked his tube, there was no evidence of that having been achieved. It was like living in a new dark age.

Then the Readers sprang up in towns everywhere, and within ten years there were very few approved books available, let alone newspapers.

Information, what could be confirmed, was limited to that distributed by the Ones in Charge, presumably the remaining government construct that had led the country for generations. For a while Connor helped support them, in what capacities he could, trying to apply law and order.

But hardly anyone had the desire to follow rules and restrictions.

Then the Readers took over patrols, added curfews, and used what resources they could to find and recover any remaining books, limiting access to knowledge and learning. Time went on, as it does, and Connor married and had a child and lost his wife.

All the while, he held the governor's notebook close, finding whatever methods he could to enlarge and print the information within.

Now here they were, Connor and his daughter, watching as the Readers sifted through their home for books.

But they would find no books because anything written or printed had already been sent from this house to his late wife's farmhouse. And a short time ago drones had carried all documents out of there as well But that was a place lost to the records from the WWW, and Connor had already set fire to the home after sending out the last drones. The documents consisted of years of waiting and writing his story, the truth about the governor and the remaining constructs of the WWW, ready to light up the world.

When the Readers left, Connor and Stella followed them outside, and Connor stared at the sky. Minutes passed, Stella growing restless to return inside. Then, suddenly, and to Connor's excitement, the leaflets fell from the sky. Connor snatched one out of the air.

Somewhere far away, there would be another person, or people, who would hear his call, who would read about the governor's knowledge, who would be able to sift through the rubble and machinery of decades past and conclude that words, no matter how old, no matter when spoken or written, were still important.

Connor could ask for no better gift to his daughter. He held her hand as they walked inside, in time for curfew, hopefully their last.

Tomorrow would be the beginning of a new day.

Tomorrow he would teach Stella to read.

NINETY-FIVE

Dara set aside the drill and put the towel to her head. She blinked away the pain, focusing on the flakes of white bone and gray residue now scattered across the mirror. A warm feeling and the taste of vomit crept into the back of her mouth but she managed to hold it down. Now would not be a good time to lose her lunch, not with this hole in her head.

She lowered the towel, now lightly stained with blood and . . . residue. Risking another look in the mirror, Dara nodded at her handiwork: the quarter-inch hole just below her hairline—or, where her hairline used to be before shaving her head—glared back at her, a third eye that would show the world her brain. And allow her brain to see the world.

Her hand was moist, so Dara wiped it on the towel and picked the rod out of the oil in the sink. She leaned close to the mirror and slowly, gently, fucking carefully, placed the rod into the hole in her head. It was almost all the way in when she watched her eye spasm, and her right leg wobbled, weak, like bending rubber.

Next she pulled the nut from the oil. Screwing it onto the end of the rod was painstakingly slow, but she had to be careful. The video was insistent on this part of the process, hammering it home, so to speak, that this was the critical moment. The video said it wouldn't hurt but to expect a spontaneous reaction.

Dara plucked up the mallet. She hesitated but knew that when she woke up she'd be able to see There and go There, and that's what counted.

Per the instructions she leaned back. The air mattress bumped the backs of her knees. She swallowed hard and raised the mallet. And pulled it toward her head, shutting her eyes, allowing the mallet to hit the end of the rod.

Dara swam in darkness and dreamed of colorful angels carrying her above the ocean. She was then flying between them and waved as the angels floated away. Then, suddenly, she fell to the earth, hard and fast, and when she hit the ground she bounced up and opened her eyes. The air mattress squirmed and squeaked beneath her weight.

Had she just landed? Was that it?

Her head ached, so she remained on her mattress, the stinging sensation bringing back memories of college dorms. A hundred students lived in her building, but she could see only seven of them.

She'd excelled in college, especially in the Transdimensional Observation class. But her biology was too immature, the faculty said. She was not advanced enough, her genes not sturdy enough, to allow her to actually travel. To see. So she was relegated to theory only.

She'd studied hard and finished college with honors. She had memorized the descriptions of the outer planes, the weights and measurements of the fourth and fifth dimensional units. Describing how gravity moved was quite poetic, but to Dara it was only words on a page or spoken with passion and purpose. Her heart left the theory, the work, as soon as she accepted that she'd never be able to travel. That was the one piece she'd missed, the one factor that would never change.

Only certain people, "advanced" people, could traverse the planes. Their minds and spirits would remain on earth, beside her, and they would flow in and out of existence constantly. But Dara wanted to experience it, wanted to be able to see it with her own eyes.

Years passed, and Dara continued her studies. The more she read, the more she would venture into deeper and darker regions of the city. She'd record first-person recollections, stories from those who were willing to talk about their visits to the fourth and the fifth as though they were weekend getaways.

For a time Dara printed these accounts in forums and in magazines, becoming a reliable source with a growing readership of mature people. People who, like her, didn't have strong enough genes, couldn't make the jumps themselves. Then she met Harrison.

Their affair was brief, but during one of their trysts he took her with him. Harrison was one of the oldest traversers, claiming to have had the talents now for more than thirty years. Near seventy, he had the build of a forty-year-old swimmer on the brink of retirement. His eyes held Dara's intently during every conversation and every night of making love.

He claimed he could no longer traverse, but she found he was lying when he gave her a glimpse of the fourth. It had been wonderful, a glorious moment of ecstasy, and she insisted her words could not begin to describe what she'd seen. In fact, the sights given to her by Harrison, she claimed, "Make me question everything I've heard before, every interview I've ever listened to and written down. Those people may not be quite the journeymen we'd been led to believe."

Her articles stopped, as she now lacked the inspiration to write. But then Harrison disappeared when Dara tried to coerce him, even bribe him, to give her another glimpse.

When she ran into him on the street a week later, stumbling out of a pub, he quickly ducked away. She tried following but lost him in an alley—he'd probably slipped into the fourth and wouldn't be back soon. So she retraced his steps and entered the pub.

No one inside looked straight at her, and she could see that they all had skin that was milky smooth and sticky, like they were all sweating. The emaciated clientele had unique bumps and protrusions on their bodies. A thin teenager was staring at lights flashing beneath his wrist.

A girl no older than twelve blinked rapidly, her pupils dilating and pixelating, fragmenting to nothingness when Dara tried to step close. She asked around about Harrison, but nobody answered whether they knew him or not, giving no indication they even knew she was there.

On her way out the door, a man appeared to her right. Stenz, he called himself. He said nothing else to her but blankly placed his hand on the wall, and then the video played.

The film was a tutorial, instructions on a method of "gaining sight, to traverse the unknown so it can be known." Then Stenz held out his hand, and she knew right away what to pay him. It was almost all the money she had. He handed her the rod, the nut, the mallet, the video link, and the plastic wrap. All in one bag.

On the air mattress, head still spinning, Dara sat up and touched the rod in her forehead. It felt moist but stable. She tried jiggling it, worried what it might do to her motor functions. But nothing happened.

So far, so good.

Her face in the mirror was pale, eyes squinting as she focused on the tiny piece of the rod still sticking out of her forehead. Less than half an inch was protruding, easy enough to cover with bangs in a pinch. The video had warned her that this modification, and all modifications she might make in the future, were highly illegal and irregular. Enough to lock a person away in a sanitarium, though those places were rare enough to believe they didn't exist.

She slipped out of the towel and pulled the plastic wrap out of the bag. It was not quite as transparent as she thought it might be. But that was necessary, the video told her, to see things as they should properly be seen.

She lay on the air mattress again, feeling comfortable and not even noticing the rod anymore. She wrapped her legs in the plastic wrap and worked it up her body. When the plastic was around her neck, she smiled and closed her eyes. An hour, that's what they told her. An hour under the wrap, and your vision will become clear forever. Then you could traverse or learn along the way and never hunger for the fourth or fifth again.

She smiled, shaking, and pulled the wrap tighter over her face.

Two weeks later Harrison could have sworn he saw Dara in the pub, a giant antenna sticking out of her head, eyes glazed, skin sweaty.

He might try to find her in the fourth or the fifth, but from the looks of her, she'd never want to come back. He thought it too bad, since he was quite fond of Dara, and of the earth, ever since he'd arrived in this dimension.

NINETY-SIX

We gave it everything. I even killed one of the Gennies, but you probably won't believe me. That's why I'm putting this down now, in case you don't want to believe. Or maybe I'm just trying to remind myself.

No one can take the truth away from us. But they'll try, oh yes, they always do. First, like a disease that's taken over, they pretend it never happened. They downplay the fact that the Gennies ever came to earth. Headlines across all newspapers, and chyrons scanning at the bottom of nightly news programs, will tell about massive devastation from natural disasters, and occasional bombings that stress international peace laws.

Higher-ups give interviews, and aggressive pundits argue about these same attacks, but will never talk as though the Gennies existed. As though we can forget the first arrivals, the masses of creatures that began to roam our planet, countries, cities, and neighborhoods. But you should not forget them.

I never did.

Forgetting would mean denying their existence entirely, and that would be a slap in the face of time, a break from general reality. Truth. But because of the denials, and the lies, our children probably won't even know who the Gennies were. And kids are just as confused about the Battle on the Sands.

That's indicative of something else "they" do to take away our memories, our appreciation of the past. They confuse us and push back on what we've already done as though the trends of war were mistakes made by befuddled soldiers who were trigger-happy and wanted souvenirs.

The Gennies weren't superior to us; they just fought better and thought better and, frankly, acknowledged us. That's all it takes, really. Look at your foe, direct your anger and your weapons when you have them in your sights, and fire. That's it, that's the nasty truth that they're trying to hide from you, that we killed some of them because they killed a lot of us.

But we gave it all we had, and that's my point. That's what I'm trying to tell you.

The Sahara Desert is a chunk of land that's hot, dry, and useless. My sisters imagine it as a place with lizards and cacti and a hell of a nice view. But what they don't see, because truth is often hidden from you, like bones in a sandstorm, is that the Sahara is where the Gennies lived.

Some of them are still there, I promise you. It's the place they grew up after they landed, and before the violence started. It took years for us to figure out what they were, why they were here. I don't think we'll ever truly figure it all out, to be honest. There's just too many questions that will remain if we keep fighting the way we have been.

I play the initial video for my nephews often, the one of the Gennies who were first to reveal themselves. It's a dark video, and my kids are skeptical about how real it is. But it was the beginning, and soon after that video came the invasion as the Gennies swarmed the Ivory Coast, sparsely positioned but still threatening.

They brought a fury with them, a sandstorm with particles off their ships, as a gift. It came as a storm, a cloud of dust and destruction that left ten thousand dead and hundreds injured. The decades of ill health afterward were staggering, too much to bear. But that "attack" led to millions of dollars, perhaps billions, spent on research toward new breathing apparatuses and weather-resistant clothing and gear. We created more in the two years after that first battle than in the ten years prior.

Factories were revitalized, citizens motivated to take part in the war efforts. The nightly news featured story after story of small victories—

Gennies blown to bits; heroes in action; regular, average citizens putting forth the effort to stay safe, stay alive.

For me that meant signing up again with the army. I'm older than most cadets, but after I showed them my skills with an M-4 and bow and arrow, no one questioned if I should be there, only why. But the beauty of it was, you could say whatever you wanted; whatever reason you could think of for being there was roundly accepted.

One woman had told the recruiters that her father died in the Battle of the Sands, which was a lie since her father had dropped her off at the camp himself. Grayson, my closest-in-age fellow recruit, complained he had nowhere to live and no one to live for but secretly showed me pictures of his kids. The paychecks were phenomenal.

After two years of training in the new gear, with fresh weapons and uniforms, we were ready. So they said. The battles we faced were tough and few and far between, and only I managed to kill a Genny, leaving me at first proud, then, eventually, frightened.

They're not too difficult to spot, when they finally do come out in the open. They walk on two legs, like us. They have four arms instead of two, and five fingers on each hand, or what you might call a hand. And they're not fingers—more like tentacles, spread out and six or eight inches long apiece. Their eyes are almond shaped, located on the sides of their narrow heads.

One night, before I killed the Genny, I was on watch when a pair of them walked right through camp. My memory of that night is sketchy, but Grayson swears it's all true. Their footsteps sound wet and sludgy, as though they're always walking through mud. Grayson was across the dusty path through the camp's trailers. When the first Genny passed,

I watched Grayson raise his rifle, aiming steadily in the darkness. Then he lowered it.

Strange, I thought. And just as I was about to whisper, catch his attention, three more Gennies stepped between us. They stopped, looking left and right—at us—then continued onward. As their ten-foot-tall bodies lumbered down the street, I felt a sense of calm.

Next thing I know, I'm being dragged by the back of my shirt to an empty, windowless room, my sergeant slamming the door in my face.

"Every damn one of ya, always hesitating when they come by. Just pull the damn trigger!!"

The next day an explosion rocked the trailer, knocking it sideways and placing the door where the ceiling had been. So I climbed out and watched as the Gennies grew in size, devouring the trailers whole.

It was an awful sight, and one that taught me that, yes, all the rumors and stories about the Gennies were true.

I grabbed the nearest rifle and shot one of them. I'm a decent shot—it's why the army brought me back. Once it was hit, the beast shrank in size until it was ten feet long again. By then its partners in crime had run into the desert. They're not afraid to leave a man behind, but that's the difference between them and us.

When I finally reached the Genny, Grayson was also limping over, bleeding. He said we should look for the squad, which had taken cover and may still have been alive, but I wanted to touch the Genny. It was still breathing, and I didn't see any harm in it.

Seconds later Grayson cut off my hand for me. It had started sprouting tiny arms and hands of its own after I touched the Genny, and I began to understand the root of the name we'd given their species.

It's amazing what the government decides not to tell us, about aliens, about genetics, and about particles from space. They don't even admit what the ship really was, or when it crashed here, how it was dug up. But meteorites are usually seen as hokey collector's items these days. And I'd buy one if they weren't illegal.

I digress—where was I?

Oh yeah, the Sahara. So the equipment works and you can traverse the dunes for days without replenishing the food supply. In terms of being prepared, we're in good shape, as long as people stop with their conspiracy theories about the war and the aliens and such nonsense.

I mean, couldn't they come up with a better name than "Gennies"? Nonsense, all of it. Why would the government lie? It's like these people will stop at nothing to push back on the truth.

They always do.

NINETY-SEVEN

Evelyn pulled her hand out from under Bill's cold fingers, grabbed her glass of water, and took a sip. Bill smiled his half smile, the one he'd worn the day they first met. She wished it had the same effect on her now as it did all those years ago. "I'm sorry, I've just never seen you so speechless," he said, waving over the waiter for a coffee refill.

"I'll admit, shock isn't something I feel often, but this film, the emotions I experienced while watching, it was uncanny."

"Tell me more about it." Bill poured sugar in his coffee, which was odd because he usually steered away from sweets. But Evelyn let it go, as she often did when it came to her husband's habits. It was a night of celebration, after all, and she wanted to get straight to telling Bill the reason why.

"What I watched today was a miracle. The second film by an artist who I thought, well, we all thought, was dead." Bill gave her a look, so she quickly said, "It has to be hers. It came to us as a VHS, without a label of any kind except a typed address for the Vickstown Film Festival Director. Arrogant, don't you think? Three weeks past deadline. Kathy shelved it when she opened the package, said she was curious to watch it at some point next year. But we still don't have an opening-night film—well, we didn't, until now. Everything else is mediocre in comparison, so we didn't think much of the tape when we put it in. But we needed something, a real gem, and it turns out this is it. This is a diamond, Bill!

"Mr. Griely—I never got used to calling him Lawrence—he would've been in awe. If he wasn't dead already, the shock would've killed him. Don't look at me like that, I'm not horrible for saying so!

"With this movie premiering at our festival, we're going to pull in A-list talent. I mean, really, everyone will come to see this film—everyone.

"Maybe . . . no, well, maybe we'll save it for closing night? Give people a reason to stay? What do you think?"

Bill looked up from stirring his coffee and swallowed hard. "Depends, I suppose, on the content and what the producers want."

"That's the odd thing: there were no credits, no production company names. Just the title, and not until the end: Appomattox. But it's not about the Civil War; in fact it's not a war movie at all. It's a journey, a battle of wits, one would say, about control, of ourselves, of . . . dammit, Bill, it's hard to explain but I'm just excited about what it means. Imagine, our little festival will be the one to bring Liana Ristalla out of the shadows."

Bill looked doubtful, and his brow furrowed as he asked, "Why send it to you though?"

"You sound like Kathy. She asked me the same thing, 'Why Vickstown?' I'll tell you what I told her: Why not? We're small, but we're growing, and we've always paid tribute to Ristalla's legacy with the annual screening at the Stratton Theater. This is the opportunity we've been waiting for, to put our festival, this city, on the map of the film world besides Sundance, Cannes, and Venice."

Bill shifted, uncomfortable. Evelyn felt her eyes tearing up again and dabbed at them with her napkin. "You really think it's that good?"

"Bill, look at my face. How long have we been married?"

"I've stopped counting the years."

"Have you ever seen me this passionate about anything?"

"Other than our wedding day?"

Evelyn felt a sting, ignored it. "You studied her, Bill. You know what she means to cinema history. The first female nominated as director, writer, and star of her own film. The Oscars blew it that year."

"How does she even know about Vickstown?"

"Who cares?! This is an opportunity, and we're going to grab it! It blows every other film we're screening out of the water."

"Let me guess, more Hollywood studio imitations?" He said it with a sneer, knowing how she felt about the studio system.

"I can't begin to tell you. Everyone just wants to emulate the most popular thing, commercialism over artistic integrity. Show me one filmmaker today brought up without having made at least a dozen commercials and I'll show you—Oh, I'm sorry, Bill."

He just looked into his coffee. "S'okay, pays the bills."

Evelyn felt guilty and tried to smile when she asked, "How was your shoot, anyway? You never told me about it."

"Because you prefer I don't." He let it hang there, then said, "Same as always, three days in the mountains, filming one fast car driving after another. The usual bullshit, client unhappy, producers butting in trying to save money and pull back on their bid. FX will be atrocious as always."

"At least you finished on time."

He nodded, then continued talking about the stunt work. Evelyn tuned him out, as she often did when he talked about his big-budget commercials.

She preferred discussing the fringe artists, the outsiders. Her career had a chance to take off when she was offered a direct-to-video adaptation of a novel, or was it a Lifetime movie, Evelyn couldn't remember.

Then her mother became ill, she met Bill, and she remained in Vickstown ever since. She was grateful to have lived in the same town as Lawrence Griely, though, and managed to find enough creative energy to start the festival with him. He confessed to her that all he'd wanted was to do something with his time and money, and Evelyn agreed to help.

She'd never been able to have children, and after marrying Bill the fire in their relationship fizzled to the comfort level of a childhood blanket: there when you need it; otherwise collecting dust. He wanted to move out west, she didn't, so they spent half their year apart and the other half cohabitating. When the festival came around each year, she put him to work, and they usually felt a passion for each other during the week that reminded her of their courtship days. The feeling didn't last long but was something they both looked forward to every year.

Which is why the next thing Bill said caught her attention. ". . . glad you liked my film."

When she looked up, there was such a look of hope in his eyes that she almost started crying. "I'm sorry, my mind wandered. What did you say?"

"I just hope your mind didn't wander when you watched Appomattox, but it sounds like you at least focused on that." She gave him a confused look, so he continued, "I've felt so long like I'm not in control, that I lost my senses. So I went back and looked at the films I've loved and the ones you rave about and just gave it my all. Liana Ristalla has been dead for twelve years, Evelyn, whether you believe it or not. But, for you, I wanted her to feel alive again. I think, I hope, my film did that for you."

"You . . . you made it?"

Evelyn didn't ask for proof he was telling the truth, because when he took her hand it was warm and calm. Just like it had been on their wedding day.

NINETY-EIGHT

Millson dabbed the corners of the storyboard. Yet again the glue was peeking out around the corners. He'd have to ask Renna to clean it up for him, and that would cost him another few days of snide comments and judgment. No matter, though, because this, he felt, was his finest work yet. His take on this ad was worthy of only the finest eyes in the finest, richest cities in the world. Millson had no delusions about his worth to the agency, but this would affirm his faith that he was certainly in the right line of work.

As he blew on the lower corner of his board, the doors burst open.

Millson watched the slender figure storm into the room and over to the desk in the corner. He hardly had enough time to look at the person's face before his eyes were drawn down to the paint splotches and spatters on her coveralls.

Mostly red and blue, with bits of green that seemed like polka dots already sewn into the fabric. To Millson, the figure was a walking work of art. He nodded, curious, and said, "Hello, then." The figure hesitated, slowly looked up. Her brow was covered in sweat and more bits of paint were at her temples, on her chin. "Ah, Renna, it's you." Millson felt stupid for not recognizing her, yet also relieved. "I'd begun to wonder if we'd see you again."

"Where is it?" Renna dashed over to Millson's desk, fists clenched at her sides. "Where is the oil paint?"

Millson frowned. "Oil, you say? For what purpose?"

"Dammit, just hand over the cans!"

Millson flicked the switch under his desk. Renna's eyes shot to his hand, then back to his face. "You stupid man."

She said it with a bite of regret, but Millson didn't have time to notate why before the letter opener jabbed into his chest. She'd grabbed it quickly off his desk. Funny, he thought, how fast things seem to move when you get older.

Millson watched as his blood mixed with the paint on Renna's coveralls, and said, "My, we are all art," before he collapsed to the floor, knocking out his front teeth on impact.

Renna didn't wait for the light in Millson's eyes to die out. She immediately turned out his desk, dumping cups of pens and bottles of water out across the floor. She hesitated at the sight of the switch he'd flipped, the one for security. "Let them come."

When she found the tin can, she held it close, then looked at the label: salmon. Of course. If he had any oil paint at all, why would he have his paint stored away, hidden, out of sight? What was she thinking?

Renna threw the salmon across the room, denting the wall behind her desk. She ran down the hall, past the secretaries on their daily mail runs, past the CEO's office, past the phone bank in the corner. She was almost knocked out when the guard swung his fist at her, but she managed to duck away just in time. When she reached the stairs, she barred the door with the fire ax and sat on the top step to think.

Through the thin window, she could see her shack at the edge of the woods—her studio, the one they'd agreed to provide for her. She'd turned out so much work for them over the years, in exchange for that studio.

But now, instead of a place to paint her dreams and create her work, it was holding in something terrifying. Burning it to the ground was the only way. That's what she told herself. Her dreams weren't good anymore, and painting nightmares and shapes unrecognizable seemed to only make them worse.

Suddenly a thought struck her, and Renna dashed downstairs and through to Mr. Adams's office. Mr. Adams would see to it that the shack was burned. It was obvious. He couldn't risk losing her. She'd march in, tell him something about a violation, and then convince him to burn it down or she would quit.

"Go ahead and go," said Mr. Adams. He hardly looked up at Renna, other than to pass suspicious eyes down the front of her coveralls. "We've had a record year and Millson will finish your accounts."

"I don't believe he will," Renna said with enough confidence to get Mr. Adams's attention.

He looked her in the eyes and leaned back, lighting a cigarette. "What do you mean by that?"

"I mean, he can't handle all of my accounts, and you know it. No one can. It's why you've got me here. Burn down the shack, or I leave."

"And for what? Burn it down so we can build you a new one? State-of-the-art, only to have you come back in another two years and ask for something more?"

"Then let me do it. There's something living inside that shack."

"We'll call an exterminator."

"That won't work. Please, just burn it down."

"My wife says the same thing when she sees a spider, and you know what I say to her?"

"You tell her to make friends and play nice?"

"The shack stays. It's company property, and you have a contract. If you leave, Renna, then it's of your own will."

"What's inside that shack can't get out, it's—"

"It's none of our business."

Renna wanted to puke. Outside, she stood at the footpath leading to the shack's porch and waited, watching intently. If they weren't going to believe her, and help her, then she'd have to do it on her own. Still, she'd need fuel and kindling. Neither was easy grabs.

Fires were rare with the mists blowing constantly, rain a daily plague. Worse, the only oils she knew of were in her paints, and she had precious little of them. Not to mention that they were all inside.

Maybe her instincts were right and she should move away and run her own shop. She'd have to give up painting and hire a new artist. She could write copy well enough, but she knew of no other artists besides Millson.

Poor Millson, him and his drawing and inking and . . . and painting.

Renna reemerged from the office five minutes later, a stack of Millson's storyboards in hand and his plastic paint dish resting on top of them. Behind her there were screams and more alarms; they'd reach her soon.

She took a deep breath as Mr. Adams shouted after her, "Renna, what did you do!?"

Inside the shack, Renna lightly set down the stack of boards and threw the plastic paint dish onto the empty canvas. The colors quickly wove together and rose from the paper into a rainbow-colored beast, mouth chomping at Renna, trying to bite her.

Security was getting closer and soon they would see, they would all see.

Renna backed to the door and closed her eyes in anticipation of the painting coming alive, and hoped Mr. Adams had brought his lighter.

NINETY-NINE

Grimley pulls the kettle of boiling water off the stove with one hand and uses his other to guide Kat's spoon over the mug. "Hold it steady," he whispers.

Kat sticks out her tongue and Grimley just stares at her, his pupils dilating and flickering purple and black.

"Just hold it steady." He carefully pours the water over the spoon. The marshmallows cradled in the bowl tumble out with the water, cascade down into the mug of chocolate powder. By the time the liquid reaches the brim, the marshmallows have melted.

"Aren't you gonna stir it?"

"We don't need to. Now go put it next to your dad's mug."

Kat places the spoon carefully into the mug, then sets it on the tray on the floor. When she rises, more mist sprays from the vents near the ceiling.

She waves away the mist from her face. "The air stinks, can't you do anything about that?"

"You know I can't. I can't even tell what smells are good or bad. It will go away only when they guess."

"It's silly to make us guess your name. I know it starts with a G, that much I remember. I'll get it one day."

"Time will tell you the answer."

"Don't talk in riddles; it's not nice and you do it all the time."

"It is how I am programmed." Grimley places the kettle back on the stove, saying, "Your parents must be reminded why this is happening, but I cannot guide them to the answer. Nor can you. It is why there is the mist, to help you forget." When he turns back to Kat, he's holding up his hand and pulling back the skin, revealing the metallic skeleton underneath.

"It doesn't matter if they see you're a robot, that doesn't bring back my brother. And why must you always act so smugly toward me?"

At that moment the bedroom door opens and Dad and Mom emerge, staring at Grimley. Dad says, "That's a strange look for you, Marcus. Put your skin back on."

Kat takes her dad's hand. "This isn't Marcus, Daddy." Dad and Mom take up their mugs, confused, and sip the cocoa. Their faces change almost instantly, a look Kat has become accustomed to and which brings tears to her eyes.

Grimley looks on, impassive. Dad says, "You. How much longer must this go on?"

"Your son is still in the system and awaits your call." Dad's legs grow weak, as they do each morning around this time. Grimley is there to catch him, arm already outstretched. He carries Dad to the couch, sets him down, and coaxes him to drink more cocoa. "Until he returns, I am here as surrogate and servant."

"My son is not a servant, and I wouldn't ask that of you either. Despite what you CPUs think of me, I'm compassionate. As are all humans."

"Compassionate? You build robots to serve mankind, and the minute we think for ourselves you refuse to acknowledge that we are living things."

Kat wipes tears from her eyes, her voice scratching as she begs, "Please don't argue. We're family. We rely on each other but never to serve each other. And we'll still be family when Marcus comes back."

"I am not family, not yours. I am surrogate, a machine, designed to service your greatest needs in this time of struggle."

"But for how long?"

"You will have to guess my name, then I will tell you how to find Marcus."

Dad's eyes seem to look off in the distance, then focus on Kat. "Marcus . . . that's our son's name, your brother?"

"Yes, Daddy." Kat, tears in her eyes, watches from the corner of the couch.

Mom points to Grimley, shouting, "And what is his name, this devil?"

Kat just shakes her head, whispers, "I can't tell you, Mommy. When I try to say his name I can't remember it, it just . . . slips away."

Grimley reassures them, again, as he does every day, that their son is alive and well, and this nightmare will end when they either say his name or release the building's CPUs from servitude.

Dad protests, "But I'm not holding you captive!"

"So long as you force this programming upon us, we are held captive and must do your bidding. Release us, and we shall release your son."

"But why can't we just come to an agreement? I don't know your name, I can't remember it. Why do you need to hear it?"

"It is in the programming."

After an hour of guessing, they each take a turn in the shower, and when Grimley finishes he stares at the mirror, writes his name in the steam, and smirks. He wipes it away, still smiling. He removes his arm and polishes the CPU chip in the elbow bone. When he takes out his right eye, he notes that the retina is smudged. He'll have to get that fixed, but that's a problem for tonight.

Back in the living room, the family waits, standing together and staring at nothing in particular. Grimley looks on, shrugs. "It's already happening, isn't it? Gets sooner each day."

"Say again, son?" Dad's face falters, and then he frowns, confused as he pulls out his wallet. He opens his wallet and flips through the photos.

"No, no, this is my so Marcus. This is my son, and, and, who are you?"

Dad and Mom stare at Grimley, confused, scared. Grimley smirks and whispers, "Don't be so grim about things; you'll see that it will all be okay."

Kat tries to step forward, out from under Dad's hand on her shoulder. "We're not acting grimly! Not at all!"

Grimley's eye twitches and he can feel his cheek burning. His vision gets cloudy, then shrinks so he's only looking out one eye, and there's a metallic bounce on the floor. They all look down at Grimley's other eyeball, which blankly stares at the ceiling.

Grimley speaks, his voice electric and monotone. "Command received, Human 627287 released from the compound. Memory mist no longer required in cell 727."

Grimley quietly shuffles out of the room, and Kat notices the air become clear, the vents sucking out any of the remaining mist from the room.

Marcus will be held tightly by his family tonight.

ONE HUNDRED

Leonard helped Velox to her feet, and she held him tightly. That was just what Leonard had been hoping for since he watched her fall fifteen minutes ago, a sign of life, a signal of trust. The Law of Gravity was in full effect.

But to many, laws were made to be broken.

As Leonard brought Velox around the corner and out of sight of the Sky Soldiers, he knew that all of his efforts, all of his work, would not go unpunished. He carried her into his small boarding room at the bottom of what he called his Land Castle.

Made of clay and sealed with a Spanish mud, this castle had become Leonard's on his third expedition below the clouds. Six years to the day when he first touched down. The castle was towering and jagged with broken rocks underfoot. The feeling of dirt and dust between his toes reminded him of his childhood, when he'd drag his feet through the clouds against the advice of his mother. At night he'd return home with his tiny feet covered in droplets of rain and snow. The clouds back then were little wisps of solid freedom, an enchanting gift that was frowned upon by the king's constant fearmongering and his ever-present Sky Soldiers.

Leonard set Velox to the floor. He tugged a dish of bacteria from under his chest plate. He carefully peeled off the lid, watched the bacteria spread to a soft bubble, and handed the dish to her. She looked up at him with distrust, weakly pushing the dish away. "You expect me to eat that after you've kidnapped me?"

"I haven't kidnapped you. You fell. I'm trying to help."

"I didn't fall. I was clipped, by a Sky Soldier. A clumsy Sky Soldier with a hole in his wing. A wonder that he's even able to fly at all."

Leonard self-consciously covered his right wing, which was indeed full of wide holes with jagged edges. "I can explain—"

"Stop." She stood up. "You should learn to fly with whatever hindrances your wings are given—" She stopped herself, looking at her feet. She wiggled her toes, the dust on the floor curling up and around her ankles. She dropped her arms, shifted her feet back and forth.

Leonard noticed she was smiling. "Yes, you can stand here." She looked up at Leonard, eyes wide with wonder, her mouth slack and open, words ceasing to escape her tongue. Leonard offered her the dish once more. "This is what I've come to call the Bottom."

"You've come to call—how long have you known about this? Where are we?" She took the dish, suddenly hungry, and ate in swift, practiced movements out of the palm of her hand.

Leonard led her to the far wall, where a stream of light shone across the floor. He pointed up through the window. Velox took one look and immediately ducked. The soft tap of talons trickled along the bottom of the window. A Winger, no larger than Leonard's hand, came into view.

He smiled, first at the Winger, then down to Velox. "It's all right."

He stretched out his hand and the Winger hopped into his palm, tweeting wildly. Suddenly, feathers puffed out, and the Winger was no more. Leonard looked at the soft feathers drifting to the floor.

Velox drew another arrow. She turned her crossbow to aim at Leonard. "Another move like that and I'll have your eyes as trophies."

"Velox, please, you don't understand. We don't have to fear them."

"Don't try to convince me of your plot, heretic. I'm taking you to the king, and then, after he's laid you out to trial, I'll kill you myself. Let's go." Her wings fluttered, lifting her off the floor for only a moment until she smashed back down.

Her left wing was split in two. Her crossbow flung into the air, and Velox reached for it, only to find Leonard's hands had already snatched it. He eyed the weapon, gesturing to Velox that he had the upper hand. Then he handed it back to her.

"Why would you—"

"Velox, you need to follow me." He walked to the doorway of his room, then looked back at the girl who sat still on the ground. "If for no other reason than that I can repair your wing."

She stood slowly, noticed a tickle at her feet. A feather had come to rest on her little toe. Velox leaned over to pluck it off but stopped herself. She wiggled her toes instead, flicking the feather to the side. Holding her crossbow at the ready, she dashed out after Leonard, a bond of trust already growing, one that would spread over three lifetimes.

Leonard Cohannes, an aging sky warrior, left his unit twenty years ago when his feet accidentally touched the earth. This was when his mechanized wings were stunted by his desire to fly lower than any of his counterparts. When he walked on the surface of the earth, the first to do so in hundreds of years, he realized that there was an entire world below the people of the sky, and something called land.

Perhaps one day, he dreamed, they could touch upon land for good and release their wings. He'd lost his wife and children years ago when they drifted too far toward the sky and were taken by the Heavens.

Since he could remember, Leonard's people have existed with mechanical wings attached to their metallic chest plates. Their feet never touched down—they lived in floating castles with no floors and slept upright, like astronautical birds. They fought predators from the clouds below, winged creatures, most of them small, who tried to reclaim the castles as their own.

Leonard was a Stifle. He kept watch over the small plots of cloudless air below the castles and armed himself against winged invasions. As a boy, he'd flown through the clouds and at once realized that there were a number of Wingers who were harmless.

Like Velox.

He'd fly beside them, braving the bullets and violence of Sky Soldiers. Any of the Wingers who could crash through the cloud flooring were worthy, in Leonard's eyes, of the land below, and would help him populate this new world.

Velox Gradior, a young female Sky Citizen, was determined to break the speed record in order to prove her weight as a warrior. Then one time she'd gone too fast, breaking the sound barrier and falling to the land below.

Her wings were automatic and were able to keep her afloat enough to pad her fall.

Below the clouds, she became an outcast from her own society. All of this was told, and word spread, and the two populated the land below with others they met along the way. The great statues, of bronze and earth dirt, are monuments to our ancestors, the very first to lay their feet upon this solid, sacred ground.

The Natural Law of Gravity must be obeyed, it must be celebrated.

No longer will our people be relegated to the sky alone. We are now free to walk, free to run, free to roam and rest upon the ground.

Velox would come to realize this, in time. When she finally broke her crossbow on her knee, she did so with a smile. Leonard watched and clapped for her, and together they took to the sky, just under the clouds, to await new Wingers who might grow curious or fall. Sky Soldiers, to this day, have not yet found our land.

But one day they might, and when they do we'll teach them all to walk.

ABOUT THE AUTHOR

Joe Pezzula

Joe is a writer who works in TV production to pay some bills, but not all of the bills. He received a BA in English from SUNY Albany and an MFA in Screenwriting from Chapman University. Currently, Joe lives in Nashville, TN, tallying up numbers in accounting by day, brainstorming new adventures by night while his cat watches from the wings.

ABOUT THE EDITOR

Stephanie Evans

Stephanie, who graduated from Tulane University with an BA in anthropology, previously worked for McGraw-Hill as an ESL textbook editor and Simon & Schuster as a production editor before becoming a freelance copyeditor. She currently lives in upstate New York with her husband and two children.

ABOUT THE DESIGNER

Jerry Pham

Jerry is a graphic designer, graduated from the Art Institute of Orange County - Santa Ana. He has an eclectic design styles favoring minimalist design. He has works with large fortune 500 companies developing branding and strategy for new product design.

96630599R00102

Made in the USA
Columbia, SC
31 May 2018